DEADLY

LISTING

ALSO BY SUSAN BUDAVARI

Merano & Bell Novels

Bargain for Life

Chain of Lies

DEADLY LISTING

A Merano & Bell Novel

SUSAN BUDAVARI

FERVENT PRESS

An Imprint of Red Coyote Press LLC

Published by Fervent Press, an imprint of Red Coyote Press LLC

Fountain Hills, Arizona

ISBN-13: 978-0-9766733-7-8

ISBN-10: 0-9766733-7-1

Library of Congress Control Number: 2016901042

Cover Design: Kästle Olson

Cover image: istock.com

Printed in the United States of America

First Edition

To all those who have helped along the way

ONE

DR. Elise Bell's heart pounded as she raced from the elevators to her father's room in the intermediate care unit of Clearview Hospital in Guilford, New Jersey.

She had managed to keep her emotions in check during the long flight from Phoenix to Newark but couldn't hold it together much longer. Tears trickled down her cheeks. She rubbed her burning eyes.

Just as she reached her father's room, a nurse with a weary expression came out the door. The curtain was drawn.

The nurse glanced in Elise's direction.

Elise caught her breath. "I'm Mr. Bell's daughter. I've just gotten into town."

"We need another couple of minutes to finish up. Then you can go in to see your father."

Elise fiddled with the buttons on her pantsuit jacket while she waited. She was in a hospital, familiar surroundings; she needed to draw on her training as a physician and stay cool and unemotional. Yet, with her father so ill, it was easier said than done. When she left her hometown four years ago, she vowed never to return. She was here now because her parents needed her. No matter what, she had to focus on them and put her personal issues aside.

After the nurse opened the curtain, Elise braced herself and went in.

Her mother, Sharon, jumped up from her chair at the bedside. "Darling, thank God you're here. I've been counting the minutes since your flight landed." She looked into Elise's eyes. "I know how hard it is for you to come back to Guilford."

Elise set her carry-on down and hugged her mother. "It's okay, Mom. How's Dad doing?" It hurt to see her mother's eyes, glassy from crying.

Sharon Bell shrugged. "They're pumping all sorts of drugs into him. I don't think Dr. Fletcher has any idea what's wrong with him."

"After you and I talked last night, I called Fletcher. We spoke for a long time. He told me about the tests he's running on Dad. He expected to have some results by this afternoon."

Elise looked down at her father's ashen face. When she caressed his forehead, she found it cool to the touch. She lifted his eyelids and was relieved to see the pupils appeared normal and responded to light. She inspected the monitors and checked his IVs.

"How does he look to you?"

Elise weighed her words. She had to be careful what she said to her mother under the circumstances. "Like I expected. His vitals are stable." She mustered a faint smile.

"The nurse just told me Dr. Fletcher's on his way down. I hope he has some news. The nurses say he's one of the best doctors here—whatever that means."

"Mom, are you okay? I know this has been very hard on you."

"I'm overwhelmed and totally exhausted. I feel like if I close my eyes, I'll never open them again. Dad's always been so strong. I depend on him for everything. I never imagined anything like this could happen."

Neither did I. "Try to think positively. He's going to get better." Elise took hold of her mother's hands and didn't let go until they stopped shaking.

"There's something else I need to tell you, Elise. No sense waiting."

"What?"

"Laura was brought in this morning." Sharon held her chest and took a deep breath. "I can't believe it. Dad and Laura both so sick." She sighed. "I got the feeling Fletcher doesn't think Laura's going to make it."

"Her heart?"

"They're not sure yet what's going on. Jeff heard her yell and got to her room just as she fell to the floor. He called nine-one-one."

"Oh, that's awful." Tears welled in Elise's eyes. Laura Kirby was not only her father's business partner at K&B Realty but also a dear family friend. Elise imagined the horror Jeff, Laura's eighteen-year-old son, must have felt witnessing his mother's collapse.

Sharon walked to the window in the back of the room. "I'm still so angry at every one of Laura's doctors."

Elise followed. "Why, Mom?"

"Her heart attack in July could've been prevented. She told all her doctors her symptoms, but they all brushed them off. Not one of them bothered to check out her heart." Sharon shook her head. "Sorry, dear, but I don't have much faith in doctors, anymore."

Elise's face darkened. "Unfortunately, some docs still don't get it that women's heart attack symptoms can be very different from men's."

"It's infuriating."

Elise placed a comforting hand on her mother's shoulder. "Don't dwell on the past. We have to focus on giving Dad and Laura all the support we can."

Sharon pursed her lips. "It's strange they both became ill at the same time. Don't you think they were exposed to something?"

"Let's wait to see what the doctors find out." Elise refused to speculate. Although her mother was a strong, intelligent woman, she tended to jump to conclusions without waiting for all the facts. Elise's stomach rumbled. She reached into her purse for some antacids before returning to her father's bedside.

Although in his mid-fifties, her father, Rick, had looked fit and much younger than his age. The two of them had always been close. Even during the lowest periods of her life, Elise felt secure knowing she could count on him being there for her. Now he looked like a pale shadow of himself. It was her turn to be there for him . . . and for her mother.

People said Elise and her dad were a lot alike. Both were slender and tall, with thick brown hair, and almond-shaped brown eyes. They shared a quick smile and determination and were survivors, a trait he sorely needed now.

Over her years of residency in internal medicine at Marivista Hospital in Scottsdale, Elise had witnessed how having a loved one suffering in the hospital could distort the thinking of a patient's family, no matter how educated they were. Now that she found herself in that position, she fought the temptation to put her head in her hands and cry. She chided herself for her weakness.

Elise's mother put her arm around her. "Earth to Elise. You look like you're in another world."

"I was thinking about things." She paused. "Has Dad been happy working with Laura?" Her father had teamed up with Laura in her real estate business after Laura's husband, Dave, died.

"He loves K&B. It was fortunate he could take early retirement from his finance job, when Laura lost Dave." Sharon sighed. "Now with house sales dropping, the business is struggling a bit, but until recently they did extremely well."

Elise studied her mother's face. The strain of the last few days had taken a toll on the fifty-three year old. She had dark circles under her eyes and deep creases around her mouth. A month ago she'd looked a lot younger when she visited Elise in Scottsdale on her way back from a Las Vegas computer show.

Her father stirred. His eyelids fluttered, and one eye flicked open and closed. Although excited, Elise spoke very slowly and deliberately. "Aw Dad, some people will do anything to get their kids to visit." She waited a few moments, hoping he might be able to engage in their usual banter. When he didn't speak, she said, "Mom called me last night to say you were here in Clearview. I flew in to see you."

Elise thought she saw the beginning of a smile on her father's face. She smoothed back his hair. "How do you feel?"

No response. Her father's eyes remained shut.

Sharon's jaw dropped. "Oh, I thought he was waking up."

Elise reached for her mother's hand. "We have to be patient. He'll come around. Try to stimulate him by speaking to him."

"Okay, I can do that. I didn't think he could hear me."

"We don't know for sure, but it may help. I always tell families to assume the patient can hear them and to talk to them."

At that moment, Dr. Fletcher appeared at the door.

He nodded to Sharon. "Good evening, Mrs. Bell." He extended his hand to Elise. "You must be Dr. Bell. It was good speaking to you last night."

"Yes. Please call me Elise." She shook his hand.

Fletcher looked different from what she expected. Despite graying hair, he appeared to be in his late-thirties. Roughly five feet eleven, a couple of inches taller than she, he had a medium build. His pale and pasty complexion was in stark contrast to large brown eyes and dark, bushy eyebrows. He looked like a stern, no nonsense person and projected an air of confidence.

Fletcher put his stethoscope to his ears and moved next to the bed. "It's Dr. Fletcher, Mr. Bell." He reached for Rick's hand.

"Do you know what he's doing?" Sharon asked Elise.

Elise whispered, "He's checking if Dad responds to his voice and pressing his nail beds to see if he reacts to pain. Now he's opening Dad's eyes to see if his pupils respond to light."

Elise watched as Fletcher continued the examination. His expression changed as he scrutinized a large red, blistered area on the top of her father's right hand between his thumb and index finger. At first glance, it seemed to Elise like dermatitis, or maybe cellulitis, but she would take a closer look at the hand later.

Fletcher went out to the nurses' station and returned holding a printout. "We've gotten some test results back." He flipped through the pages. "Cardiac enzymes are okay, so Mr. Bell hasn't had a heart attack. All the cultures we ran are negative, so it doesn't look like any type of common infection. It's not alcohol poisoning, and his urine drug screen is negative. The MRI of his brain was normal, and the latest EEG shows no seizure activity." He looked up at Elise. "We'll continue to give him supportive care and start looking for zebras now."

"What do you mean zebras?" Sharon asked.

Elise smiled. "They always tell medical students: 'When you hear hoof beats, think horses, not zebras.' What that means is, first eliminate the common causes, then start looking for more obscure things—unusual diagnoses."

Fletcher nodded. "We originally wrote off most of your husband's symptoms as due to the high alcohol content in his blood. Now that the alcohol's out of his system and he hasn't recovered, we think something else is going on. One thing I'm concerned about is the arrhythmia we've detected. I'll be consulting later today with some outside specialists. Do you have any questions?"

"How much longer will my husband need all those tubes?"

"Until he can take fluid and medications by mouth. We've got to keep him well hydrated. He's had seizures so we're giving him anti-epileptic drugs which, based on the most recent EEG, appear to be working."

"I see."

"Could he have some sort of viral encephalitis?" Elise asked.

Fletcher shook his head, but before he could explain, his pager sounded. He glanced at it. "Excuse me. I need to get this." He picked up the phone on the table next to the bed and keyed in some numbers.

"Fletcher." He rubbed his forehead as he listened to the caller.

"Put on a 100% non-rebreather mask, get a portable chest X-ray, and an ECG," he ordered. "Also get a stat CBC, electrolytes, cardiac enzymes, serum lactate and ABG. Run normal saline wide open to try to bring her pressure up. Make sure the code cart is in the room. I'll be right there."

Elise leaned toward Fletcher and whispered, "Is it about Laura . . . Mrs. Kirby?"

From the look in his eyes, she knew the answer.

"I'll be back as soon as I can."

Sharon tapped Elise on her arm. "Aren't you going along to help?"

"I wish I could, but I'm not licensed in New Jersey. Anyway, it's not a good idea for physicians to take care of their family or friends. We just can't be objective."

"I guess you're right."

"It's frustrating for me too, Mom, but we have to have faith and rely on Dr. Fletcher."

"I hope he won't let Laura down like all her other doctors have."

TWO

"WHAT'S going on here, Lynn?" Dr. Fletcher asked the redheaded nurse standing in the middle of the group working on Laura Kirby.

The nurse looked up. "Mrs. Kirby's pressure's been low all afternoon. She became unresponsive, so we called the code at 6:25 p.m."

Fletcher checked the monitor. "Give her a milligram of atropine." He turned to the nurse standing directly behind him. "Barb, let Mrs. Kirby's son know what's happening."

Fletcher observed the patient's breathing for a few moments. "Let's intubate her."

He took off his jacket and rolled up his sleeves. Within seconds, he successfully inserted the tube into Laura's throat. Then just as her oxygen saturations stabilized, a nurse shouted, "She doesn't have a pulse!"

Fletcher looked up at the cardiac monitor. "Start chest compressions. Get the epi ready. Somebody hand me the paddles and charge the defibrillator."

Holding the paddles, he yelled, "Clear!" and shocked Laura. Her body bounced on the bed. She lay motionless.

"Okay, keep going with the chest compressions."

DESPITE frantic efforts over the next thirty minutes they couldn't elicit a response. Finally, Fletcher said, "We've lost her." He looked up at the clock. "Time of death 7:08 p.m."

He took a deep breath and wiped his forehead. "I'll go talk to her son."

"Before you leave, Dr. Fletcher," Lynn said, "take a look at Mrs. Kirby's right hand. I've never seen anything like it."

ELISE sat by her father's bedside when Dr. Fletcher entered the room an hour later. She stood. "How's Mrs. Kirby?"

Fletcher motioned for Elise to follow him. He spoke slowly, with compassion in his voice. "I'm sorry, the news is bad."

A chill ran through her body. "What happened?"

"Cardiogenic shock. We coded her for thirty minutes but couldn't get a rhythm back. Her cardiac function was poor coming in. She didn't have much reserve. I'm very sorry."

Elise cupped her head in her hands and fought her sobs. After a few moments she regained her composure. But her eyes welled with tears. "No matter how much you prepare yourself, the finality is hard." She shook her head. "How's her son Jeff, taking it?"

"I sat with him for a while. He said he realized that ever since his mother's heart attack in July, she could have another one. He seems to be holding up, but he'll need support. I don't think it's all registered yet. Does he have any family nearby?"

"Unfortunately, no. Laura's sister lives in Minneapolis. I'm sure she'll come and help out. Jeff is close to Laura's fiancé, Tim Dixon, who lives in town."

Elise rubbed her left hand against her cheek. "I'm worried how my mother's going to take this. She was antsy and went down to the cafeteria a while ago. She should be back any minute."

"Don't let her draw conclusions about your father's outcome based on what's happened with Mrs. Kirby. His general health is excellent—hers wasn't."

"I'll remind my mother of that."

"The family gave permission for a post-mortem. Maybe we'll learn something that'll help with your father's treatment."

"You think their illnesses might be related?"

"We haven't ruled that out," Fletcher said.

As Fletcher started to leave, Elise asked, "What's next for my dad?"

"We'll continue supportive therapy and see whether his condition improves over the next twenty-four to forty-eight hours. If it doesn't, we may need to transfer him to a tertiary care center like University Hospital. Maybe they can figure out what's going on."

Elise felt a deep frown settle on her face. Before she could say anything, Fletcher added, "Let's hold off on all decisions until after we get the autopsy results. We'll put a rush on them."

"Maybe this isn't an isolated occurrence. Have you checked for reports of similar cases locally?"

Fletcher stared at Elise for a moment before answering. "I called the New York and New Jersey Health departments and the CDC, but I came up empty. It might be a good idea for you to retrace your father and Mrs. Kirby's steps over the last week. Find out if they were exposed to anything that might've made them sick."

Elise began to say she'd do that but stopped when she spotted her mother at the door.

Fletcher spoke first. "Mrs. Bell. Could I have a word with you?"

"Dr. Fletcher. How's Laura?"

Elise took her mother's hands. "I'm sorry, Mom. We've lost Laura."

Sharon's expression froze.

"We tried everything," Fletcher said, "but . . . we weren't able to save her. She had a weak heart. I'm so sorry, Mrs. Bell."

Sharon began to weep. Elise reached out to her mother and pulled her close. When Sharon finally spoke, she said, "Poor Laura. I can't believe it."

"I'm so sorry, Mom. Laura was very sick. This was just too much for her heart to take."

"I know that, but I didn't expect it. I kept on hoping . . ."

Fletcher said, "I'm afraid I have to leave now." He handed Elise his card. "Call me if you need me. My sincere condolences."

Elise put her arm around her mother and led her to a chair. She filled her in on what Fletcher had said and waited patiently until her mother became a bit calmer. "Do you want to go to see Jeff now?"

Sharon nodded then mumbled, "I shouldn't have said anything. When will I learn?"

"What do you mean, Mom?"

"Last week I remarked to your father how well everything was going. I tempted fate."

"Oh, you don't really believe that. Nothing you did caused this."

"It seems as good a reason as any for all this happening."

Elise shook her head and moved closer to her father. She took a good look at his hands. The condition of his right hand below the thumb and first finger concerned her. There was an abrasion with surrounding swelling and redness, and signs of blistering. Could it be a severe allergic or contact dermatitis? She snapped some pictures with her cell phone, kissed her father's cheek, and followed her mother out of the room.

ELISE and Sharon found out from Laura's nurse that Jeff and Tim Dixon, Laura's fiancé, were meeting with hospital staff about funeral arrangements. They spotted Jeff at the door of the conference room saying good-bye to the chaplain and nurse supervisor and waited for him to finish.

Jeff waved them inside the room. Elise saw the grief in his eyes and hugged him. Sharon followed suit.

He gently pulled away. "I can't believe Mom's gone. It happened so fast." His eyelids were red and puffy. "Tim's been with me all day. He gestured to a slim, gray-haired man who looked to be in his late-fifties, seated at the conference room table.

Sharon whispered, "Elise, you remember Tim."

"Of course." She extended her hand to him. "Sorry to see you under these terrible circumstances."

Elise and Sharon took places at the table on either side of Jeff and across from Tim.

"I'm just overwhelmed." Heavy creases marked Tim's pale face. "I had lunch with Laura and Rick yesterday. They both seemed fine. Now Laura's gone, and Rick is fighting for his life."

Jeff broke the silence with a rush of words. "Mom's cries woke me this morning." His voice trembled but he kept up the pace. "When she collapsed I called nine-one-one right away."

Sharon touched Jeff's hand. "Take a breath, Jeff."

He inhaled deeply and began speaking again, his voice more controlled. "While the paramedics got Mom settled, I called K&B and left a message for Mr. Bell. Then I called you, Mrs. Bell." He paused for a moment. "It blew my mind when you told me Mr. Bell was in the hospital." He swallowed. "I hope he's doing okay."

"He's holding his own, Jeff," Elise said.

Jeff stared ahead "I think Mom had a feeling she was going to die."

"What do you mean?" Elise and Sharon asked in unison, both wide-eyed.

"When I got home Monday night and passed her bedroom door, I heard her crying. She jumped and shrieked when I entered the room . . . almost like she was afraid for her life. I asked her what was going on. She said it was nothing, but I wasn't so sure. She got angry when I asked her again, so I kept quiet. She handed me the insurance policy she took out after my dad died. I'm the beneficiary."

"What did she say?" Elise asked.

"Put it in a safe place. For when you need it."

"Do you have any idea if something happened earlier in the day that upset her?"

"No." Jeff shook his head. "She downplayed the whole thing. Said she'd been meaning to give me the policy and had just come across it when she was straightening her drawer." He shrugged. "I thought there was more to it."

"What do you mean?"

"All that talk about insurance policies, one for me as beneficiary and another for Mr. Bell. Almost like she thought I was going to need them soon."

Elise looked at Tim and waited to see if he would add anything. He just shook his head.

Sharon said to Elise, "When Dad and Laura became partners they took out reciprocal policies to protect the business. In case either one of them died, the money was supposed to help tide the other one over."

"That's what Mom told me," Jeff said.

"What about last night? How was she then?" Elise asked.

"I dunno. I got home real late. Her bedroom door was closed. Her room was dark so I figured she was sleeping."

"Now that I think of it," Tim piped in, "both Rick and Laura were fidgety at lunch yesterday, and kept glancing at each other more than usual. It didn't register with me until now." He rubbed his eyes. "We were talking finances. That's enough to make anyone uneasy, but maybe it was more than that. Neither of them seemed sick or said anything to make me think there was any trouble though."

"Were they having financial problems?" Elise asked.

Tim shook his head. "The business is solid. Things were a little slower this year because of the economy, and also Laura was out sick. But they were optimistic everything would work out."

Sharon took Jeff's hands. "I loved your mother very much. I'm so sorry. You can count on us for anything—anything at all."

Jeff blushed and whispered, "Thanks."

Elise said, "Jeff, do you want to come to our house tonight?"

"Thanks, but no. I'm staying with Tim tonight. My Aunt Deanna's flying in from Minneapolis tomorrow morning. She's going to help me take care of things at the house."

After exchanging parting hugs with Jeff and Tim, Elise and Sharon headed over to see Laura. They stopped at the nurses' station and a nurse escorted them to Laura's room.

They found her draped in a white sheet up to her neck. The intubation tube was still in her mouth, but not connected to anything. While her mother stood next to the bed looking at Laura, Elise located a pair of plastic gloves and slipped them on. She went over to the opposite side of the bed and lowered the sheet. After a quick look at Laura's head, neck and upper body, she carefully examined her right hand and arm. The hand was red, blistered, and swollen, more than her father's was, but in the same way. Irritation had spread up the wrist. It was unlike anything Elise had seen before. She snapped some shots with her cell phone then carefully folded Laura's hands on her abdomen and pulled up the sheet.

She disposed of the gloves and joined hands with her mother. The two women said a prayer for Laura. They spent another ten minutes in the room then left. The condition of Laura's hand dominated Elise's thoughts. She wondered what the autopsy would reveal.

Elise made a decision. "I can't stand by without doing anything. I'm taking Fletcher's suggestion and retracing Laura and Dad's steps over the last week. I'll start with K&B in the morning and look through their desks. Hopefully, I'll find some clue to what happened to them."

"I know how you feel Elise, but couldn't you do more good

by helping treat Dad? It's driving me crazy they still don't know what's wrong with him."

"I'll do what I can, but I still want to find out what Dad and Laura did in the last week. I assume they keep their records on their office computers."

"Yes. I set up the programs for them." Sharon frowned and cast her eyes downward. "If only Dad had taken this week off as he planned, none of this would have happened!"

"We'll never know. Best to put that out of your mind."

"You're right." She sighed. "Keeping busy will help get me through the next few days."

"Tomorrow, I'll go check on where they were last week. You visit with Dad."

"I'm going with you. I won't take no for an answer." Sharon stared at Elise. "Ever since I got my real estate license last year I've been spending a couple of evenings a week and some weekends at K&B. I know exactly where Dad keeps everything. It'll save time."

Elise knew it didn't pay to argue with her mother. She wouldn't win this battle.

THREE

ELISE rose before 6:00 a.m. despite getting to bed well after midnight and tossing and turning for at least another hour. She threw on a pair of jeans, a shirt, and sweater. The clothes she'd brought with her proved perfect for the early November warm spell in New Jersey. She joined her mother for coffee and the two women were ready to leave by six-thirty.

As her mother pulled out of the driveway, Elise noticed a dark full-sized sedan parked across the road and caught a glimpse of a man in the driver's seat puffing on a cigarette. He slouched down out of view. "Do you know who that is? I think he's watching us."

Sharon shook her head. "He's probably a worker killing time before going to one of the neighbors. The houses on the street are all showing their age. Everyone's remodeling these days."

Elise observed her family home as they drove past. Other than a lighter stain on the redwood siding of the two-story house, the outside looked pretty much the same as it had when she left four years ago. The extreme anxiety she expected to feel at being back home hadn't materialized, at least not yet.

While her mother drove slowly up Mountain Boulevard toward her father's office, Elise admired the red, copper, and yellow fall foliage of the oak, ash, and tulip trees lining the roads. Many new commercial buildings had sprung up during the time she'd been away.

At the K&B Realty sign, Sharon turned into the parking lot, pulling up near the entrance of the brick office building. There was only one other vehicle in the lot. Sharon said the car belonged to Sam Peters, the night security guard.

Before her mother could put a key in the lock, Sam appeared at the door and opened it from the inside for them. "Good morning, Mrs. Bell. You're out really early."

"Good morning, Sam. We'll only be here for a couple of hours." She quickly added, "This is my daughter, Elise."

"Oh yes, the doctor from Arizona." He tipped his head. "Do you need my help with anything?"

"No, but thanks."

"In case I don't see you on the way out, have a nice day ladies." He locked the door and walked away.

When he was out of earshot, Elise whispered, "I guess Sam hasn't heard about Laura."

"I'm glad. I can't talk about it, yet."

They headed for the wing that housed the K&B suite of offices. The clicking sound of their heels on the tile floor resounded in the empty building. Sharon unlocked the door to the suite and turned on the lights in the reception area. "We only have a receptionist on weekends now. During the week we see clients by appointment."

Elise followed Sharon across the carpeted floor. Both women dropped their sweaters on an armchair outside her father's office.

"Let's do Dad's desk first," Sharon said. "Then can you go through Laura's things by yourself? I can't handle that."

Elise nodded, turned on the light, and looked around. "I've never seen Dad's new furniture. I remember you saying he selected it by himself." She smiled. "Very professional—shiny and neat.

Nice desk and conference table."

Elise ran her fingers along the side of the desk as she walked around to the back. She sat on a plush brown leather chair.

"Your father's always had good taste."

"I see he jots appointments on the desk calendar." Elise flipped through the pages. "Does he keep a schedule on his computer or cell phone?"

"No. He still prefers paper. Check the center drawer. I stopped in here late on Tuesday night. I was so wound up after the hospital I knew I wouldn't be able to sleep. I looked up their appointments for the week and cancelled all but one, a woman who's supposed to come in at ten today."

"Then one of us will have to wait around for her. What's her name?" Elise asked.

"Lenz." Sharon rubbed her temples. "Stacy Lenz."

"You can go to the hospital when we finish up. I'll stay and make some calls then catch a taxi after I finish with the woman."

"Okay."

Elise thought for a moment. "I'll list the places that both Dad and Laura went in the last week and whom they saw."

"If what they have is contagious, only one had to be exposed."

"I've thought of that, but it's unlikely they have something contagious. Jeff, Tim, and you are okay. You were all exposed to Dad and Laura." When her mother made a face, Elise added, "Okay. We can keep track of the places they went separately in case any of you become sick later on."

"That makes more sense. It'll be less likely we'll miss something."

Elise saw a flashing light on the telephone. "Better check the messages."

"Okay." Sharon reached for the phone. "Why don't you have a look at their client profiles? They're on the computer."

"How do I get to them?"

Sharon pointed to an icon on the computer desktop. "Double-click on this. It'll bring up all the files. They're searchable by client name, location, and date. You can also browse through them."

"What's the password?"

"Bonanza. I'll bet you can figure out where that came from."

"I used to love to sit next to Dad when I was a kid and watch the *Bonanza* reruns. That show was a favorite of his."

"I bought him the DVDs."

Elise chuckled. "Lucky for you. Now you can see them whenever you want."

Sharon punched in the numbers to get to voice mail. "Fourteen messages. All left since Tuesday night." She jotted notes on a pad then checked the caller ID list.

"Anything interesting?" Elise asked when Sharon put the receiver down.

"A few new inquiries about houses. The rest just follow-up calls." Sharon ran her finger down the list. "The Lenz woman called. She'll be here at nine instead of ten. I would've liked to reschedule her to next week, but unfortunately, her phone number doesn't show up."

"Anyway, nine's better than ten. I'll be able to get to the hospital earlier. Anything else?"

Looking at the list, Sharon added, "These names aren't familiar to me: Babish, Graham Brown, Theresa Rothe, and Gladys Stiegl." Sharon shook her head. "I take that back. I know Brown. He's a lawyer. And Tim called too." Sharon handed the paper to Elise. "I'd better get back to Theresa Rothe today. She said she's changed her mind about selling her home and wants to cancel the listing."

Elise leaned back in her chair staring at the ceiling. She tried to sort out the best way to go about things.

Sharon picked up the desk calendar and began working her

way through the pages. "This shouldn't take very long. Then we can get started on client profiles."

"We have to figure out what to ask everyone," Elise said. "It's going to be tricky to get information from people without alarming them."

"If something's out there that'll make them sick, people have to know," Sharon snapped.

"Sure, if it turns out there's something to tell them."

A little while later Elise asked, "Do you remember Matt Merano?"

"Of course. He had such a crush on you."

"Are you serious? We were just good friends." Elise smiled.

"After you left, he asked about you for months."

"You never said anything."

"There was no reason to."

"I was thinking of calling him for some advice," Elise said. "He's had lots of experience conducting police investigations. Maybe he can give us some pointers on how to figure this out."

"Didn't you know he's not a policeman anymore?"

"No? What happened?"

"He became a private investigator around the time he got married. I didn't realize you'd lost touch with him."

Elise found it amusing to think Matt might've once had a crush on her. She'd always liked him a lot but more as a brother than a boyfriend. "Last time I spoke to Matt was when I ran out of Dad's party four years ago. We talked in the parking lot. He saw how upset I was and tried to calm me down. He was very nice to me."

She thought back to the night of her father's fiftieth birthday party. At the time, she was in her last year of medical school in Philadelphia and had come back to Guilford for the celebration. The Guilford Firehouse was decorated with bright streamers. Arthur Penman, the father of her deceased classmate,

Steve, walked to the podium to do his part in "roasting" her father. Elise remembered the incident as clearly as if it had just happened. She felt a knot developing in her stomach. *Would she ever get over that night?*

Arthur Penman had been drinking. His speech slurred as he went on and on about her father's taxes—how you could judge a man by his taxes. Elise recalled how surprised she had been to see everyone laughing at the drivel. At the time, she thought many people were tipsy judging by all the empty wine and beer bottles around. She hadn't found Arthur's remarks funny.

The expression on Arthur's face changed. "Rick's a good father. Even though he's the father of a murderer." He'd pointed to her. "His prized daughter murdered my only son. She abandoned him when he needed her." Penman then sobbed, "Am I still a father, if my only child is dead?"

A hush came over the room. The audience seemed to be waiting for a humorous punch line. They squirmed in their seats. All they got was more ranting from a disturbed man.

Elise remembered her face flushing. How many people in the room knew of Steve's suicide years back and that Arthur's deep sadness was behind his bizarre behavior? If not, they would have had no idea what was happening.

Arthur's sobs had reverberated in the microphone. Her father stepped up to the podium, wrapped his arm around Arthur's shoulder and said, "That's enough for now. Let's give someone else a chance at the mike." Turning to Elise's mother, he fired, "Sharon, please come up here."

Her mother, arms outstretched in an expression of bewilderment, had hurried to the podium as her father eased Arthur down. Sharon signaled to the DJ. "Some music, please. Time to dance. We'll get back to the roast in just a short while."

People got up from their seats. Whispers broke the hush in the room. Her father struggled with Arthur, who continued to spew hateful remarks about Elise. Only when Mrs. Penman took hold of her husband's arm, did he stop raving. Elise was sure Steve's mother hadn't seen her standing close by. People openly gawked at Elise. Humiliation overwhelmed her.

Mrs. Penman apologized to Elise's parents. "Arthur still hasn't found a way to cope with losing Steve." She took Sharon's hand. "Please tell Elise, Arthur didn't mean what he said. I'm so ashamed. I can't face her to tell her myself." A sob escaped. "I'll call you tomorrow." Mrs. Penman steered her husband through the crowd and out the front of the hall. Elise could still hear Arthur Penman shouting her name as they left.

Elise decided to leave the party, to leave Guilford and never come back. She grabbed her purse, mouthed to her parents she was leaving, and headed for the rear door.

Matt intercepted her on the way to her car.

"Please wait up," he'd called out to her. She'd faced him and saw the sadness in his eyes. "For what it's worth," he said, "everybody knows what Penman said is pure garbage. If anyone is responsible for what happened to Steve, it certainly isn't you. Steve's father was selfish and distant. Steve had turned to him for help but his father pushed him away."

Elise remembered her words to Matt. "Thanks for trying. I have to get out of here. This will always hang over me if I'm in Guilford." She'd reached for Matt's hands. "You were always special to me. I hope you get everything you want out of life." She let go of his hands and opened her arms to give him a quick hug goodbye. He had bent down and kissed her, his mouth afire. She broke away as gently as she could. "Be happy. I'm going to try to be, and I'm going to stay as far away from here as I can get."

"Elise, please remember you can always count on me." He had remained by her side until she'd convinced him she was capable of driving. He walked her to her car. As she got behind the wheel she thought she saw tears in his eyes.

Over the past four years Elise had replayed that evening many times in her mind. Why hadn't she thought more about that last conversation with Matt and his reaction?

The sound of her mother's voice jolted her.

"You do know Matt's wife died, don't you?" Sharon said, without looking up.

"I had no idea. You'd told me that he married Kara Parsons, but I don't remember you saying anything much about them after that. What happened to her?"

"Flu. Everyone was shocked. She was so healthy. Only twenty-seven."

"It could have been H1N1, a strain of the swine flu. It's often the cause when young, healthy people die of the flu. Matt must have been devastated."

Sharon nodded. "He took it very badly."

"I can imagine. I'm going to call him today."

Elise stood and walked around the desk. She watched over her mother's shoulder as Sharon resumed what she'd been doing.

"I see Dad didn't work last weekend."

Sharon looked up. "It was Halloween, and both he and Laura took it off. It's usually a slow weekend. We had a relaxing couple of days."

"Do anything special?"

"No. Just worked around the house. Saturday night we drove over to Culbertsville for dinner to celebrate Dad's birthday."

"Did he have any problem with the dinner?"

"Problem? Like food poisoning?"

"That or anything else. I'm just trying to see if we've overlooked anything obvious."

"I can't think of anything. It was a delicious dinner. We both felt fine."

"Did Dad tell you I called him on Monday? To wish him a happy birthday."

"No. I'm surprised he didn't."

"It was about eight-thirty in the morning, your time. I'd just come off overnight call and had a little free time before morning rounds. He sounded happy to hear from me. Pretty excited about the feature article *The Sentinel* had done on K&B."

"Yeah, it was a good article. Laura's idea to drum up some business."

"Come to think of it, while we were talking, he put me on hold to take another call. He said it was someone who'd seen the article."

"Little did he know what would happen in the next couple of days."

"That brings me back to Monday evening. I know we talked about it on the phone Tuesday night, but I want to be sure I got everything straight."

"What didn't you understand?"

"You said that things went sour Monday evening. That Dad was upset when he got home. Right?"

"Yes, very upset."

"Something must've happened during the day to change his mood. He was upbeat when I spoke to him in the morning."

"His mood was foul at six o'clock when he got home. The first thing he did was reach for the bottle of gin, pour half a glass, and start sipping."

"I don't remember Dad ever drinking much."

"That's why I asked him what was going on. He just stared back at me without answering. Told me to stop nagging and walked away."

"That doesn't sound at all like Dad. Didn't you try to find out what was wrong?"

"He wouldn't talk. I thought of calling Laura, but didn't want to stir up things further. We are all entitled to an occasional bad day, even if it's on our birthday."

Elise sighed. "Come to think of it, Jeff said something was troubling Laura on Monday night, too."

Sharon nodded.

"Anything else unusual happen that night?"

"Not that I recall." Sharon tapped her fingers on her lips. "A woman called Dad right after he got home. The agency calls are forwarded to our house after hours, and I answered the phone and handed it to him. I heard him set a time for them to meet in the morning."

"Do you think she had anything to do with his being upset?"

Sharon shrugged. "I doubt it. Probably just a new client."

"Go on."

"He said he didn't want dinner. I left him alone. Around ten I knocked on the door of the den. He said through the door I should go to bed. He'd be up soon. He sounded a little better to me. I was really tired, so I went upstairs. When I awoke in the morning, he was gone. His side of the bed hadn't been slept in."

"Did you call him at work on Tuesday?"

"Yes, briefly from the office of one of my customers. I still take freelance programming jobs. Dad was expecting a client to arrive any moment. He sounded okay."

"Has he ever acted like that before?"

Sharon shook her head. "I didn't know what to make of it. I just decided to let it go and give him a chance to work things out. I figured he'd explain when he was ready."

"Was Dad under financial strain?"

"Not that I know of."

"Any special problems at work?"

"Not really. With Laura back, things were much easier for him."

"Is he into anything new?"

"What do you mean?"

"Oh, I don't know: clubs, new hobbies or interests, new friends?"

"Nothing, as far as I know."

Elise nodded. "Okay, how was Tuesday night?"

"He acted the same way as on Monday night. Maybe he

25

kept it together during the day, but the strange behavior resurfaced by the time he got home. He started on the gin minutes after he walked in the door. I made up my mind I had to talk to him." Sharon looked down at her hands and up at Elise. She took a deep breath.

"What is it, Mom?"

"I haven't told you everything. Dad made me promise. I feel like I'm betraying him."

"If you know something that might help us figure out what happened to him, now's the time to tell me." Elise kept her voice polite but firm.

"Tuesday night I pressed him about what was wrong. After a lot of prodding, he finally said, 'I'm in a little trouble. But I'll work it out.' He looked at me with pleading eyes and added, 'Keep this to yourself.'"

"Did he say what kind of *trouble*?"

Sharon shook her head.

"Tell me again everything you remember about that night."

"When he got home he seemed pretty agitated, just like the night before. He went right to the den."

"Where were you?"

"I stayed in the den with him for a while. After he told me about the trouble and was adamant that I not ask him any questions, I went to the kitchen."

"Was he hostile or just upset with what had happened?"

"Just upset."

"What did you say to each other?"

"Not much. A little later he came into the kitchen. He said he wasn't feeling well and was going to lie down. I told him I'd let him know when dinner was ready."

"Anything else?"

"Twenty minutes later I went upstairs to get him. I found him lying on the bathroom floor in a puddle of vomit. I checked for his pulse then turned him on his side and called nine-one-one. The

EMTs took us to the Emergency Room at Clearview."

"How was he while you were waiting for the EMTs?"

"He drifted in and out of consciousness. Every so often he would start shaking badly and vomit. By the time we left the house, he couldn't have had much left in his stomach."

"How did he look?"

"Bad. Pale and strange-looking."

"Did he speak at all?"

"A few words here and there. But they didn't make sense. One moment he had chills, the next he was sweating profusely. He was uncoordinated. He could never have stood on his own."

"Do you remember anything he said?"

"No, his sentences started okay but quickly turned to gibberish. At first I thought he'd just had way too much to drink. Maybe that he had alcohol poisoning."

"I understand why you thought that."

"It really scared me. I could hardly wait for the EMTs to arrive. They started an IV and took him out on a stretcher."

"One last question. Did you notice any irritation on his hand?"

"His hand?"

"The right hand."

"His right hand?"

Elise nodded.

"I saw him scratching his hand when he first came home, but I didn't make too much of it. I remember telling him money might be coming his way." Sharon thought for a moment. "Something was coming his way for sure, but it wasn't money," she muttered.

"I don't get it."

Sharon looked puzzled for a moment then smiled. "Oh, there's an old saying that if your palm itches, you'll come into some money."

Elise nodded. "But did you actually see the top of his hand, not only his palm?"

"I guess not. He didn't make an issue of it, so I didn't pay attention to it."

Seeing her mother's agitation increasing as the conversation went on, Elise ended it. "We can talk about this later, Mom. I'll need to get into Laura's desk."

"The key's taped under the inkwell. Her office door is open."

WHEN Elise and Sharon finished compiling the list of names and places, Sharon put on her sweater and hugged Elise goodbye. "Call me if you change your mind and want me to pick you up."

"Thanks, but I'm sure I can get a taxi. While I'm waiting for the Lenz woman to show up, I'll check on my patients in Scottsdale and also try to reach Matt."

Elise felt an excitement and trepidation saying Matt's name. The real test of how well she could cope with being back in Guilford would soon begin.

FOUR

ELISE found Matt's website and jotted down his direct line. While she was anxious to offer him her condolences and to enlist his help, she worried he might bring up their encounter on the night of her father's party four years ago. She wasn't sure how she'd handle that.

After a few minutes, she mustered the courage to call him. He answered on the third ring.

"Merano."

Despite the queasy feeling in her stomach, she projected confidence when she spoke. "Good morning, Matt, it's a ghost from your past: Elise Bell."

"Elise. Well, I'll be damned. It's been a long time."

He sounded happy to hear from her. She felt relief. "Yes. It has been."

"You were really upset the last time I saw you. I—"

"It's good to hear your voice."

"Are you in town?"

"Yes. I came back because my father's in Clearview Hospital." Elise paused. "I just learned about your wife. How are you doing?"

"Hanging in there. You didn't know?"

"I had no idea before today. My mother told me when I said I was going to call you."

"It's almost a year now."

"My mother said it was the flu."

"Yeah. Respiratory failure in the end. It took me for a loop. Kara was in tip-top shape, went to the gym all the time, ate healthy."

"Do you mind if I ask what happened?"

"It's okay. Right after Thanksgiving she complained about some aches and pains, said she was nauseous. I didn't think anything of it at first. But then she started coughing a lot and became short of breath just walking around the house. She didn't want to go, but when she developed a fever I took her to the hospital. Her breathing got so bad they had to put her on a ventilator. It was horrible. The doctors tried hard but they couldn't save her."

Elise groped for words. She said softly, "I'm so sorry."

"You know, I still dream she's alive. Crazy, isn't it?"

"Everyone has those kinds of dreams. I did when Steve Penman died." Steve's name slipped out of her mouth before she realized it had.

"Steve." Matt sighed. "We've lost a lot of friends from high school."

"Yeah," Elise lamented.

Matt's voice strengthened. "So how's the doctor's life these days?"

"I'm working hard as a resident at Marivista Hospital in Scottsdale. Everything's going well in my life. At least it was until my father took sick. He and his business partner, Laura Kirby, were admitted to Clearview, my father on Tuesday night, Laura the next morning."

"How are they doing?"

"Not well, I'm afraid." She filled him in.

"I'm sorry to hear that."

"It's not clear yet if my father and Laura's illnesses are related, but I think they could be. That's why I called you."

"Wait. Do you think someone tried to kill them?"

"I'm not sure."

"What do the docs say happened?"

"They don't really know what's going on with my father. They've ruled out the usual medical causes."

"Had Laura ever had heart problems before?"

"Yes. She had a heart attack in July."

"So, what's suspicious about a second heart attack?"

"Nothing, unless this episode was triggered by something external."

"What do you mean? Do you have anything specific in mind?"

"Right now it's mostly gut feeling but I've learned to trust my gut. There are some things that bother me."

"Like what?"

"According to Laura's son, Jeff, Laura was unusually jittery Monday night and acted strangely."

"How old is the son?"

"Eighteen."

"Losing a parent is tough, especially at that age. Maybe he's just having trouble accepting his mother's death and looking for an explanation."

"She gave him an insurance policy in case something happened to her. Let's assume she had a reason to be worried."

"Is there anyone who might want to harm her or your father?"

"Not that I know of."

"One of the first things to do is look for a motive."

"Yeah, I know. I thought you'd say that."

"Let's back up for a moment. What makes you think the same thing put both of them in the hospital?"

"Timing and both being very upset beforehand." She

related what her mother had told her about her father's behavior. "When my mother pressed him on Tuesday evening, he reluctantly admitted he was in some kind of trouble but wouldn't say what it was. Jeff told us his mother seemed scared. Laura wasn't neurotic and neither is my father."

"So you think something bad may have happened that upset both of them?"

"It's possible. I spoke to my dad Monday morning. He was in a good mood. According to my mother, by the evening, that had completely changed."

"I remember your Dad from when he coached our middle school soccer team. Nothing rattled him. We all liked him a lot."

"On Monday and Tuesday evenings he acted strangely. My mother said he drank a lot. That's unusual for him. When he was admitted to the hospital on Tuesday night, at first they suspected alcohol poisoning."

"That didn't pan out?"

"Tests ruled it out. Dad's blood alcohol level was up, but not high enough to explain his condition. He awoke briefly. They pumped him with lots of fluid. Got the alcohol out of his system. The doctors decided something else had to be going on."

"Bottom line—you want me to look into this?"

"Yes. Originally, I thought I'd be able to figure it all out by myself. That all I had to do was check into where they'd been recently and whom they'd seen. I'm in their office now. I've gone through their records, but I have no idea what to do next. I want to hire you to investigate and to protect us if need be."

The line went quiet for a few moments. Then Matt asked, "Are they going to autopsy Mrs. Kirby?"

"It's underway. We should have preliminary results pretty soon. For now, I need to know if you'll help us."

"Sure, Elise. I'll do everything I can. I've got to be honest with you. I might not be able to come up with much." Matt cleared his throat. "It seems to me, it could turn out there are simple medical reasons for their illnesses, nothing more."

"But what if that's not the case? I don't want to chance it."

"Okay. Have you spoken to the police?"

"No. They're not involved—at least, not yet." Elise wiped beads of sweat from her forehead with a tissue. "I may have jumped the gun by calling you, but I don't want to risk missing anything that could be important later on. Instinct tells me we can't just rely on the police anyway."

"Why do you say that?"

"Bad memories from how the Guilford police handled Steve Penman's suicide."

While Elise couldn't see the expression on Matt's face, she interpreted his lack of protest to mean he agreed with her. She imagined him shifting in his seat debating how to respond.

"Tell you what," he finally said, "come to my office so we can talk some more. Hold on for a second, I'll set up a time for us to meet."

After a couple of minutes, during which Elise heard muffled sounds of pages flipping and people talking in the background, Matt came back on the line. "It looks like I'm booked all day, but I can see you tonight after six. How's that?"

"I'll be there. Is there anything I should bring?"

Without hesitation, Matt said, "I'll need to look at where your father and Mrs. Kirby went last week, whom they saw. And quiz your mother again about possible enemies."

"Mom and I gathered quite a bit of information this morning. Fortunately, both my father and Laura kept good records."

"Okay. Don't speak to anyone about this until after we meet tonight."

"Actually, we planned to call a few of their clients, but I wanted your advice on what to say to them. For business reasons, we have to get back to them pretty quickly."

"We'll review what you found then decide what needs to be

done. I have several really good guys working for me. I'll start by assigning two: Jerry Sanders and Al Jenkins. We served together on the Guilford Police Force. They can start tomorrow morning. We'll handle the calls."

"Before they do anything, I'll want them to talk to my mother. She's familiar with everything going on at K&B. She'll be able to advise them and show them any files they need to see."

"Okay."

"Thanks, Matt. I really appreciate this."

She gave him her and her mother's phone numbers, discussed fees, and hung up. She then called the medical resident in Scottsdale who was covering for her and was relieved to find everything was going smoothly with her patients.

Elise looked around Laura's office, not quite sure what she hoped to find. She had already gone through Laura's calendar and checked off items versus the master list.

In the top center drawer there were rubber-banded piles of small white papers with handwritten notes scribbled on them. Elise felt uncomfortable as she began reading Laura's notes even though all were business-related: names, addresses, and budgets.

None of the notes seemed pertinent. She could always go back through them later if anything popped up to warrant it.

Elise spent another half hour going through Laura's office. By the time she checked her watch, it was a quarter to nine. She realized Stacy Lenz would be arriving soon. She decided to arrange for a taxi to take her to the hospital.

Just as Elise finished speaking with the taxi dispatcher, she heard a cough from the direction of the door. She looked up to see a woman with long blonde hair, standing in the doorway, sipping coffee from a paper cup.

Elise assumed the woman was Stacy Lenz. She was approximately Elise's age and about the same height, but fairer in complexion and a few pounds heavier. She wore a stylish charcoal suit. While she had a sweet smile, there was something unnerving about it. Elise wondered how long she'd been watching her and listening to her conversation.

"Hello. I didn't mean to startle you," the woman said. "The door in the hallway was unlocked so I walked in. I heard you talking so I headed to your office and waited. I didn't want to disturb you. I have an appointment with Mr. Bell. Is he in?"

Elise came out from behind the desk. "I'm his daughter, Elise Bell. You must be Stacy Lenz. Please have a seat." Elise pulled out a chair for her.

The woman nodded and sat down.

Elise went behind Laura's desk. "Unfortunately, my father can't meet with you this morning. We weren't able to contact you to let you know."

"Oh, that's too bad. I was anxious to see what he found for me. What about Mrs. Kirby?"

"I'm afraid she's not available either." Elise paused and then made a quick decision to add, "How well do you and Mrs. Kirby know each other?"

"I'm a new client and just met her briefly on Tuesday. Nice lady. She's also trying to find some houses and condos for me. I live in New York City now with a friend but have started a lab job in New Jersey. I really hate to leave the city, but I need to move closer to work."

Elise took a deep breath. "I have some very sad news about Mrs. Kirby." Elise looked down for a moment. "She passed away yesterday evening."

"Oh, I'm so sorry to hear that. What happened?"

"It appears to have been a heart attack."

"That's really terrible."

"Yes. She was a very close friend." Elise folded her hands together and sighed. "We're extremely upset, as you can well imagine."

Stacy nodded and bowed her head.

"If you'll give me your number, I'll ask my father to

contact you when he returns to the office."

Stacy sat silently for a moment before speaking. "I don't mean to be insensitive, but do you have any idea when he'll be able to see me?"

"Probably sometime in the middle of next week."

"That should work. I'll call him then. I hope he's doing okay under the circumstances."

"I'll tell him to expect your call. I'm sorry you had to make the trip here for nothing."

Stacy stood. With some hesitation she said, "I hope you won't think I'm nosy, but I couldn't help overhearing you call for a taxi to Clearview Hospital."

"Yes." Elise stared back at her.

"I'm going past there. I can drop you off. That way, I won't feel bad I inconvenienced you."

"That's nice of you, but my taxi's already on the way." Elise rose and gently motioned for Stacy to make her way to the door. "Here, let me take your cup," Elise offered. She placed the empty cup in the wastebasket under Laura's desk.

"Really, Ms. Bell, I'd be glad to drop you at the hospital. I'm sure you could cancel the cab. They're always late starting out."

Elise deliberated for a moment. "Okay. Thank you." She called and cancelled the cab.

On the way out to the parking lot, Elise asked Stacy, "Have you been in this part of the country long?"

"I moved from Indiana a couple of years ago. When I finished graduate school."

"Do you like living in a big city like New York?"

"I love the excitement and hustle of the city and am sorry to have to leave."

"You'll find things a lot quieter out here."

Stacy smiled. "This is my car." She unlocked the doors of the white BMW 530 sedan. Elise got in on the passenger side.

A beep startled Elise. "What a weird sound."

"It's a custom security system. The car cost me a lot. I'd hate to have it stolen." She held up crossed fingers.

As Elise fastened her seatbelt, she realized she was more on edge than she'd thought.

Stacy started the car and pulled out of the parking lot.

Elise observed the deluxe instrument panel. On her salary as a medical resident, this price-range car wasn't something she'd be able to afford anytime soon, not that she'd ever spend so much on transportation.

During the ride, Stacy talked non-stop. When she tried to prod Elise about her father, Elise changed the subject. "How did you happen to select K&B Realty? There are several real estate agencies in Guilford."

"The write-up in the local paper. The article was quite flattering."

By the time they'd arrived at the hospital, Elise knew more about Stacy's life than she felt she needed to or wanted to. On the other hand, Elise had put to rest her uneasy feelings about the woman. She was quite surprised how charming and outgoing Stacy had proven to be, so unlike the other lab scientists Elise knew.

"HOW'S Dad doing?" Elise said as she entered her father's room.

"Not much change, I'm afraid."

Elise checked the monitors and IVs then examined her father's head, neck, and hands before pulling up a chair next to her mother at his bedside.

"Did you finish everything you planned to?" her mother asked.

"Just about. I also called Matt and made an appointment to talk to him at six. I'll need a ride home later to borrow Dad's car."

"Sure. Did the Lenz woman show up?"

"Yes. Strange woman. She overheard me calling a taxi and

insisted on bringing me here."

"That was nice of her. Why did you call her 'strange'?"

"She seemed much too interested in what I was doing and where I was going. Talked a lot. But I have to admit, by the time we said goodbye, she'd won me over."

"Did you tell her about Laura?"

"Yes. She asked for Laura when I said Dad couldn't keep the appointment."

"What was her reaction?"

"Nothing special. She didn't know Laura, so there wasn't much for her to say.

"Is she young?"

"Late twenties, I'd guess. Well-dressed, expensive clothes, expensive car. She drove a white BMW, a 530."

"A 530? So?"

"Let's say—seventy thousand dollars-worth of car."

"Oh. Well, if she can afford a car like that, she sounds like a good prospect. Where did you leave things with her?"

"She's going to call Dad next week."

"I hope he's recovered by then."

Elise nodded. "Has Dr. Fletcher been here today?"

"Not yet."

"I'm going to ask the nurse to page him to find out when he can stop by to give us an update."

THE young man sat for a moment to quiet his nerves. He rehearsed what he'd say one more time then called Clearview Hospital. When an operator answered, he said in a deep voice, "I'd like to know the condition of one of your patients, a Mr. Bell."

"Are you family?" the operator asked.

"I'm a cousin from out-of-state."

"Well, I can put you through to his room. His wife is accepting calls for him."

"No, I don't want to disturb them."

"Would you like me to connect you with the nurses' station on the floor? They can help you."

"Uh, no, I'll call Mrs. Bell at home later. One more thing, I also wanted to ask about Mrs. Laura Kirby."

"Let me put you on hold for a moment." When the woman came back on the line, she said, "The family has asked us to direct calls from family to the Kirby home."

Before hanging up, he asked, "Is Mr. Bell still in room one-fifty? I want to make sure my card and flowers reach him."

"No, he's in two-twelve."

Immediately after disconnecting, the caller entered another number.

A man picked up on the first ring. "Yeah."

"It looks like one's down. The other one's not taking calls so must not be doing too well." He related what he had found out.

"Damn it! I can't trust her or her boyfriend to finish anything. We'll have to handle this ourselves. I'll pick you up on Saturday morning. It will be easier to do what we need to when there's a skeleton staff on the weekend." The line went dead before the caller could say a word in reply.

FIVE

AROUND one o'clock, two cars drove along Hillcrest Road. After passing the intersection with Passaic Road, the first car, a blue Camry, turned right onto an asphalt driveway. Moments later the second car, a white BMW, swung off the main road at the same spot. It kept to the right past the fork in the road and proceeded onto a rough and winding crushed stone driveway enclosed by large boulders and tall pine trees. At the end of the long driveway, a large white frame colonial with a black shingle roof stood in a wide cleared area. The car stopped in front of the garage, and Stacy Lenz got out.

She unlocked the front door and walked into the living room. A white pillow leaning against the arm of the gold velvet sofa caught her eye, and she picked it up. When she spotted the straw-colored hairs on the white pillowcase, she grimaced. She hurled the pillow back on to the sofa and rushed across the room to the hallway.

She knocked on the door of the studio. "Grigor, it's me,"

"Come in."

She pushed the door open and stood in the doorway. "A blue Camry turned into the driveway ahead of me. It went to the house next door. Have you seen anyone walking around outside?"

The tall, slim man, dressed in a painter's smock over jeans, put his brush down on the stool next to his easel and slowly turned toward her. "No."

Her mouth dropped open when she saw his face. His left eye was swollen half-closed, his forehead and cheeks covered with bloody scratches.

"What happened to you, Grigor?" She rushed to him, gently caressed his face, and smoothed his coarse blond hair.

"When I got here, Sergei was spread out on the sofa waiting for me."

"I saw the filthy pillow he left there."

"He started cursing me, saying he should never have brought me here from Ukraine. All the money he wasted on me . . . sending me for training. That I'm just a—"

"He's an idiot. Without your paintings, what would he have to sell? What set him off this time?"

"He asked if those people that broke in here are taken care of. The real estate agents. I said everything was under control. Then he starts punching me. He screams not to lie to him." Grigor stared at her. "What happened? You said—"

"The woman's dead. The guy's circling the drain. There's nothing to worry about."

"What went wrong?"

"No matter. I will finish the guy off," she snapped. "Neither of them would've talked anyway. I'm positive of that. I watched the video playback very carefully and listened to their every word. They were too scared. They did not want to bring attention to themselves." She took a breath. "Sergei's paranoid. So I did what he wanted. The guy's as good as dead."

Grigor gestured wildly. "He called me a careless drunk, smacked me and said I could have ruined the whole operation with the big payoff only days away."

"Couldn't you have stopped him? You're bigger than he is and younger." She struggled to hold her cool. *Don't yell at him.* If only she'd seen the video surveillance before Sergei. She would have taken care of the matter quietly. Sergei would never have known."

"Before he left, he tried to brush off that he'd given me a beating. Said he'd make it up to me after the job is done. Yeah, sure. I had it with that *svoloch*."

"We have to play it smart. The deliveries are set for Sunday night, and by Monday morning, none of this will matter. Be patient."

Grigor slouched. "You know I hate violence. That swine pointed a gun at me. I thought he was going to kill me."

She didn't like the pain she saw in his eyes, the crystal blue eyes she'd fell in love with the day they'd met in that little restaurant in Manhattan. He had appeared strong and confident. If only she'd known the truth. She should have taken a clue when his eyes misted as he told her he'd sworn off violence after seeing a young child caught in a shootout years before in Kiev. Since that day, he claimed he hadn't raised a fist or touched a weapon. She was sure there was more to it than he admitted.

Men always sought her out, but she had never before felt such a strong instant attraction. She went with Grigor when he invited her to his apartment for a drink. He'd told her he restored paintings. He bragged his unique techniques set his work above anyone in the field in the entire world. She'd believed his every word. When he introduced her to Sergei, she found out just how Grigor made his money. But by then, she didn't care what he did; she only cared about being with him.

Grigor's ranting brought her back to the present.

"If you don't protect yourself, the next time you may not be so lucky." The wounded look in his eyes made her stop scolding him. "I need to find out how much Sergei told any of the bosses about those Realtors. Then once this deal is over, I promise you we'll get rid of Sergei. He won't get another chance to hurt you."

Grigor looked down at the floor.

She took a deep breath, and exhaled slowly as she paced back and forth. "An accidental overdose, that's it. He's still shooting up, isn't he?" One thing she'd never do is become addicted to drugs. She despised anyone who had.

He nodded. "Sergei says he's not, but he hides his stuff in the towel rack in the bathroom. He shoots up there because there are no cameras."

"What he needs is some special heroin."

"That could get us in hot water with the big bosses," he muttered.

She stared at Grigor and said nothing for a moment. "Those bosses Sergei always threatens us with, whoever they are, if they knew he was into drugs, he'd be dead already." She ran her hand across her throat. "He's dispensable. They'll close their eyes as long as they get their cut and nothing points back to them."

"I still think we take a big chance to kill him." Fear resonated in Grigor's voice.

Her temper rose. She waited until she calmed down before saying more. "Look, it's time for us to leave here. With the money we've saved, and with what we get on Monday, there'll be enough for us to go anywhere we want. We'll get a new start. There will be no one telling us what to do or when to do it."

Grigor slowly smiled. "That will be good."

"Sergei makes the delivery Sunday night and comes back here afterwards, so we'll take care of him then." Stacy nodded.

"Where will you get the dope?"

"I have my sources. You needn't worry about anything. Leave this all to me."

She watched as Grigor wiped his forehead and tossed the tissue into the wastebasket. He wrapped his arms around her and softly kissed her lips. "*Dorogaya*, I hate that loser almost as much as I love you. Forgive me. Sergei's gotten into my soul and poisoned it."

"Relax." She gently freed herself from his embrace. "I'll

take care of everything. Have I ever let you down?" The sound of her own words comforted her. She threw Grigor an air kiss as she inched away from him. "My love, I promise you it'll all work out. Let me go and erase the surveillance video, and then show me where Sergei keeps his stuff."

SIX

It took Elise less than twenty minutes to drive from Clearview Hospital to Matt's offices.

Merano Enterprises occupied the east wing of the first floor of a new professional building in the center of the business district of Morrisville. From the upscale look of the building, Elise assumed Matt's business did well.

She parked in one of the customer spaces in front of his entrance, rang the doorbell, and was immediately buzzed in.

Elise told the receptionist she had a six o'clock appointment. The young woman gave her a friendly smile and said Matt would be right out.

He emerged through the door on the right and walked over to her. Elise was surprised to feel a tingle run through her. He looked the same as she remembered: tall, fit, with a shy smile, mouth full of white, straight teeth, and a dimple in the center of his broad chin. His thick, dark brown hair looked freshly cut. He wore a light blue shirt and khakis.

His face brightened the moment their eyes met. He opened his arms and warmly embraced her. The minute his hands touched her shoulders, it brought back memories of his kiss goodbye that night four years ago.

After a few moments Matt released her and stepped back. "Let me look at you."

She turned around slowly, modeling for him.

"Boy, you look terrific. You haven't changed a bit except for the hair. It's not as long as it used to be."

She ran her fingers through her hair. "I keep it short for low maintenance. With my hours at the hospital, I have to save time wherever I can."

"When do you finish your training?"

"I complete my residency next May, but I may be doing a chief resident year."

"In Scottsdale?"

"Most likely there. At Marivista Hospital. That's where I am now."

"Well, what then?"

"Not sure yet. Maybe specialize."

Matt nodded. "Let's not stand out here. Come inside to my office. I know you're anxious to talk about your father's situation then get back to the hospital."

"Thanks, Matt. I appreciate your making time to see me today."

Elise followed him, pausing briefly to admire the photographs on the paneled walls along the corridor leading to his office. "Looks like you've done a lot of traveling."

"Yeah, that part's been fantastic. Actually, it's one of the reasons I went into business for myself—so I could go where I pleased, when I pleased. Kara and I did a lot in the short time we had together. If I'd stayed on the police force, none of it would have been possible."

They entered Matt's office, and he pulled out a chair for her. Once she was seated, he walked behind the massive mahogany desk. Elise watched as he eased himself into a black leather executive chair, and as he did, his eyes briefly focused on a gold-framed wedding photo of his late wife and him.

"Nice place you have here," Elise said.

"It's my office and my home."

"What do you mean?"

"After Kara died, I gave up our apartment and put a sofa bed, a TV, and a microwave in the back office here. I did it to save some money while I decide where I really want to live. It's taken me more time to decide than I expected."

"That can't be too comfortable."

"It's okay for now. It puts a snag in my quest to become a gourmet cook, but I don't have that much free time, anyway. I spend a lot of hours on the job."

Elise nodded and chuckled, not sure how serious he was about the gourmet part, but Matt had revealed a lot more about where he was in his life than he might have suspected. She shifted her attention to the rectangular brass paperweight, which had Double-Em in quotation marks on it. She picked it up. "Seeing this brings back many memories. Does anyone call you Double-Em any more, the way they did in high school?"

"Nope. Hardly anyone still around who'd remember that old nickname."

She put the paperweight down.

Matt smiled and reached for a notebook and pen then focused his eyes on Elise. "Before we get started, I thought you might have questions about my business. Is there anything you'd like to know?"

"I wondered what type of cases you usually handle."

Matt leaned back in his chair. "Guilford hasn't changed too much over the time you've been away. Our population is at fourteen thousand now, and we still have a low crime rate compared to the surrounding Central Jersey towns. But we see some of everything. I've dealt with cheating husbands and wives, employee thefts, vandalism, robberies, drugs, cyber bullying, blackmail, and even the occasional homicide. We're the USA today." He smiled and moved forward in his chair. "Between my time on the Guilford police and my private cases, I've investigated most everything, and my solve rate is top-notch. You can check me out on the Internet and with the BBB." Matt stopped and smiled again. "I guess that's TMI."

"You've sold me. I'm ready to start now." She smiled. "I'm here because I'm unable to sort things out. I hoped to figure out what made my father and his partner sick. I thought I'd be able to put the pieces together. I do that kind of thing every day at the hospital when I make a diagnosis."

"So you thought my job's a snap," Matt said, pouting his lips.

"Well, I found out there's much more to detective work than I suspected. And I should leave it to the experts."

Matt's eyes twinkled. "That's why they pay me the big bucks. I wish." He laughed. "For sure, what I do isn't always straightforward. And it always takes a lot of digging and attention to details."

Elise folded her hands. "To tell you the truth, I don't even know where to go from here."

"Since we spoke earlier, have you figured out what you'd actually like me to do?"

"My father and Laura were afraid of something. As I said on the phone, he grudgingly admitted to my mother he was in trouble. But he refused to say what the trouble was. Maybe you can find out."

Matt fiddled with his pen. "Hmm. You realize that the trouble he referred to may have nothing to do with their illnesses."

"But, what if it does?" Elise sensed Matt thought she was way off track, that this was simply a medical situation, something for physicians to handle, not something that required a private detective.

"Okay, let's talk about this." Matt thought for a moment. "Here's a 'what if.' What if something is found in Laura's autopsy that suggests attempted murder? The police will be called in by the hospital. I could see a role for me then. Things with the police can move slowly, and you don't want the trail to get cold. I still have a few buddies with the Guilford police, so I'd be able to keep up with what they do."

"Okay." Elise relaxed a little.

"What we'd do then is check out your Dad and his partner. Maybe there's something you're not aware of? Maybe even something they weren't aware of? Does that make sense?"

"Of course."

"I've got to level with you. As I always warn my clients, you'll need to prepare yourself because if the police get involved, they're going to poke into everything."

"What do you mean?"

"First they'll look for someone who had a motive to harm your father and Laura. A lot of the time, it turns out the guilty parties are close relatives or friends. So the police will question your mother, family friends, and business associates. They'll look closely at Laura's son. They might go easy on you, since you don't live locally. I bet they'll go after your mother first." He paused. "I'm telling you this because no matter how much I caution families, they're always surprised at how the police act when they get involved."

Elise listened carefully and nodded. "Matt, I know I may be jumping the gun, but I'd like to proceed as if we knew there was a murder and an attempted murder. If we find out the cause is medical or accidental, or whatever, and no crime is involved, we can stop everything. I'll apologize for wasting your time."

"Okay, Elise. It's your dime. I'd wait, but if you want us to get started, we will."

"Thanks, Matt. That's a big relief for me." Elise debated for a moment and then decided to say more. "After working with patients for years, I've developed a certain instinct that tells me to keep looking—that there's something out of the ordinary behind the patient's illness. My instinct tells me that's what we're facing here and we need to keep looking."

Matt nodded. "Now, is there anything I should know before we go any further? I don't want to be hit by surprises down the road."

"We don't have any big secrets, at least none that I know of. As far as motive, I can't think of any reason anyone would want to harm either my father or Laura." Elise had to admit that living over two-thousand miles away from her parents and Laura for the last four years, she really didn't know much about their everyday lives at present, but she felt that nothing substantial had changed.

"Some of the most frequent motives behind murder are sex, money, revenge, and drugs. Think hard. Is there anything at all along those lines that might rouse police suspicions?"

Elise remained silent for a few moments and then said, "Well, there's one thing that may look suspicious, but I know it's not meaningful." She told him about the insurance policies."

Matt shook his head. "I don't think that's a problem. Having those kinds of policies is standard business practice. Your father wouldn't be viewed as a serious suspect for that alone. It would be a bit far-fetched for him to make himself deathly sick as a cover, unless his getting sick was an accident."

"I'm sure he had nothing to do with this. Anyway, my family has substantial assets so it wouldn't impact their lifestyle even if the business went under."

"What about jealousy?"

Elise dismissed that as an issue.

Matt bowed his head and then looked up at Elise. "Sometimes it's hard to imagine our parents in certain situations, but there are affairs even in marriages where things look fine on the surface. Stuff happens when people work closely together."

"Not here. My mother loved Laura. If she had the slightest suspicion something was going on between Laura and my father,

I'd have gotten wind of it. Anyway, Laura and Tim Dixon, K&B's accountant, were engaged earlier this year."

"Do you know much about Tim?"

"He's been a family friend for as long as I can remember. He lost his wife to cancer years ago. They had no children."

"I'd like to talk to him."

Elise nodded. "That shouldn't be a problem."

"Any chance your mother is involved with someone?"

"That never occurred to me." Elise sat up straight in her chair and adjusted her earring while pondering the possibility. "I seriously doubt it."

"At any rate, you need to prepare her for a police investigation. Let her know they'll scrutinize her private life. Find out if she's keeping anything from you."

"I'll talk with her."

Matt rubbed his forehead. "What kind of kid is Laura's son?"

"What are you thinking?"

"Has he ever been in any trouble? Any involvement at all with drugs? It's a pretty widespread problem in high schools these days."

"No drug issues that I know off. Jeff's a great kid. He and Laura were very close."

Matt drew his lips tightly together and nodded slowly. "Something occurred to me. This is probably obvious, but have the doctors contacted the CDC and the health department to check for any outbreaks?"

"My father's doctor has. So far, he hasn't learned of anything."

"Let me know if he does." Matt jotted a few notes on his pad and then looked up. "For now, we'll start some background searches. You said you compiled a list of the places your father and Mrs. Kirby went in the last week."

Elise gave Matt the list.

He looked it over. "To start, I'll get Al and Jerry working on this list. They should be able to go through it pretty quickly. In the detective business, ninety percent of the effort is legwork, and these guys are two of the best in the business."

SEVEN

ELISE'S meeting with Matt ended by nine o'clock. They'd talked for almost three hours, breaking only to eat the sandwiches Matt ordered in. She felt a renewed closeness to him when he picked up the telephone to place the food order and whispered to her, "You still like tuna, red onions and tomato on toasted dark rye, and iced tea?" She nodded and smiled.

By the time Elise left Matt's office, she felt assured hiring him had been the right thing to do. They agreed on how he would proceed and how they'd keep each other informed. It had been really nice to see him again.

When she arrived at her parents' house she called the hospital. Her father was resting, and her mother was just about to leave for home.

Elise grabbed a diet soda from the refrigerator and went to the den to use the computer. The room, with its crown moldings, built-in walnut bookcases, and brick fireplace, always made Elise feel warm and secure. She logged onto the hospital server in Scottsdale and checked her e-mail.

Her mother walked in a short time later. She pulled over a chair and sat down beside Elise. "I wanted to catch up with you before I head up to bed. How did things go with Matt?"

"Very well. He's going to help."

"Is he a one-man operation?"

"No. He has three ex-policemen working for him full-time and brings in contract PIs when he needs extra help on a case. His fees are reasonable under the circumstances."

"Money is the least of my worries. What matters is that we work with someone who's not only competent but cares about us." Sharon sliced the air with her right hand for emphasis. "We have to do everything possible to get to the bottom of this. We owe it to Laura."

"And to Dad."

Sharon nodded.

"I think Matt will do a thorough job." Elise reached for her soda and took a sip. "In the morning, two of his men will begin working on the list we compiled. They'll call you before they start."

Sharon leaned back in her chair. "Did you talk about his wife?"

Elise nodded. "Briefly. It's obvious he's still hurting. But he's totally professional and controls his emotions. He kept our conversation focused on Dad and Laura."

"Did he have any idea what might have happened to them?"

"No. I wouldn't expect him to. He has nothing to go on at this point. I told him Dad confided in you he was in some kind of trouble."

"Oh—" Sharon crinkled her brow.

"Mom, I had to. We can't keep any information from him that might help his investigation."

Sharon exhaled. "Of course, Matt needed to know."

"Just so you're prepared, once Laura's autopsy results are back, if there's anything suspicious, the hospital will notify the police."

"I get the feeling you think that's what will happen."

Elise nodded. "I do. I began leaning in that direction after you told me Dad admitted he was in some kind of trouble and Jeff said Laura seemed afraid for her life."

"I see."

Elise shrugged. "Maybe, Dr. Fletcher will find out what's made them ill, and that'll be it. But for now there remains the possibility of something criminal." Elise moved her chair back and away from the computer to face her mother. "All that said, I still can't imagine who'd want to hurt Dad or Laura. Can you?"

Sharon shook her head. She stood and started pacing. "Are we in danger, Elise?"

"I don't think so." Elise wished she could be more confident that was true. "Let's just not do anything foolhardy. It pays not to take any unnecessary risks."

"What do you mean?"

"As Grandma told you and you told me: don't walk down any dark alleys alone at night."

"Are you being flippant with me?"

"No, Mom. Honestly, I'm trying to lighten things." Elise waited a moment. "You're a careful person. Just continue being careful. Perhaps, even a little more vigilant than before."

Sharon sat and faced Elise. "Why can't we just call the police? Maybe it's better if they get involved right away. At least they could provide protection."

"Matt's going to protect us, so don't worry about that part. Even if we call the police, they won't do anything unless they're convinced there's been a crime. Anyway there's a good side and a negative side to having them on the scene."

"What could be negative?"

Elise repeated Matt's warnings about the potential invasive nature of usual police procedure.

"That's scary."

"In the short term, don't be surprised if they focus in on Laura's life insurance policy and Dad as beneficiary."

"But Elise, why would Dad risk killing himself in the process?"

"They could say to cast suspicion away from himself or maybe, he accidentally injured himself."

"That's absurd."

"Yes, you and I know that. But the police don't. It's a sizeable amount of money, and they may check the business out with Tim and find it wasn't doing so well. They could think Dad was strapped and desperate for money."

"Dad and I have all the money we need. Both of us had very lucrative stock options from our companies, which fortunately, we cashed in when the stocks were at their high point. They alone have made us financially independent. That angle is totally off-base."

"As I said, you and I know this, but the police don't. In doing their job they could cause us unnecessary grief. They'll snoop around and could make wild assertions. Even say Dad and Laura were having an affair and you were jealous and wanted to get rid of her and hurt him. Or that you were having an affair and wanted to eliminate Dad."

"No way. You know that," Sharon said indignantly. She took a deep breath and frowned. "I get the picture, and I don't like it. How on earth am I supposed to prove something like that is untrue?"

"We'll face it, if, and when, we have to."

"Dad and Laura were business partners who cared for each other like family. There was no romance. Both would frown at the suggestion if they could. And me, an affair? I should be so lucky." Sharon cracked a slight smile.

"I know. I feel awful that we might have to endure such an inquisition, but it could happen." Elise looked directly at her mother. There was a question she needed to ask and might as well get it over with. "Is there anything embarrassing they could dredge up about you or Dad? Tell me now, if there is."

"Absolutely nothing. We lead very dull lives—no intrigue, no affairs, no enemies we know of. We go to work, come home, go to sleep, and get up and go back to work. We're as dull as they come and that's just fine with us."

Elise smiled sympathetically. "It's been a long time since we talked about it, but I know Dad and you were college sweethearts. You've been lucky. Things have been good for you over the years, haven't they? I've been absorbed in my own life, and you're inclined to release information on a need to know basis."

"Need to know basis, hmm. Strange to hear you say that, but," Sharon looked up and nodded, "it's probably true. Elise, you know how Dad and I met."

"All I remember is that it was at Rutgers. You'd just started, and Dad was a junior."

A shy smile appeared on Sharon's face. "Yes, I was eighteen and a first semester student in applied mathematics. Dad was a year older but in his third year, majoring in business. He walked up to me in the hallway and asked if I'd like to participate in a study for his finance class. My initial thought was that he was trying to come on to me. But when I took a good look at him, I decided he was sincere, and I instantly knew we'd get to know each other much better in the days to come."

"I guess you had a touch of ESP."

"Maybe. We were going steady by the end of the year and married when I finished college. By then Dad was in his second year of graduate school."

"You worked so Dad could finish school."

"I took a job with a small computer company in Morrisville. The computer field was taking off. I'd been there just over a year, everything was going great, and I learned I was two months pregnant with you."

"So I was a surprise."

"It was good news, but in those days firms didn't always

look kindly on pregnant female employees. I made it clear to my manager that I intended to pursue a career and would be back at my desk after a six-month maternity leave."

"And I'm sure you were."

"Absolutely. I always took my work seriously, and when I give my word, I keep it." She cleared her throat. "I've sometimes felt I shortchanged you by doing that, but I'm happy to say you've managed to turn out okay. Much more than okay, in fact."

Elise took her mother's hand. "I never felt neglected."

Sharon's eyes welled. "Thank you. You do realize my working has helped us accumulate quite a nest egg."

"If I play devil's advocate for a moment, someone might speculate that if Dad were planning to leave you for Laura or somebody else, you would want to prevent losing half that money."

"They could say lots of things, but none of them would be true."

"I don't doubt you for a moment. I can only hope we never have to deal with any of this."

"You know, Elise, it's terrible to have your friend die, worry about losing your husband, and then be afraid the police are going to drag you over the coals. To be truthful, this conversation is really disturbing to me." She looked away. "I'm going to sleep now."

"Better to be forewarned and prepared. If I made you uncomfortable, just think how bad a police interrogation would be if it took you by surprise."

"It just isn't fair." Sharon shook her head and stood. "I have to stop this now. It's been a long day. Tomorrow will be even longer. I'm helping Deanna and Jeff prepare for Laura's funeral service on Saturday."

"Where is it being held?"

"Guilford Funeral Home. There'll be a notice in the morning papers."

Elise nodded.

"Good night, dear."

"I'm going to work a little longer. Talk to you in the morning."

Feeling guilty at having upset her mother, Elise jumped up and gave her a warm hug. "I love you, Mom. We'll help each other deal with anything they throw at us."

Sharon nodded and left the room. Elise rubbed her eyes and resolved to get back to work. She set about finding case reports where the patients presented with the same symptoms as Laura and her father.

Hours later, after weeding through a large amount of material, she felt no closer to figuring out what could have made her father and Laura sick. Without more specific information, she found it impossible to whittle it all down to real possibilities.

While she'd have to wait for the autopsy results, she was determined to keep after Fletcher and make sure he did everything possible to improve her father's chances for recovery. *Keep it together, Elise. A lot depends on you.*

EIGHT

"**ANYTHING** new with Dad?" Elise asked as she entered her father's hospital room on Friday morning and greeted her mother with a hug.

"There's some good news. His nurse told me he said a few words during the night."

Elise's face lit up. "Wonderful." She made a grand gesture crossing her fingers. "It shouldn't be long before we have him back."

Sharon's eyes clouded with tears. "By the way, some results from Laura's autopsy have come in. Dr. Fletcher said to have the nurse page him when you get here and he'll come over with the toxicologist."

"Terrific. I'll take a peek at Dad while you speak to the nurse."

A feeling of sadness came over Elise as she looked down at her father. Despite his having made some improvement since she arrived, her once youthful father now looked frail and elderly. Even with the best outcome she could hope for, life might never be the same for him.

Thoughts of her father's mortality consumed Elise. Her friends warned her that losing a parent packs a double wallop. Not only do you no longer have someone you loved, but you also realize you're moving closer to the front of the line as the advance sentinels are taken out.

Her father's progress was largely dependent on whether he developed liver or kidney failure. If test results indicated liver damage, the liver could repair itself if the destruction wasn't too widespread. Looking up at the monitors for his vitals, she was pleased to see that everything seemed stable.

Elise picked up his right hand and lifted the dressing to examine the inflamed area. The tissue damage was extensive. Just yesterday it seemed no more than a very nasty abrasion. She inspected the area carefully, but couldn't find visible cuts or needle marks. Whatever caused the damage and swelling probably was absorbed through the skin on contact. Either by accident or as a result of an intentional act, something toxic had come in contact with her father's right hand. Whatever "it" was, it continued to do local damage. But could it be responsible for his illness? She'd have to make sure Fletcher had a dermatologist look at the area.

The sound of her mother's voice interrupted her thoughts.

"Drs. Fletcher and Patel will be right over. How do things look to you?"

"I was worried about Dad's kidneys. Fortunately his urine output is good, so it doesn't look like his kidneys took too much of a hit." Elise refastened the bandage.

There was a soft knock at the door. Elise looked up to see Dr. Fletcher and a short, dark-complexioned man standing in the doorway.

"Good morning, Mrs. Bell, Dr. Bell. I'd like to introduce Dr. Patel," Fletcher said. "He's a toxicologist associated with State University. I've asked him to consult on Mr. Bell's case."

Elise and Sharon shook hands with Dr. Patel.

The first thing Elise noticed about Patel was his slight build. She guessed him to be about five feet four inches tall and not more than one hundred thirty pounds. He was clean-shaven and wore clear plastic-framed glasses that accentuated his aquiline nose. Somewhere in his mid-forties, she assumed from his appearance and name, he was from India. His accent suggested he'd been educated in British schools.

Fletcher immediately got down to business. "Let's go to a quiet area to talk."

He led the way to a meeting room at the end of the floor. Inside, off to the side of the room, two pair of chairs faced each other. Fletcher motioned in that direction.

When they were all seated, Fletcher leaned forward and made eye contact with Elise and Sharon. "As expected, we found that Mrs. Kirby's death was due to a massive MI, but the autopsy also suggested poisoning, at least as a contributing factor."

Sharon gasped. "Did I understand you right? You actually believe someone killed Laura?"

Dr. Patel responded to her in a slow and deliberate manner. "Please, don't rush to conclusions. We don't know yet if the poisoning was accidental, self-inflicted, or the result of a criminal act. Dr. Fletcher wanted to inform you of the preliminary findings."

Elise pursed her lips. "How do you think the poison entered her system?"

"Through her skin," Fletcher said.

"Through the skin of her right hand? Elise asked.

Patel nodded. "As a precaution, we've alerted the Guilford Police. They will make the determination if a crime has been committed."

"Have you identified the substance?" Elise asked.

"The agent is nothing that shows up on the standard tox screens," Patel said. "I have an idea of the class of compound but prefer not to say more until I have additional facts."

"We test for sixty substances, and it's not one of the sixty," Fletcher interjected. "We've sent rush samples to an outside lab for identification. Once we know exactly what substance is involved, we'll have a better idea how she may have been exposed. Unfortunately, since it happened more than twenty-four hours ago, there's a chance there won't be enough residual."

"If Mrs. Kirby was purposely poisoned," Elise said, "don't we have to assume my father was as well, and that his life may still be in danger?" She stared at Patel and Fletcher. While neither answered immediately, she thought she saw confirmation in Patel's eyes. Maybe he'd say more if she caught him alone later.

Fletcher rubbed the bridge of his nose. "I see some poisonings in my practice, but very few turn out to be intentional. Most resolve themselves to accidental exposures."

"What are you thinking is the case here?" Elise asked.

"It's too early to conclude anything. Let's wait until all the results are in." He turned to Patel. "Is there anything you want to add?"

"I agree it's premature to voice a definite opinion. In India, I saw a large number of poisonings. Some were accidental, some self-afflicted, but a significant number were murder attempts. I'm sure the police will look into all possibilities. Frankly, I believe the key lies in analyzing how Mrs. Kirby's right hand became so severely damaged."

"Since the damage is on top of the hand, it doesn't look like it's from touching something," Elise said. "What I find puzzling is, since my father is left-handed, it would be more likely he'd injure his left hand."

Patel nodded. "I wondered about a needle puncture. I looked hard for one on Mrs. Kirby's hand but could not find any. I also checked for cuts and bruises. There were several on both her palms."

"Laura liked to garden," Sharon said. "She didn't always wear gloves. That could account for the scratches and cuts."

"I examined Mr. Bell's hands too, but his skin looked pretty much intact, except for a small paper cut," Patel said.

Elise looked down at her right hand and moved it around.

"I wonder if they could have been exposed through a handshake."

"The same idea actually occurred to me," Patel said.

Sharon interjected, "Did the autopsy show anything that will help you treat my husband?"

"Nothing specific, but rest reassured Mrs. Bell, your husband went into this in good health and is making progress," Fletcher said. "Had Mrs. Kirby not had such a weak heart, we feel she would have survived. As long as Mr. Bell continues to show signs of waking up, his prognosis is very good."

Fletcher and Patel stood.

"I'm sorry, but I have another appointment," Fletcher said. As he and Dr. Patel walked toward the door, he added, "I'll contact you once the full tox report is in."

"Dr. Patel, could you remain for a few moments? I have some questions," Elise said.

Patel looked over at Fletcher.

After some hesitation, Fletcher nodded his approval.

"I need to tell Dr. Fletcher something, but will be right back." Patel followed Fletcher from the room.

When Patel returned, Sharon excused herself, leaving Elise alone with Patel. Once he was seated, Elise asked, "Can you please tell me what's going on here?"

Patel folded his hands in front of him, looked down at them for several moments, and then up at Elise. "What I'd like to do first is review what we know."

"Certainly."

"Since your father and Mrs. Kirby became ill about the same time, the first inclination was to look for a common exposure to viral or bacterial pathogens. Dr. Fletcher has systematically ruled these out, as well as other usual causes of illness matching their symptoms. It is possible their illnesses are unrelated and their admittance at the same time is coincidental."

Elise nodded vigorously, not from agreement, but to encourage Patel to get to the point. His professorial posture was making her nervous.

"Mrs. Kirby had a weak heart and was on digoxin. At first we thought she might have digoxin toxicity, something unrelated to your father's illness."

Because of Patel's peculiar way of speaking, Elise feared getting caught up in his words and losing the meaning. "Do you actually think their illnesses are unrelated?"

"It is too early to be sure. We are evaluating both avenues of possibility."

"I bet they're related. They both had the same G.I. and neurological symptoms, plus swollen right hands. There are few such coincidences."

"Perhaps. It remains to be established if the condition of their right hands is significant. It may or may not be related to their illnesses," Patel emphasized.

"Has there been a dermatology consult yet?"

"Dr. Fletcher has arranged for one," Patel said. "I have a few questions for you."

"Please, go ahead." *And speed up.*

"Does your father use salves or herbal preparations?"

"I don't think so. Why do you ask?"

"In my country, herbal medicines are used widely. I have seen many cases where people have suffered from using too much of various natural substances they view as harmless."

"I doubt my father uses any herbal preparations. If something like that is responsible for his illness, I can't imagine how it happened."

"I do not have a theory about that yet. I will raise the subject with Dr. Fletcher, and we will come up with a plan to approach this. I have one more question. Do you think someone might have purposely tried to harm him?"

"Do you mean tried to poison him?" Elise shook her head. "I don't know of anyone who'd have a reason to." She could feel her face flush as she spoke. "What makes you ask?"

"Please, Dr. Bell, I didn't mean to upset you. There can be accidental exposures, and there can be sinister exposures. It is prudent to evaluate whether there are any circumstances that make one or the other more likely."

Elise felt Patel was keeping information from her. "Well, have there been any random poisonings around Guilford?"

"I am not aware of any."

She stared directly into Patel's eyes. She had trouble reading him. "Then, wouldn't it make more sense to look for an accidental poisoning by some common chemical?"

"We've considered that along with a host of other things. This is not a simple case."

Elise felt like they were dancing around in circles. "I'm starting to feel you're not leveling with me, that information is purposely being kept from me."

Patel shook his head. "I don't want you to think I'm being devious. Please listen to what I have to say and think about it."

Elise nodded.

"In my country, murders have been committed by paid assassins using subcutaneous injection of lethal substances. The condition of the tissue in Mrs. Kirby's hand, and in your father's to some extent, resembles the condition of skin I've seen in poisonings where certain agents were used."

"What types of agents?"

"Rather than rattle off names, I want to check my records and do some research."

"So you've actually seen such poisonings yourself?"

"Yes. That is why Dr. Fletcher asked me to consult. But this is not India, and circumstances are different," Patel said. "I want to be sure not to propose anything that does not make sense in this environment. So, before I go looking for anything sinister, we must be sure that this hasn't happened as a result of something accidental."

"Like?"

When he finally spoke, Patel's voice was very calm. "For example, people have died from too much ephedrine in preparations that did not list it as an ingredient. This type of problem goes back to alternative medicines not being regulated and inspected. While there are many high-quality preparations, substandard products do sneak through, and people unwittingly use them and do harm to themselves. I call these the 'self-injured.'"

Elise searched her memory. Had her parents ever mentioned using any homeopathic or naturopathic meds? No, she was certain they hadn't. They shopped only at the major retail pharmacies.

"It is even worse with beauty creams and salves," Patel droned on. "With the Internet it is easy to acquire substances from anywhere in the world, some of which may be substandard, dangerous, and could even be put to ill use."

"I understand. Getting back to my father and Mrs. Kirby, I think we can eliminate their using herbal preparations or salves as a potential cause, but I'll double-check with my mother." Elise rubbed her eyes. She felt a headache coming on. She found Patel's speech pattern exhausting. "Dr. Patel, we keep on circling around the idea someone killed Mrs. Kirby and tried to kill my father. I've no clue who'd want to do such a thing, but if there were someone, why on earth would they use poison?"

"The advantage of poisoning is that it often goes undetected. Since we have reason to suspect poisoning, I have alerted the proper authorities." Patel lifted his glasses and rubbed his left eyelid. "From my experience, the first thing the authorities do is look at family and close friends as suspects. Unless it appears necessary, we try to avoid subjecting anyone to scrutiny."

"That makes sense. It also tells me you think foul play is a distinct possibility here and it's necessary to bring the police in."

Patel nodded. "Once we have the final results of the post mortem on Mrs. Kirby, we will know more. There are indications she sustained the kind of damage to brain and gastrointestinal tract indicative of specific kinds of poisoning. When Dr. Fletcher prescreened Mrs. Kirby's preliminary autopsy results and spotted something disturbing, he called me in to look at the results and asked me to examine your father again. Dr. Fletcher knows I was involved in solving so-called handshake assassinations, where criminals injected their victims with lethal preparations, usually during street encounters. But, Dr. Fletcher is very cautious. He does not like to jump to conclusions."

Elise nodded.

"Based on those investigations I suspect certain agents may be involved. We will only know if I am right if very specific assays are performed, and there are only a few labs in the region that run those highly specialized tests."

"Dr. Fletcher had expressed concern there might not be enough residue to test at this point," Elise said. "Can you use the serum taken when Laura and my father were first admitted to the hospital?"

"Dr. Fletcher contacted the hospital lab to preserve those samples should we need them."

Elise stood, took a few paces, and stopped behind her chair, resting her hands on the top. "Exactly why do you suspect the agents you do?"

"The clinical symptoms are classic, and the nature of the damage to Mrs. Kirby's internal organs resembles the pattern I've seen before."

"If this had been known from the start, would you have treated Mrs. Kirby or my father any differently?"

"Absolutely not. Unfortunately, there are no antidotes available to us. We would have followed the same procedure." Patel adjusted his glasses. "Right now we have to wait for the confirmatory results and for your father to recover. The rest is up to the police."

"What's the next step?"

"I've contacted colleagues in India who know a great deal

about these toxic agents. They are familiar with occurrences some years ago and will know if any new methods are being used to dispense the poisons. Once I hear back from them, I will share what I learn."

"How long will it take to get a response from them?"

"A day at most."

Elise extended her hand to Patel. "I'm hopeful we can quickly get to the bottom of this terrible situation."

Once Patel left the room, Elise broke into a cold sweat. She took a tissue from her purse and wiped her face. The stress had gotten to her. She felt powerless and inadequate. She couldn't accept that her only recourse was to wait: wait for her father to improve; wait for the test results to come in; wait for answers from Patel and Fletcher. What nagged at her was now that Laura was dead, if someone actually had tried to poison her father, would he try again? Would the person or persons come after Jeff, her mother, or her?

Elise's thoughts turned to Matt. She reached for her cell phone. Maybe talking everything over with him would calm her down.

After Elise finished telling Matt about the autopsy results, he said, "I'll get a man up to the hospital to watch your father's room until we can get a police guard."

"Do you think Jeff could be in danger?"

"It's unlikely, but let's play it safe. I'll have someone keep an eye on the Kirby house. How are you doing, Elise?"

"I'm okay."

On the spur of the moment, Elise invited Matt to dinner at her parents' home. While she doubted she was afraid for her safety, she wondered if that was the reason she always seemed to want Matt around. She quickly admitted to herself that fear played only a small part, if any at all.

NINE

THAT evening, while Elise put the final touches on dinner, her mother and Matt sat on easy chairs facing each other in the living room of the Bell home.

After a few minutes of small talk, Matt said, "Elise filled me in on everything you told her about how Mr. Bell acted on Monday and Tuesday night. It made me wonder if there's any chance the trouble he mentioned could possibly involve crime of some sort. Would there be any reason he'd hesitate to go to the police?"

"I've given it some thought and I could only come up with one thing. I know he wouldn't want to chance doing anything to jeopardize his broker's license. He just got it last year. Laura sponsored him. The rules in New Jersey are very strict. He could lose his license if he were involved in any criminal activity." Sharon shifted in her seat. "Believe me, this is all conjecture. I have no reason at all to suspect that could actually be an issue."

"Okay. Let's put it aside for now then. What about money? Have you and your husband had any recent financial problems?"

"No. None."

Matt nodded. "I hope I won't make you uncomfortable but I have to ask a personal question."

"Go ahead. Ask me anything you need to."

"Have either you or your husband ever been involved with anyone outside your marriage?"

Sharon blushed. "I certainly have not. I have no reason to believe Rick has either."

"Was his relationship with Laura more than just business? Some people have speculated about that."

"Rick and Laura were simply good friends and trusted business partners. I would stake my life on that, Matt. Laura was like a sister to both of us."

Tears formed in Sharon's eyes and Matt decided he'd asked enough for now. "Thanks, Sharon. You've told me everything I need to know."

She glanced at her watch. "Elise should have dinner ready. Let's go join her."

ELISE and Matt sat at the square glass kitchen table in front of a large picture window. Sodium lights flooded the back yard, and several times during the evening Elise caught herself mindlessly staring out the window watching the tree branches sway in the wind. Memories of childhood parties held in the back yard flashed through her mind. Much happier times than now.

Elise served a casserole prepared from shrimp, rice, and assorted vegetables she'd found in the refrigerator. One stroke short of a potluck dinner.

Earlier, when her mother and Matt had come to the dinner table after their talk, Sharon helped herself to a plateful and said she was returning to the den to take care of the mail and to catch up on some phone calls. Elise wanted to be alone with Matt and appreciated her mother's consideration.

Matt finished two helpings of the casserole and raved about the delights of home cooking. "I don't get to cook much these days. That's something I sort of miss with my current digs. One day I'll cook for you. I'm a champion soup-maker."

"Really?"

"Yep. I tell no lies."

"Well that gives me lots of ideas for your Christmas present." She laughed.

Their conversation had been lively. Elise filled him in on everything she'd learned from Fletcher and Patel earlier in the day, and Matt updated her on what his investigation had uncovered. Despite the circumstances that brought about their evening together, Elise realized how glad she was for Matt's company and marveled about the new things she had learned about him.

After they'd finished their coffees, Matt refilled their wineglasses. Elise raised her glass and took a sip. She leaned back in her chair and savored the taste of the chardonnay.

"Anything else on your mind? I'll listen," Matt said.

"I guess I really could use a sympathetic ear. I'm so tired and edgy . . . not sleeping well. I've been having a hard time concentrating and getting my head around what's happening. Now with Laura's autopsy . . ." She shrugged. "I keep wondering if someone actually tried to kill my father and Laura, or was this all a terrible accident? One minute I think the worst, and then the next minute I tell myself it's just not possible." She shook her head. "Bad things like this don't happen to people like us."

"I know everything's confusing at this point." Matt leaned forward, resting his elbow on the table. "I give you my word we won't stop looking until we find out what happened to your dad and Laura, and why."

Elise stared into space. She tried to push from her mind the visions of Laura lying dead in the hospital.

"I'm sorry it was this unfortunate situation that brought us together again, but grateful that it has," Matt said.

Elise did not respond. While she heard Matt's words, her thoughts at that moment were dominated by the realization Laura may have actually been murdered. When that possibility had first occurred to her, it was less frightening, because it was hypothetical. Now it seemed all too possible.

"I often thought about you and wondered how you were," Matt went on.

Elise snapped out of her thoughts and locked eyes with him. "Why didn't you call me?" She was surprised by her own words. Why was she so reluctant to admit her feelings for Matt?

Matt appeared puzzled. "I figured you didn't want to hear from me. I knew you were hurting. I didn't want to be a reminder of everything in Guilford that made you leave. And once Kara and I started seeing each other, well . . ."

Elise nodded. "You did the right thing. I probably would've treated you badly. When I left . . . when I ran away, I wanted to forget everything about this place. Sever all connections except those with my parents and a few of our closest family friends."

"Did that include forgetting me? Do you still feel that way?" Matt asked softly.

"Never you, Matt. Honestly, I was even afraid to come back to Guilford when my mother told me my father was ill and that they needed me. I didn't know what I'd have to face. Now the strongest feeling I have is helplessness. Laura's gone. I might still lose my father. A killer could be out there. It makes all my worries about self-preservation and past hurts seem unbelievably selfish." She slowly raised her glass and took a gulp of wine.

"I'm sorry, Elise, for being insensitive."

"No, you're certainly not insensitive. You're not caught up in all the same emotions I am. You can focus on what might've been and how you'd like things to be."

"It's not every day someone very important to you— someone you thought was more than just a good friend—runs out of a party and totally disappears from your life for years." Matt averted his eyes.

Elise stared at the troubled expression on his face and felt the need to make him understand. "I was ashamed I got so upset—

that I took the words of a drunken man seriously—a man filled with guilt who wanted to shift blame to someone else."

Matt nodded. "The way I saw it, Arthur Penman was the guilty party, not you, and whatever he said didn't matter at all. I couldn't imagine why it got to you so much."

"But I *was* guilty. I had let Steve down."

"Why do you think that?"

"I watched out for my own interests. I made a choice between sticking around and helping Steve or thinking only of myself and protecting my future. I left for college and didn't concern myself with any possible consequences. When I left town, I put Steve out of my mind. Or at least I tried to."

"Things aren't that clear-cut. You were just eighteen when it all happened. You're looking back on a teenager's world through adult eyes. You shouldn't feel guilty. No one is responsible for making another person happy at any cost. There's no glory in sacrifice."

"I know that now. But knowing something intellectually doesn't prevent my having an emotional reaction." Elise shook her head. "Just before my father took sick, I was convinced I was doing well. It had been a long time since I'd thought about Steve. Coming home has brought everything back."

"Maybe now you can try to get it all out, confront it, and finally put it behind you. Maybe, if we talk it will help."

Elise stood, grabbed her glass and the empty wine bottle, and walked to the sink. She spilled out the remaining wine and rinsed her glass. After standing there for a moment, she turned toward Matt. "I realize it may not be fair of me to ask, but . . ."

Matt jumped to his feet before Elise could finish her thought and rushed over to her. He took her hands. "Promise me if you think I can help in any way, you'll let me. And no more running away."

Elise searched his eyes. He looked like a lovesick puppy. *Dear Matt.* After a moment passed, she slowly slipped her hands out from under his and decided she'd said enough.

"Are you all right?"

"I'll be okay. I know it. Thank you for listening."

Elise bowed her head and rubbed her eyes, then looked up and took a deep breath. "Let's talk about other things."

Matt locked eyes with her and nodded.

She collected her thoughts and said, "I asked my mother if there was ever anything between Dad and Laura. She snickered and said Laura was deeply in love with Tim Dixon and they were planning to get married next year."

"So, as far as she's concerned, your father and Laura were never more than business partners," Matt said emphasizing *never* as he headed back to his chair and sat down.

"My mother was adamant."

"Well, then I guess we should cross that concern off the list," Matt said. "Next I need to contact Tim and see when we can get together."

"I'll call him tomorrow and tell him to expect to hear from you."

"I also need to ask Jeff some questions. Do you want to arrange that, too?"

"Sure. I'd like to find out how he's doing." Elise glanced at her watch. "I can call him now. It's only nine. I'm sure he and his aunt Deanna are still up."

Elise took the phone from the kitchen wall and carried it to the table. She sat and punched in the Kirbys' number, staring at Matt while she waited for Jeff to pick up. How lucky she was to have Matt here. But it wasn't the right time to rekindle a romance that never really got started and one that would be complicated by a long distance relationship. Maybe, when her father was well again, and this dreadful situation cleared up, then . . .

Jeff came on the line.

"It's Elise. Do you have time to talk?"

"Yeah. I was just going through Mom's things."

"Oh. How are you doing?"

"Okay, I guess. These last few days have been bad. It's hard to get used to Mom being gone."

"I'm so sorry."

Elise waited for Jeff to speak. When he didn't say anything, she began, "Jeff, I've been doing a lot of thinking . . . and a number of things just don't make sense to me." Elise paused for a moment to give Jeff a chance to say something.

"I know what you mean. What do you wanna do?"

"I've asked an old friend of mine, Matt Merano, to help us find out what happened to your mom and my dad."

"Matt, the cop?"

"He's now a private investigator."

"Why'd you get him involved? Shouldn't the cops be enough, Dr. E?"

"I certainly hope so, but we want to help speed things up and make sure nothing is missed."

"Oh."

"Don't you agree?"

"Yeah, I . . . I guess."

"Actually, Matt wants to talk to you as soon as possible."

"You wanna come over now?" Jeff asked. "I don't go to bed 'til after midnight."

Elise put Jeff on hold and turned to Matt. "Are you game to go over to talk to Jeff now?"

"Sure."

"Okay." Elise brought Jeff back on the line and said, "We'll be at your house in half an hour." She hung up.

"Let's ask your mother to come along rather than stay here alone. She can keep Jeff's aunt occupied while we talk to him."

TEN

MATT offered to drive to the Kirby home. As they rode along, Elise thought about the holidays and special occasions her family had spent together with the Kirbys. Laura had been present at every Bell family event as far back as she could remember. With Laura gone, her parents' lives would majorly change. A sudden chill ran through her. She buttoned the top of her jacket although she knew that wouldn't help.

After passing Guilford High School, Matt took the next left onto the Kirbys' street. The houses all had brick fronts and dated back to the sixties. In the moonlight, the large sprawling fir trees seemed to unify the structures and created a peaceful look to the neighborhood. A nice place to live.

The Kirbys' house was the fourth on the right, midway down the street, which ended in a cul-de-sac. The outdoor lights were all on, making the house easy to spot. The surrounding homes looked dark by comparison, the occupants most likely settling in for the night to prepare for an early start the next morning. Laura had been friendly with the neighbors and undoubtedly her death had given them pause. While saddened, life for them would go on unaltered, whereas the lives of one eighteen-year-old and those of the Kirby and Bell families would never be the same.

Matt pulled into the driveway, and they all got out without saying a word. Elise looked around trying to spot the man Matt had watching the house. She wondered if he might be in one of the parked cars sitting across the street.

When Sharon rang the bell, Laura's sister, Deanna, opened the door and invited them in. They exchanged pleasantries, and Elise and Sharon went to the living room. Matt stayed behind to talk to Deanna.

Elise remembered how Laura had music playing and coffee brewing every time they visited, no matter the time of day or night. The coffee aroma would be the first thing to hit Elise's senses when she stepped through the door. The absence of both the music and the familiar smells underscored Laura's absence. Elise and her mother exchanged sad, knowing looks.

When they entered the softly lit living room, Jeff sat on the sofa shuffling through a pile of papers on the cocktail table in front of him.

"Hi, Mrs. Bell and Dr. E." He stood and walked around the table toward them. Sharon wrapped her arms around Jeff. After a long moment, she let go and stepped aside.

Elise gave Jeff a warm hug. She noticed how thin and pale he looked. "How ya doing, Jeff?"

"Lousy. I half-expected Mom to be standing there in back of you."

"I'm so sorry," Elise whispered.

Matt and Deanna entered the room a few minutes later.

Elise gestured toward Matt. "Jeff, you remember Matt Merano."

"Hi, Jeff." Matt extended his hand. "I'm really sorry about your mom."

"Thanks, Mr. Merano. I remember when you came to speak to my class about drugs."

Matt nodded and smiled. "Please call me Matt."

Elise said, "I know it's been a tough day for you, Jeff.

We'll only stay a short while."

"We're going to do our best to find out what happened to your mom and Mr. Bell," Matt said.

"Mom was the best. No way did she deserve what happened to her."

Elise waited patiently for Jeff to finish then said, "Matt has some questions. Where would you like to talk?"

Jeff led Matt and Elise to his mother's bedroom while Sharon stayed behind in the living room with Deanna. On the way, Matt told Elise that Deanna had spoken to Laura on Saturday and everything was perfectly fine then as far as Deanna knew.

The last time Elise had been inside the Kirbys' master bedroom, Dave, Laura's husband, was still alive. She glanced around looking for changes. The walls were now lighter in color. She thought the three-piece rosewood bedroom set was the same, but the carpet and the oak desk in the corner by the window were new. Laura's touch showed in the way all the neatly framed photographs of the Kirby family were lined up chronologically. The earlier photos featured Dave prominently; the later ones were just of Laura and a growing Jeff. Elise focused on a photo of her father and an elated Laura at the official opening of K&B Realty. When she looked over at Jeff's face all she could think of was the grief he must feel with the loss of his mother.

Matt spoke first. "Jeff, I know this isn't easy for you, so I'll try not to ask too many questions."

"Go ahead, Matt, it doesn't matter. I want to help."

Jeff and Elise sat down at the foot of the bed, and Matt pulled over a chair to face them.

"First off, I want you to know one of my men, Al Jenkins, is watching your house as a precaution," Matt said. "I've already told your aunt."

"You think someone's after us?"

"No, but we'd rather be careful and not take any chances."

"Geez. What should we do, if something happens?"

"If you need Al, turn the lights on and off three times. He'll come running. But call nine-one-one first if you feel you're not safe." Matt took a card from his pocket and wrote on it. "I've put Al's cell phone number on the back."

After Jeff placed the card in his shirt pocket, Matt said, "Had your mom been unusually worried recently?"

Jeff shook his head. "Before Monday night everything was great. She was really happy to be back at work. Something must've happened because she was crying and seemed scared, when I came home that night."

"Did you ask her what was wrong?"

"Yeah, but she wouldn't say. I told Dr. E and Mrs. Bell, she just wanted me to know about her insurance policy. Like in case something happened to her."

"Did you think that was strange?"

"Yeah, but . . ." He shrugged. "She always worried a lot, so I didn't make too much of it."

"Elise told me about two policies: one where you're the beneficiary and the other where Mr. Bell is. Do you know how much your policy is for?"

"Five hundred thousand dollars." Jeff looked away from Matt when he answered.

Elise noticed Matt's eyes widen and feared what his next question would be. She signaled him to go easy.

Jeff fidgeted a little and stood. "I'll be right back. I need a glass of water. Anyone want anything?"

Matt and Elise shook their heads.

When Jeff left the room, Elise said, "I hope you're not thinking he did something to his mother to get the insurance money?"

Matt leaned back in his chair. "It occurred to me. It has to occur to the police, too."

"No way. Not Jeff. He was totally devoted to Laura. If the police question him, so be it, but I'm not going to be party to accusing him of anything."

"Relax. You'll do him a favor if you prepare him."

Elise ran her hands through her hair. "Okay, I'll say something to him, later."

Jeff returned and plopped down beside Elise. "Sorry, I was really thirsty. Do you have any other questions?"

Matt rubbed his temples. "Did your mom ever mention problems with anyone?"

"Not to me. Sometimes she complained about clients but nothing special." Jeff scratched the side of his face as he spoke.

"Who were her closest friends?"

"Mrs. Bell and Tim Dixon. Tim spent a lot of time here when Mom was sick. They were getting married."

"Tim's been close to Laura and my parents for years," Elise interjected. "I think I mentioned to you he lost his wife quite a while ago to breast cancer. Really nice guy."

"Jeff, is there anything else I should know about, like money problems, arguments with neighbors, strange phone calls, bad behavior? Anything out of the ordinary?" Matt asked.

"Bad behavior? Huh?"

"What I meant was, was your mom drinking or gambling?"

"Mom? Hell, no! She was a girl scout." Tears welled in Jeff's eyes. He wiped them with his bare hands.

"Did she see any therapists or doctors regularly?"

"Only a heart doctor, since her heart attack. It used to be a Dr. Leiberman, but he retired. She started seeing his partner, but I don't remember his name."

Matt jotted some notes on his pad. "Besides her job, did your mom have any hobbies?"

Elise said, "Laura was active in the Guilford Garden Club."

"Garden club?" Matt turned to Jeff. "Did your mom still garden?"

"Yeah. She grew roses and flowers in the summer. She has herbs in the kitchen."

"Anything exotic?"

"Just stuff for cooking."

"We'll take a look at them." Matt paused. "How about social, religious, or political groups?"

"She was into local politics for a while but gave up on that."

"Do you know why?"

"She worked a lot and I guess, didn't have time."

"Was that the only reason?"

"She said the people were impossible. Thought they were all idiots or crooks and didn't want to waste her time on them."

Matt glanced at Elise. "What about your father? Was he into politics too?"

"For a short time. Maybe two, three years ago. He used to tell me about things. Then one day he stopped. I assumed he got busy at work and gave it up."

Matt wrote something down and then turned his attention back to Jeff. "Was your mom close to her sister?"

"Yeah. Aunt Deanna lives far away but they kept in touch by phone and e-mail."

Matt glanced at Elise then back at Jeff. "Can I take a look at your mom's computer?"

"Sure. It's in the den."

On the way out of the bedroom, Matt pointed to a digital camera on top of the dresser. "Is that your mom's?"

Jeff picked it up. "Yeah. Tim gave it to her. He thought it would make things easier for her at work." Jeff moved his hands up and down the body of the camera as if removing invisible dust.

"Easier?"

"Mom used to take videos of the houses she looked at. They're called virtual tours. She uploaded them to her work computer and then to the K&B website. Sometimes she edited them at home first. I helped her set up editing software on her desktop." He inspected the camera. "The memory card is missing.

She must have just uploaded some stuff. We can take a look." Jeff led them to Laura's computer. He fired up the machine and then explained the file setup to Matt. When Matt began opening the files, Elise gestured for Jeff to join her on the den sofa. She decided to try to broach the subject of the police investigation.

Jeff sat down next to her.

"Now that the police are getting involved, they'll probably interview everyone close to your mother. Including you."

"Yeah, I know."

"They usually look first at the family until they rule them out as suspects." She watched Jeff for a reaction.

His face turned a scarlet red.

"Jeff, what's wrong?"

"You think they're going to suspect me because of Mom's big insurance policy."

"It could happen," Elise sensed Matt was listening to her conversation with Jeff.

"I would never hurt Mom. I don't give a damn about money." Jeff stood and clenched his fists by his sides.

Matt turned around and started to say something, but stopped when Elise began speaking.

In a forceful voice, she said, "I know you didn't do anything, Jeff, but the police don't know you the way I do. They may think the worst."

Matt interjected, "Jeff, the police will want to figure out what happened. They have a standard procedure. First they look at close family and friends for motives such as money."

Jeff locked eyes with Elise. "Do you think I could ever harm my mom?"

"Absolutely, not." Elise felt bad that she might have hurt Jeff, but it was important to prepare him.

"I didn't." Jeff sat and buried his head in his hands. "I couldn't. She was everything. I'm not afraid of the police. Let them ask me anything and get it over with. I don't want them wasting time on me while the real bad guy gets away."

Elise hugged Jeff. "That's the right attitude. I'm proud of you."

Matt turned back to the screen. After several moments he said, "I've been checking the files from last Monday. Take a look at this one. It's Laura describing a house she's in."

Elise and Jeff leaned over Matt's shoulder to watch a section of Laura's video. The clock showed the recording started at five minutes after one o'clock.

Matt turned up the volume.

On the computer screen, the camera panned the front of a house while Laura described the attributes. "This Hillcrest Road home is a white frame two-story colonial on five acres built in 1969. The owner, Mrs. Theresa Rothe, rents out the property for $2500 a month."

The video moved inside while Laura continued, "The kitchen is sixteen by twelve and adjoins the oversized three-car garage. The kitchen has a retro look. There's a large white porcelain double sink, a twenty-five cubic foot white refrigerator, bottom freezer, a white, thirty inch electric stove, and two sections, top and bottom, of three-high, white-washed wooden cabinets with a red ceramic tile counter top."

As the camera focused in on the countertop, a man could be heard speaking in an agitated voice, "Uh oh. I don't like the looks of what I just saw in the studio."

Laura sounded surprised. "What are you talking about Rick?"

"We have to get out of here before anyone knows we've been inside."

"Why? Rothe told us to check out the house. I don't want to lose this listing!"

"This place is trouble."

"Hey, quit it, Rick. Are you trying to scare me? Oh dammit, I've picked up all this babble on the video."

The display went black. "It stops here," Matt said.

"Creepy. I never saw that video," Jeff said. "Mom must have uploaded it Monday night. She didn't have time to edit it."

"Yikes." Elise gulped.

"So what do you think?" Matt asked.

Elise shrugged.

Matt checked his notebook. "Laura and your father met Mrs. Rothe at her home at four o'clock on Monday according to the information you gave me."

"Their appointment with her was scheduled for one o'clock," Elise said. "It didn't happen, but Mom and I have no idea why not, and we don't know where they were at one."

"Probably, Hillcrest Road," Matt said. "If they went somewhere else and wanted to keep it secret, they wouldn't have put anything about the original appointment in the office files," he added. "Laura could have erased the video, but didn't. She had to have had a reason to keep it."

"How likely is it that they'd go to the wrong address and get inside?"

"Making a mistake could happen. The street numbers are funny in that part of town," Matt said. "But finding the house unlocked, that's unlikely."

"They wouldn't break in. I'm sure of that. This whole thing doesn't make sense," Elise said. "At any rate, wherever they were, it's likely it was close to Mrs. Rothe's house."

"We'll check out the area."

"The more I think about it, Monday night Mom was very upset," Jeff remarked. "Do you think something bad happened to them in there?"

"They were okay at four because they met with Mrs. Rothe," Elise said.

Matt nodded. "I'll send a man out to Hillcrest Road in the morning. There can't be too many houses near Mrs. Rothe's home." Turning to Jeff, he asked, "Do you mind if I take copies of some files?"

"It's okay with me. I can give you a thumb drive to use." Jeff took a drive from the desk and handed it to Matt. "If you're finished with me, I think I'll crash. Look around as much as you want, take anything you need." Jeff left the room.

"Poor kid. This must be awful for him." After Matt copied the files, he inspected each of the photographs in the room and opened all the drawers and closets, checking the contents carefully but not taking anything.

He glanced at his watch and remarked, "It's getting late. Let's go, Dr. E, so these people can get some sleep."

"Hey, Matt, stop that." She feigned anger.

"Stop what?"

"Don't pretend."

Matt chuckled and whispered, "I couldn't resist calling you Dr. E after I heard Jeff do it. It's kinda cute. Does it really bother you?"

"Not really, I suppose. But Jeff's the only one who calls me that."

"If you let me call you Dr. E, then you can call me Double-Em, anytime you like."

"Hmm. Dr. E. and Double-Em, private investigators. Sounds catchy to me." She chuckled. "It's a deal."

"It's good to hear you laugh. Not much to laugh about these days." They left the bedroom and headed toward the kitchen.

Matt used his cell phone to photograph the plants in the kitchen. Then they returned to the living room to say goodnight to Jeff's aunt.

Deanna accompanied them to the front door and stepped outside, closing the door behind her. "I want to get Jeff out of harm's way. He may not be in any danger here, but I owe it to my sister to protect him in every way I can. He's coming back with me to Minneapolis."

"Is that what he wants?" Elise asked.

"I feel certain it is. Before I even had a chance to suggest it, Jeff asked me if he could stay at my house for a while." Deanna reached into her pocket and held out a business card. "Here's my address and telephone number in case you need to contact either of us."

Elise reached for the card. "When do you plan to leave?"

"Once we handle everything for Laura and get the house closed up," Deanna said. "It shouldn't take more than a week."

"So soon?" Sharon lamented. "Let us know if there's anything we can do to help you."

Deanna nodded.

"What if the police need to speak to Jeff?" Matt asked.

"We'll work it out," Deanna said. "I've already discussed it with Detective Wilhelm."

"Wilhelm?" Elise asked.

"Yes, he's been assigned as lead detective to the case. He called today, and I told him our plans. He thought it was a good idea."

"We'll see you at Laura's service in the morning," Sharon said.

Deanna waved as they headed toward the car.

When Matt unlocked the car doors, Sharon went ahead and got into the back seat.

Elise reached out for Matt's arm, "Do you know Wilhelm?"

"Unfortunately, I do."

"What does that mean?"

Matt didn't answer immediately. "It's better if you make up your own mind."

"Okay, but . . ."

"I went easy on Jeff. The police won't. Wilhelm will grill him once he finds out about the insurance policy."

"But, Jeff loved his mother."

"Come on, Elise. You read newspapers and watch TV. A week doesn't go by without a *devoted* son or daughter doing terrible things to a parent and often for a lot less than half a million dollars."

"You think he tried to kill my father too? I don't believe it. Not Jeff."

Matt shrugged. "What you and I think doesn't matter."

ELEVEN

SHORTLY after 7:00 a.m. on Saturday morning, a frumpy, middle-aged woman dressed in light blue scrubs walked past the service elevator on the second floor of Clearview Hospital. With a stooped posture and deliberate steps, she pushed a small cart loaded with a blood pressure gauge, thermometers, and assorted small instruments. In her right hand she held a yellow pad. When she reached the nursing station, she said good morning to the nurses. The night shift nurses, absorbed in reporting to their day shift replacements, nodded without looking up.

Some strands of her long, fine, brown hair fell forward as she walked. She paused for a moment to push the hairs behind her ear, looked down at her pad and up at the room numbers. When she reached room 212, she checked to be sure no one was watching her and then quickly turned her cart into the room and closed the door behind her.

The woman surveyed the surroundings. She parked her cart, glared at the sleeping patient then walked to the bathroom in the back of the room to make sure it was empty. She returned and drew the privacy curtain. To make space for her cart she maneuvered a crash cart over to the right. For several moments she watched the door then withdrew a syringe filled with a colorless fluid from her pants pocket. Before she could inject the contents into the patient's IV, a man opened the door, pushed the curtain aside and yelled, "Hey, wait a minute. What are you doing here?" He hurried toward her.

She reacted quickly, hurling the syringe at him. The needle lodged in his upper arm. It stopped him in his tracks. She slammed her cart into him knocking him to the floor then ducked around the foot of the bed and out the door as it closed behind her.

Matt got to his feet, confident he'd stopped the woman before she could harm Rick Bell. With a tissue, he pulled out the syringe from his arm and pushed up his shirt sleeve. A droplet of blood remained on his skin, but the surrounding area looked fine. The syringe was still full. He sighed with relief. He'd deal with his arm later. He placed the syringe on the table and checked Rick Bell. The man hadn't stirred despite all the commotion. Matt buzzed for the nurse who came within moments.

He checked her nametag. "Alice, did you see a woman in scrubs just run out of here?"

"No. Why?"

"I'm Matt Merano, a private investigator. I was hired by Mr. Bell's family to protect him. I stopped someone in an attendant's uniform from injecting a liquid into Mr. Bell's IV line."

"Oh, no. What did she look like?"

"Medium build, fiftyish with brown hair. About five-five, wearing blue scrubs."

The nurse shook her head. "No one like that went by the nurses' station in the last few minutes."

"Is there any other way off the floor than the elevator?"

"Just the stairs. The service elevator is out-of-order."

"I could tell the woman wasn't a nurse and was trying to do something she shouldn't be. I called out to her and she stopped. We scuffled, and she ran from the room. I'm going to try to find her. Please don't leave Mr. Bell alone until I get back. Don't touch anything."

The nurse checked Rick then reached for the phone. "I'll call Security. They'll know what to do." She glanced at Matt. "Do you know your arm's bleeding?"

"I'm okay." Matt took a tissue from his pocket and applied pressure to the bleeding area as he dashed out the door.

Matt checked the corridor west of the nurses' station, asking anyone he encountered whether they'd seen a woman in blue scrubs. Then he ran to the stairwell. Looking up the stairs, he spotted a physician on his way down from the third floor. "Did a woman pass you on the stairs?"

"No. I just walked down from the fifth floor. There was no one else on the stairs."

Matt turned and ran down to the first floor. He carefully inspected the nearby rooms, the hallway and the lobby. No one had seen the attendant. He ran out to the street and looked around. No sign of her.

Cursing under his breath, Matt took the elevator back up to the second floor. When he got out, a man from Security stopped him and asked him who he was. The guard then escorted Matt back to Rick Bell's room to speak to his boss. A tall, African-American man in his late thirties, stood next to the nurse at the door. Matt gave his name and said, "I was hired by the family to guard Mr. Bell."

"Larry Jackson, Security. Alice, here, said someone tried to attack her patient. Would you mind showing me your credentials?"

Matt handed Jackson his identification.

Jackson glanced at Matt's ID and handed it right back to him. "Thanks. I've called the police, and they should be here any minute. Alice assures me Mr. Bell wasn't hurt, despite the mess in here. Tell me what happened."

Matt caught his breath. He explained what had occurred and pointed to the syringe. "Leave this here. The police will need it as evidence. Maybe they can get some prints."

"You should go down to the Emergency Department and tell them you've had a needle stick," the nurse said. "You don't know what's in that syringe. There's a protocol we have to follow because of the danger of AIDS and hepatitis contamination."

"I will go . . . later."

The nurse rolled her eyes and turned to Jackson. "The woman who did this couldn't have been a real hospital attendant. They aren't allowed to give injections."

"That's the point, I think she was trying to kill Mr. Bell," Matt snapped.

"When I got here," Jackson said, "I closed off the stairs and left one of my men at the nurses' station to watch the elevator and wait for the police."

"Yeah, your man stopped me on my way back here."

"So far we haven't seen anyone fitting the description you provided," Jackson said. "Maybe the woman is hiding somewhere on this floor."

"Can we look at the surveillance footage for the floor?"

Jackson stared at Matt. "I called down to have them get it ready for the police when they arrive."

"Try the ladies room," the nurse said.

"Matt nodded and waved for Jackson to follow him.

They went across the hall to the ladies room. Matt patted his waist for his gun.

Standing off to the right and leaning over, Jackson knocked on the door. "Security. Please come out." Silence. He turned the handle and cautiously pushed the door open. The room was empty.

"I did a quick check of the floor, but it pays to look again," Matt said to Jackson. "You take the right side, and I'll take the left."

Of the six patient rooms on Matt's side of the hall, two were empty, and four had occupants in them. No one had seen the attendant.

As Matt came out from the last room, a stylish blonde in a

print sheath entered the elevator across from the nurses' station. Matt caught a glimpse of her back as the elevator door closed.

Matt rushed up to the security guard at the nurses' station. "Did you check the woman who just went into the elevator?

"You mean the blonde?" The guard shook his head.

"Where did she come from?" Matt asked.

The guard put his hand to his chin and looked up and down the hall. "Probably from the room next to the men's room. She doesn't fit the description I got so I didn't stop her."

Matt grimaced. "Anyone else go by?"

"Only a kid . . . about eighteen, nineteen. He came out of the waiting room and asked what was going on. I guess he heard the ruckus. When I didn't tell him anything, he mumbled something and left."

Matt shook his head. "I'll be right back." He headed down the hall.

TWELVE

A lanky young man in a brown windbreaker and green and white striped woolen cap hurried out the hospital's service entrance. He looked around the parking area and then signaled to the driver of a black sedan. The car pulled up, and he got in.

"You're out fast, Viktor. How'd it go?"

"It didn't."

"Why not?"

"When I passed the waiting room, there was lots of noise. I got close to the nurses' station and overheard them saying a woman tried to off the patient in room two-twelve. Some dude walked in and fought with her, but she got away. I waited a little then tried to find out more from the security guard, but he wouldn't tell me anything. So I left."

"Didn't you try to get into the real estate guy's room?"

"No. I'm not stupid. Police will be swarming there any minute."

"What happened to the real estate guy?"

"I don't know. Nothing I guess."

"So you're telling me you saw nothing?"

"I got out as fast as I could. I wasn't going to stick around and take a chance they'd stop me and ask questions."

"But you're sure it's the real estate guy she went after? Right?"

The younger man nodded. "Yeah, had to be. His room's two-twelve, and that was the room they talked about. The guy in there is in a coma or something."

"Listen, you little punk. You either know something or you don't. Was it his room?" He smacked the younger man on the side of his head.

"Hey, quit it, Unc. It was the real estate guy's room. They called him Mr. Bell. Bell was the real estate guy's name, right?"

Sergei nodded. "Who saw you?"

"Just the security guy, but he didn't pay any attention to me. The jerk thought he was too good to even talk to me."

Sergei frowned.

"So what do ya think?"

"It had to be Stacy. She probably tried to finish Bell off to save that idiot Grigor. She bungles things as bad as that drunk." Sergei's nostrils flared as he spoke. "Okay, let's get out of here. I've got more important business to take care of."

"So Unc, I've done my part. You gonna give me back my IOU?"

"Not a chance. Your marker isn't squared, yet."

THIRTEEN

THE slender blonde hurried from the building. When she reached the curb in front of the hospital entrance, a white sedan swung over and stopped. She jumped in.

"Everything taken care of?" The driver pulled out into traffic.

"No," she barked.

"What'd you mean?"

"Some guy walked in on me when I went to dose the IV."

"A cop?"

"No. He would have had to identify himself as one if he was."

"How did you get away?"

"Jabbed him and knocked him over with the cart. I hid in the men's room. I dumped the scrubs and wig and walked right out to the elevator without anyone stopping me."

"You were lucky."

"It was good planning, not luck." Anger filled her voice.

What're you going to do now?"

"Don't worry. I'll take care of it."

"How'd the Bell guy look?"

"He was out of it."

"You know what I think?"

"What?" she snapped.

"Just like you said, the real estate guy's no threat. It'll all be over before he even wakes up. Tell Sergei he's dead. After we get our money, we get out. Move on. Start over again."

She stared directly ahead, oblivious to the noises around her. "Yeah. Bell's not in any shape to do anything. Even if he said something, nobody would pay attention to him. They'd figure he's hallucinating." She tapped her lips with her finger and moved her head up and down.

"Then we'll go?"

"Yes, soon. Acting quickly is the only thing that'll let us pull it off. If we hang around, something'll go wrong. But there's still the matter of Sergei."

"One way or the other, we need to get rid of him."

"I'm going to pick up some stuff and then swing over to the house tomorrow early, to take care of things," she said. "If we're lucky, Sergei will be history by Monday."

"It can't be soon enough."

"I have to make sure he keeps a clear head until the delivery tomorrow night. He'll find his reward waiting for him when he gets back from Princeton."

"I know the one thing he loves more than smack is money," Grigor said. "He'll wait until the delivery's made and he's been paid before he gets high."

"And once we know he's taken care of, we leave." She felt better now that decisions were made. "With Sergei gone, the bosses won't be any the wiser for days. They might send someone around to check things out at some point, but by then it won't matter. We'll be long gone."

She stared out the window as she mulled over what she needed to do next.

"What about the cops?" Grigor asked.

"I've figured that part out. They'll find a note in Sergei's pocket to spark their interest. That, together with the evidence they uncover from the wig and syringe, should convince them Sergei's their man."

"They'd have to be really dumb to miss all those clues you're handing them."

Stacy smirked at his remark. "You're right there."

"So where should we go?"

She heard Grigor's words, but it took a moment for them to register. "Somewhere warm where we don't need passports. I already have picture IDs for us."

"You do?" Grigor's face lit up. "Do I get a new name?"

"Yes, my love. You're Stan Alexander. I'm Marie Alexander."

"Stan and Marie. I like it. When did you get the IDs?"

"Right after I heard about the real estate agents getting into the house. I figured we might have to leave town fast and would need IDs for the airport."

"That was smart." Grigor sounded genuinely impressed. At the red light he cupped her face in his hands and gave her a quick kiss.

"I've always wanted to go to Hawaii," she said. "I've dreamed about the place for as long as I can remember but never had the money and time to go."

"I know a spot: a beautiful little island. I once saw it on a travelogue. So many different plants there. Enough to keep you busy for years, or at least until we get tired of the place, and decide to go someplace better."

"I'll call around to see how soon we can get flights out of here. We'll need to go with different airlines and fly from different cities. We'll meet up in Honolulu."

"Why separate flights?" Grigor asked.

"In case the police catch on quicker than we think and are on the lookout for a couple traveling together."

"Yeah, you're right. But it will take the fun out of the trip."

"It's better to take precautions. We'll have lots of time together once we get there."

"Okay, we do it your way. How are you going to pay for the tickets?"

"With Marie's pre-paid credit card. I'll put ten-thousand dollars on it. That should be enough for a start. We have to buy round trips. One-way tickets always raise a red flag."

"What about our cars?"

"I've lined up buyers."

"You've thought of everything. What should I do?" Grigor asked.

"Pack the stuff in the apartment. Take only the essentials. Dump the rest."

"Where will you be?

"I'll go to the bank the minute we hit the City, and get cash. And also clear out my things from the lab. This afternoon no one will be there so it's a good time to do it."

"I have to wait until Monday to empty my studio. Don't want to tip Sergei off."

"Yes. Monday. We'll take care of everything else before Monday.

"Good. Tonight, we celebrate."

Celebrate what? A lot could still go wrong. For a moment she thought about saying just that. "Let's not rush things. We'll have a lot to celebrate when all this is over. It'll be worth the wait. I promise you."

FOURTEEN

MATT dashed down the corridor to the men's room and carefully pushed the door open. He looked around. *Empty.* The trash bin caught his eye. The lid was slightly off-center. He removed the lid and looked inside the bin. At the bottom of the fresh plastic liner lay a wig and scrubs.

He returned to the nurses' station looking for Jackson. He found him talking to the security guard. "The men's room should be closed to the public. There's a wig and scrubs in the trash bin. I think they were worn by the attendant. The police will need them as evidence."

"Okay, I'll lock the door and put up an out of order sign," Jackson said. "I checked out the rest of the rooms on the floor. *Nada.*"

"I'm beginning to think the blonde we saw leaving could've been the attendant," Matt said. "It's too bad we didn't get to look more closely at her."

"The guard was just telling me about her," Jackson said. "I think you may be right."

"So where are the police?"

Jackson looked at his watch. "I don't know. They should've been here by now."

Matt shook his head and looked up at the elevator position indicator. The elevator was stopped at the first floor. "I'm probably spinning my wheels, but I'm going to look some more. Maybe the blonde hasn't left the hospital grounds yet." He ran down the stairs and rechecked the first floor. He then walked out the main entrance, looked up and down the street, and ran around to the parking lot. No sign of the blonde in the tight dress anywhere.

Matt wondered if the person who just tried to kill Rick Bell, could also be the one who murdered Laura. And if so, why?

FIFTEEN

ELISE looked around the filled chapel on Saturday morning and estimated there were over a hundred people gathered for Laura's memorial service. Most had known her for many years and spoke in glowing terms about her life and contributions. Although deeply saddened by her sudden death, they celebrated her life and recounted the joy she brought to so many.

It occurred to Elise that one of the nice things about a small town like Guilford was that people rallied around each other in time of sorrow.

She'd been afraid that with so many old friends and their families assembled, someone was bound to bring up Steve Penman's name. Or even worse, his parents might come to the service. Fortunately, neither happened.

As soon as the service ended, Elise and Sharon spoke with Deanna and Jeff for a few minutes, made their apologies, and headed to the hospital, arriving shortly after noon.

When they stepped out of the second-floor elevator, Elise spotted Matt standing across from her father's room talking to a uniformed police officer. The expression on Matt's face told her something bad had happened.

He ended his conversation and hurried over to them.

"Mrs. Bell, Elise, please come with me so we can talk for a moment."

Once they were seated in a private corner of the waiting area, Matt told them what the attendant had tried to do.

Both women gasped.

"Is my father okay?"

Matt nodded. "He wasn't touched."

"Were you hurt?" Elise asked.

"The attendant stabbed me in the arm with the syringe."

"You need to go to the ER to get yourself checked," A chill ran through Elise's body at the thought that Matt might be injured. "Let me see your arm."

Matt pushed up his sleeve and pointed to the spot where the needle stuck his arm.

Elise examined the area and was relieved to see that it wasn't inflamed. "Since we have no idea what was in the syringe, you have to assume the worst, especially after what's happened to my dad and Laura."

"I'm okay, but I'll have it looked at. I promise."

"Don't neglect it," Sharon reproached Matt.

"Who could the attendant be?" Elise asked. "Did they catch anything in the surveillance footage?"

"I don't know. The police have looked at it but they aren't saying."

"Are you even sure it was a *she*?"

"The movement was like a woman, but I can't be one hundred percent sure. A while later, we spotted a blonde in street clothes leaving the floor. It might've been her. "

"Whoever it was, they don't work in a hospital or they'd know only RNs administer the IVs and add meds to them. Attendants aren't allowed to," Elise said. "Anyone at all familiar with hospital procedure wouldn't have dressed as an attendant . . . unless they weren't able to get their hands on a nurse's uniform."

Sharon buried her head in her hands. "This is unbelievable.

My whole life I thought this kind of thing only happened in movies, never to people like us! We didn't do anything to deserve this."

Elise placed her hand on her mother's shoulder and turned to Matt. "Thank God you came into the room. I shudder to think what would've happened to my father if you hadn't been here."

"We started round the clock protection for him yesterday evening. I took the first shift this morning. I was on the phone in the hall when I saw the attendant enter your father's room. I went right over. One of my men is at his door now."

"What about the police?" Sharon asked. "Why aren't they doing anything?"

"With what just happened, they should agree to station an officer at your husband's door, but we can't count on it."

Sharon lips trembled. "Do you think the killer will come back here, or after us?"

"We don't know. As a precaution, we'll provide protection for Mr. Bell and for both of you. I'll stay close-by a large part of the time. When I can't be around, one of my best men will be."

"Matt, can you stay at our house tonight?" Elise asked. "We have a comfortable guest room."

"That's a good idea. I'll take care of a few things at the office and pick up some clothes. Don't leave the hospital on your own. I'll come back by eight."

"Please stop at the ER on your way out," Elise said.

"Don't worry. Everything will be okay."

Elise wasn't so sure of that.

SIXTEEN

WHEN Elise glanced at the door of her father's room, she saw a tall, dark-haired man standing there. She and her mother had been engrossed in conversation at her father's bedside and had been unaware of his presence. Had he been eavesdropping on their conversation? Had they said anything they wouldn't want overheard?

"I'm Detective Paul Wilhelm of the Guilford Police. I'm the lead detective on the Kirby case. I'd like to speak with you folks."

"Oh, please come in," Sharon said. "I'm Sharon Bell, Mr. Bell's wife, and this is our daughter, Dr. Elise Bell. We're glad to see you. We were wondering when someone from the police would come."

They all shook hands.

While her mother conversed with Wilhelm, Elise studied him. He appeared to be in his late forties, about six feet tall, in good physical condition, although slightly overweight. His brown hair was mixed with gray at the temples; his face heavy creased from excessive sun exposure. With the exception of a broad nose, his features were angular. He had what looked like to her a perpetual scowl on his face. She did not find him at all sympathetic and took an instant dislike to him.

Elise asked, "Could you fill us in on what you've found out so far?"

"We've just started the investigation. Late yesterday Dr. Fletcher filed a report after preliminary autopsy results came in. The M.E. classified Mrs. Kirby's death as undetermined, but I'm sure you know that already." Wilhelm looked down at the pad in his hand and flipped it open. "Drs. Fletcher and Patel are our main contacts."

"Someone tried to kill my father this morning. If it weren't for Matt Merano, a private investigator we hired, my father might not be alive now."

"I've reviewed Mr. Merano's statement. We're checking into everything. If there was an actual attempt on your father's life, we'll take appropriate action. Right now I'm assigned to the Kirby case, and that's what I'm here about."

"What do you mean 'if'? It's clear someone tried to murder my father."

"We deal in evidence, ma'am. Until we've completed our investigation and have an analysis of the syringe contents, let's reserve judgment."

"At any rate, rather than take chances with his safety, why isn't there a police guard for my father? When are you going to assign someone?"

"Miss Bell, the appropriate action will be taken at the appropriate time. I'm here to gather information about Mrs. Kirby. If the lead detective on your father's case thinks it's warranted, then an officer will be sent to guard him. In the meantime, if you're concerned, make sure someone's always with him. I know you're already working with Merano, and he's got someone at the door now."

"It's Dr. Bell, Detective Wilhelm." Elise didn't like Wilhelm's adversarial manner.

"Right." Wilhelm grimaced.

"We had to hire private protection because the police weren't on the scene. Since it's a police matter now, I think a police officer should be guarding my father."

"My advice stands," Wilhelm snapped.

Elise refused to be put off by Wilhelm's snarky attitude and behavior. She thought for a moment. "Have you spoken with Dr. Patel yet? He had definite views on what may have happened to my father and to Mrs. Kirby."

"Briefly. I'm scheduled to meet with him later today."

"I see," Elise mumbled.

Before she could get another word out, Wilhelm said to her mother, "Mrs. Bell, I'd like to ask you a few questions. Privately, if you don't mind."

Sharon looked over to Elise before responding. After Elise nodded to her, Sharon responded to Wilhelm, "Sure, Detective."

"We can go to a meeting room to talk or do it here. What do you prefer?"

"Let's sit here and talk. I don't want to leave my husband's room." She turned to Elise. "Is that okay with you?"

"Of course, Mom." Elise addressed Detective Wilhelm. "I would like to have a word with my mother. Could you please excuse us for a moment?"

Detective Wilhelm nodded. His look remained cold.

Elise took her mother aside. Out of Wilhelm's earshot she whispered, "If any of his questions trouble you, you don't have to answer them. Either signal me or just tell him you want to have your lawyer present. I don't trust him."

"Okay. But do you really think a lawyer will be necessary?"

"Hopefully not. Just be careful. Matt warned me the police might get aggressive. They generally assume someone close to the victim committed the crime."

Sharon nodded to Elise then walked up to Wilhelm and told him she was ready.

They pulled two chairs to the back of the room. and sat down to talk.

Wilhelm asked Sharon if she minded if he recorded their conversation. She said she preferred he didn't.

He did not press the issue. He proceeded to question her. "How long have you known Mrs. Kirby?"

"More than thirty years. We've been especially close in recent years, ever since her husband died, and she and my husband became partners in K&B Realty."

"I heard that Mrs. Kirby could be a difficult person. Did you get along well?"

"I don't know where you heard she was difficult. It's not true. She was a lovely person and a dear friend."

"Were you jealous of all the time she spent alone with your husband?"

"What kind of question is that?" Sharon glared at Wilhelm. "They were business partners."

"Some women are less understanding than you seem to be."

Sharon pursed her lips at Wilhelm's remark.

"Do you know of anyone who might've wanted to harm Mrs. Kirby?"

"No. I can't think of anyone who'd have a reason to."

"Think hard, is there anyone who had any kind of disagreement with her: any lawsuits, sour business deals, disgruntled employees?"

Sharon shook her head.

"Any ex-boyfriends, ex-husbands, jilted lovers?"

"No."

"Tell me again, how well did you get on with Mrs. Kirby?"

"We were best of friends."

"No arguments about anything, ever?"

Sharon shook her head.

"Was she even better friends with your husband?"

"They were business partners and got along well." She

paused and took a breath. "The way you phrase your questions, I get the impression you're trying to imply something negative."

"I'm just trying to find the truth and get the bad guys, whoever they are."

Sharon shrugged. "My husband and Dave Kirby, Laura's late husband, were good friends. Dave and Laura ran a successful real estate business. Soon after Dave died, my husband took early retirement and joined Laura at Kirby Realty. They renamed the business K&B Realty, for Kirby and Bell."

"Oh, yeah? Did they spend a lot of time together alone?"

"Of course," Sharon barked at Wilhelm. "For the third time, they worked together. They were business partners."

"Did you ever suspect there was something going on between them?"

"No. Mrs. Kirby was engaged to Tim Dixon."

"Tim Dixon, that's their accountant, right? So he'd know the business finances."

"Yes, Mr. Dixon is their accountant." She took a breath. "Detective Wilhelm, why are you insinuating there was a romantic relationship between Laura and my husband?"

"Why does it upset you if there's nothing there?"

"I don't believe in wasting time. What else do you want to know?"

"As I understand it, your husband stands to get a large sum of money from an insurance policy he had on Mrs. Kirby's life."

"He and Laura had reciprocal policies, but I imagine you already know all about that."

"I do, and I also know that if he dies you stand to get that money and also the money from the reciprocal policy on his life, since Mrs. Kirby is already dead."

"What do you mean?"

"Don't pretend you didn't know the policy on your husband's life doesn't go to Laura's son, but goes to you if Laura dies before your husband? You collect on two policies: Mrs.

Kirby's and your husband's."

Sharon caught her breath. "I didn't know that. What I knew was they each took out a policy to make it easier for the surviving partner to keep the business afloat in case one of them died. It's news to me that I'm the secondary beneficiary on my husband's policy. At any rate, that's irrelevant, if true."

"Can you prove that?"

"What are you talking about? My husband is alive and hopefully will soon fully recover. And anyway, by the same . . ." She stopped mid-sentence. "Never mind."

"Let me help you out. Were you going to say that by the same token, Jeff Kirby would've collected on two policies if your husband died first?"

"No, I was not going to say that. I was going to say that if you do your job and protect my husband, there'll be no more loss of life." Sharon stood.

"Now, don't get offended, Mrs. Bell. Sit down and chill a little. I'm only doing my job."

"Try to be less insulting." Sharon moved her chair back and away from Wilhelm before sitting down again. "Are you finished with your questions?"

"No, I'm just getting started." Wilhelm looked down at his pad, flipped a few pages and then said, "Speaking of Jeff Kirby, I understand Mrs. Kirby's had a hard time with him."

"What do you mean?"

"The kid's gotten into a lot of trouble."

"What trouble? I don't know where you got that idea. Jeff's a terrific kid. He's been a tremendous help to Laura. She depended on him during her recent illness, and he came through for her. He keeps out of trouble. He works hard and does very well at school."

"According to my records, he banged up her car pretty good."

"Oh, that. He was in an accident, and the car was damaged. But it wasn't his fault. Somebody sideswiped him."

"Yeah, but he went ballistic at the scene and tried to attack the other person."

"You're exaggerating. He was upset because his mother's car was damaged. Laura was very sick at the time, and Jeff didn't want to add to her worries. He also realized he could've been seriously hurt as a result of the other driver's carelessness. The other driver was issued a ticket."

"Before that he was brought in for underage drinking and public intoxication."

Sharon took a breath. "That was a one-time thing years ago. He promised it would never happen again and it hasn't. Cut him some slack."

Wilhelm grimaced. "How often have you seen Jeff Kirby in the last few years?"

"All the time. My husband and I often have dinner with Laura and Jeff, and celebrate holidays together. My husband, daughter, and I know Jeff very well, and we all think he's a wonderful young man."

"Does he get angry and rant a lot?"

"I have never seen him lose his temper."

A skeptical look crossed Wilhelm's face. He waved a hand and said, "All right. Enough of that." He lowered his head slightly and scratched his forehead. He then looked up and locked eyes with Sharon. "Now, how long is it that you've been married to Mr. Bell?"

"Over thirty years. We married the year I graduated from college."

"College sweethearts Do you still get along well? Any fights, separations, court orders?"

"We get along very well and always have. No fights, no separations, no gossip, et cetera, et cetera. Sorry if that disappoints you."

"No need to be snippy, ma'am." Wilhelm stared straight at Sharon for a moment. "Do either you or your husband have any enemies who might want to harm him or Mrs. Kirby?"

"You asked me that before, and I said no."

"What about big debts, do you know if she had any?"

"None that I know of."

"What about your husband?"

"None. I know that for certain."

"No mortgage?"

"We own our house free and clear and have no outstanding debts."

"Does your husband gamble, take drugs, go to prostitutes?'

"No, no, no." Sharon peered angrily at Wilhelm. "You're being so rude. Why are you doing this?"

Detective Wilhelm gazed at Sharon in silence. He made a face, snarled and said, "Okay, Mrs. Bell. That's enough for now. Thanks. I'll speak to your daughter next."

Without a word to Wilhelm, Sharon stood and walked over to Elise. "It's your turn with Mister Personality. You were right. The guy's a jerk."

Elise reached for her mother's hands, and gave them a reassuring squeeze then went to the back of the room to take a seat facing Wilhelm. "Okay, Detective Wilhelm, I'm ready."

"I'll be brief with you since you live out of town. Do you mind if I record our conversation?"

"I do mind. Please don't."

"All right, I won't." Wilhelm cleared his throat before proceeding. "To your knowledge, did your father and Mrs. Kirby fight a lot?"

"To the contrary, they got along very well."

"What about Laura and your mother?"

"Devoted friends."

"Wasn't your mother bothered by the large amount of time your father and Laura spent together . . . alone?"

"It wasn't an issue."

"So everybody got along fine. Is that what you want me to

believe?"

"That's how it was."

Wilhelm sneered. "You and your mother get riled easily. Short tempers, both of you."

Only when speaking to jerks. Elise fixed her eyes on Wilhelm and waited for his next question.

"Okay, Doctor, do you know of anyone who'd want to hurt either Mrs. Kirby or your father? Any enemies, disgruntled clients, employees, neighbors?"

"I can't think of anyone."

"How well do you know Jeff Kirby?"

"Very well. I've known him since he was a baby."

"Was he always trouble?"

"Jeff was never trouble or in trouble. He's always been a good kid and devoted to his mother."

"You haven't lived in Guilford for years, so you really don't know what he's been like as a teenager."

"Our families are close, and my parents tell me about Jeff all the time. They've never said anything negative about him. They've always remarked what a wonderful young man he is."

Wilhelm flared his nostrils. "I'm running late for my next appointment, so I'll let you go for now. I'll probably have more questions later on."

"I have a question for you."

"Go ahead."

"Did the hospital surveillance footage help in identifying the person who tried to harm my father?"

"There's nothing to report at this point."

"I see. How do you plan to update us when you do find out something?"

"I'll get back to you on that." He stood and left the room.

"A real charmer," Elise said to her mother. "Not only do we have to watch out for the criminals, but we have to duck to avoid abuse by the cops."

"He made me feel like a criminal."

Elise shook her head.

"He sent several accusations my way," Sharon said, "and was really on Jeff's case. He brought up his car accident and the time he got drunk. He raised the point that had Dad died before Laura, Jeff would've benefited from both his and Laura's insurance policies. Do you think he's going to go after Jeff?"

"Not if I can do anything about it. I know Jeff's innocent, and if need be, we'll help him prove it." Elise had a feeling that proving Jeff's innocence might not be so easy to do.

SEVENTEEN

LATER that afternoon Jerry Sanders called Matt to let him know where he stood on his search for the house in Laura Kirby's video. "According to the County Assessor's maps, Matt, there are eight land parcels between seven and eight-hundred Hillcrest Road. I've checked them all out."

"Okay."

"This area of town is a maze. Tall evergreens, long hidden driveways, no numbers. Lots of cover. I would have had a hard time finding the damn houses without a map of the lots."

"Cut to the chase, Jerry."

"Eliminated six of the houses right away. That left seven-sixty-seven, according to the map, Rothe's house, and seven-fifty-seven, the house on the adjoining lot. The two have a common access coming off Hillcrest Road, and then the driveway splits. Funny thing, there's a rope around a tree trunk where the road diverges. I went left to seven-sixty-seven first. No one home, so I looked in the windows. Definitely wasn't the place in the video."

"Elise read in the K&B file that Mrs. Rothe wrapped a rope around the tree so Rick Bell and Laura Kirby could easily find the house."

"The house off to the right, seven-fifty-seven, matches the

description we have. It's a two-story white colonial. Blinds were drawn. I rang the doorbell. No answer right away, but I kept ringing. Finally, a guy with a heavy accent started shouting from behind the door. I leaned on the bell until he opened up. He was an angry dude."

"Did he threaten to call the police?"

"Nope. And I wondered about that," Jerry said. "He seemed really nervous, not afraid, just nervous. Tall, thin, pale guy in his thirties. Sloppily dressed, reeked of turpentine."

"A painter?"

"Yes, as in artist, not house painter."

"What kind of accent?"

"Not sure. I'm not too good with accents. Eastern European, maybe Russian."

"So?"

"He'd been roughed up. Scratches all over his face, puffy left eye."

"What did you tell him?"

"I picked a name out of the air. Asked for Don Pritchard. Anyway, the guy says he doesn't know any Pritchard. Tells me he minds his own business. Has no idea where anybody lives. I thought I'd give it a shot to try to get a look inside. I asked him if I could use the bathroom. He stared at me like I was crazy and shut the door in my face."

"Doesn't like strangers," Matt said.

"Very unfriendly.

"What have you found out about him?"

"Nothing yet. We're waiting to get a glimpse of his car license plate when he leaves. Judging from his bruises, somebody's really mad at him. All the more reason to think something could be going on in there."

"Who's listed as the property owner?"

"According to the tax records, ATR Associates. We're checking who's behind the name."

"Okay. Where do you stand with the K&B client list?"

"Started calling people after we checked with Mrs. Bell. Told them we're following up on Bell's calls since he'll be out of the office until next week. Nobody's asked for Mrs. Kirby yet. So far, we've got nothing."

"Well, keep watching the house."

"Al's on watch until my son Chris gets here. I take over tomorrow morning. We'll keep tabs on whoever comes and goes."

EIGHTEEN

SUNDAY afternoon at three, Stacy let herself in the front door of the Hillcrest Road house and locked it. She immediately went to the office to check the surveillance video and stop the recording.

Sergei was expected at six, so she had time, but it was better to play it safe and do what she needed to right away. He was always looking to catch her and Grigor at something and might show up earlier. In fact, she was convinced the video surveillance system was there to keep tabs on Grigor and her more than it was to guard against break-ins. Otherwise, Sergei would have upgraded the ancient equipment by now.

She grabbed her purse and walked down the hall to the bathroom, locking the door behind her. She'd rehearsed everything in her mind until satisfied all the details had been figured out. Even if Sergei arrived unexpectedly, her being in the bathroom wouldn't arouse his suspicions. The dolt often wisecracked about what broads do in the bathroom. *Her time there would be well spent.*

She put on latex gloves and removed the large chrome towel bar from its holder. Sergei had no idea Grigor and she knew he kept his paraphernalia inside the hollow cavity of the bar. She took the fitting off the end and removed a syringe, plastic tube, razor blade, and a glass vial with Sergei's cut heroin. She took a glassine envelope containing a custom heroin mix from her purse and compared its color against the vial contents. Convinced Sergei wouldn't notice the difference, she emptied the vial down the toilet and substituted the new batch of heroin. *Sergei will get a real kick from this.* She chuckled as she put everything back the way it had been.

She closed the bar and snapped it back in place, then positioned the towels. So far everything had gone smoothly. Now what she had to do was make sure Sergei didn't shoot up before he went on the deliveries to Princeton that evening.

Stacy studied her reflection in the mirror as she stretched to relieve the tension in her back. Her flushed face surprised her. Small beads of perspiration ran down her forehead. She splashed her face with water and dabbed it dry with a soft hand towel. The cool water felt good.

Once the paintings changed hands, she counted on Sergei returning to the house to celebrate by shooting up. Soon he'd no longer be a threat to Grigor and an annoyance to her. No more of his ugly face, foul mouth, lying, and lustful looks to put up with.

After flushing the toilet, she took a slow, thorough look around the bathroom to make sure no telltale signs of her handiwork remained.

She returned to the living room, took a seat on the sofa, and began thumbing through the scientific journals she'd brought with her to pass the hours until Sergei left for Princeton.

Her mind wandered. How ironic, after all her training as a scientist, and her gift for research, she was now doing this. Her father could never have envisioned her engaged in this life. He had dreamed of her becoming a famous biochemist, making great contributions to the world of science. She would have completed her doctorate at Tarson if not for that weasel Enbright and his jealous admin scheming behind her back. Gwen the bitch.

"Whatever you do," her father used to say, "strive to be the very best there is." What would he think of her now? Would he appreciate her fearlessness? She was collecting on the debt society owed him. He'd always toed the line. What did it get him? Illness and an early death. Not her. *Destroy your enemies before they can destroy you.* She would never be a victim.

After the sale of these paintings closed, there'd be enough money for her and Grigor to do all the things they'd ever wanted to. She'd pulled this deal off. Sergei couldn't have done it without her contacts with the art dealers and her ability to manipulate the banking system. After Monday, she'd even have the option to pursue her research, if she chose to. This time, without having to kowtow to someone like Enbright, who stifled her creativity.

That jerk, Sergei, didn't appreciate how vital Grigor was to everything. Without Grigor's knowledge of art, and skills as a painter, Sergei would have nothing to peddle. Sergei had stolen the two originals, but he could only sell those once. Fortunately, there were enough corrupt dealers and dishonest clients around who desired famous paintings and were willing to close their eyes to the fact they might be buying stolen goods. And even more dealers not savvy enough to know the masterpiece they were buying was an original "Kuchma." She smiled to herself.

She felt fury building inside her when she thought of how Sergei treated Grigor, how he felt free to vent his anger on him. One day, during one of his rages, Sergei could kill Grigor. She had to keep him safe. Even had she not loved Grigor, and not wanted to protect him, Sergei had to go. She'd hated him from the first day Grigor introduced them.

The transactions with the galleries would be over by midnight and all funds transferred by start of business Monday. The financial arrangements were secure.

A key clicked in the front door. *Sergei.* She psyched herself up for a little play-acting. "Grigor, finally," she called out before the door opened.

Sergei stuck his head in the door. "Stacy, it's me, not Grigor."

"Damn. I've been waiting for him. We planned to meet here before four in case you needed anything for tonight. I was a little early." She looked down at her watch. "He's never on time." She raised her arms in mock annoyance.

"A drunken loser," Sergei mumbled under his breath.

"What?"

"Nothing." He shook his head from side to side the way he did when trying to decide something. Through clenched teeth he said, "What the hell. All those no-talent artists think they're something special. Better than everyone else. Your pretty boyfriend is just like all the rest of them. Marches along, ignores advice. Look at all the trouble he's caused us."

"You're right." By agreeing with Sergei, she hoped to keep him from talking about the real estate agents and avoid any possible confrontation.

Sergei jolted, eyes open wide.

Her supporting remark appeared to throw him off guard. She continued. "Grigor thinks I'm on earth to shield him from life's inconveniences. He always expects me to protect him, keep him from getting his hands dirty." She grimaced for Sergei's benefit. If she were lucky, he didn't know about yesterday morning's mishap at the hospital and would never find out.

Sergei fired back, "I tried to help him, get him to take responsibility."

"What do you mean?"

"That's why I wanted *him* to eliminate those real estate agents. Make sure they didn't foul up anything. He made the trouble, so he should fix it. And he pawned that off on you."

"Oh, *you* wanted to wake him up to the real world?" *It was not an order coming down from the higher-ups.* "Well, you're right. He has to step up and do his part. He has to correct his own mistakes."

"You're a beautiful, smart woman. You're wasting yourself on him. He's second rate. One step away from being a washed up drunk. You and I set up a great con, with a really big payday, and we had to worry if he could stay sober long enough to finish his part of the deal on time. You're a pro. You could do much better."

Stacy wanted to scream. Sergei had no right to criticize Grigor. He was a revolting druggie, the lowest of the low. She bit her lip to keep from telling him off. Instead, she asked, "Everything's set, isn't it?"

"Yeah. The deliveries are arranged starting at nine tonight with payment locked in."

"So everyone, including Grigor, came through and in time." *Without Grigor's paintings, there would be nothing to sell, you idiot.*

"Yeah, but only because I kept on Grigor's tail, or he'd have screwed everything up."

"Look, bottom-line, what matters is that things go off as planned. Once the deal's done, there'll be no more pressure. We'll get off each other's cases. You'll see."

Sergei stepped slowly towards her. His lips quivered. With an exaggerated motion, he stretched out his arms and wrapped them around her as if to comfort her. "Yes, soon it will be done."

Although disgusted by his closeness, she didn't resist the embrace. It served a purpose. Unfortunately, they were about the same height so she had to endure his hot breath on her face. When he made a move to start kissing her, she eased herself away. "There may be a time for that, but it's not now. I'm not a player. If one day I end things with Grigor, then . . ."

"You can count on me. I hold nothing against you. I've always liked you. You're clever and have real talent. I've gone easy on Grigor because of you." He took a breath and locked eyes with her. "I've even forgiven you for disappointing me." He smiled, exposing his mouth of crooked yellow teeth. She doubted he'd ever been to a dentist.

"Huh? What are you talking about?" *Oh, no. Here it comes.*

"You've botched up eliminating those nosy real estate agents."

She seethed. "They haven't caused any trouble, have they? The deal's going off as planned."

"The guy could still be a problem."

"No way. He's as good as dead. There's nothing he could say or do that would matter, anyway."

Sergei started to protest and then seemed to change his mind. "Okay, I'll take your word for that, but you had better be right."

"I am right. You'll never have any trouble from him. Sergei, you won't have any problems from Grigor or me, anymore, either. Friends?"

"Yeah, *druzh'ya.*"

She reached into her purse and took out her cell phone. "Grigor must have gone to the apartment, instead of coming here. He always forgets where we're supposed to meet." She punched in the number and gestured when Grigor answered. "Sure enough, he's at the apartment," she whispered to Sergei.

"Grigor, I'm at the house. Why aren't you here?" She paused, as if waiting for an answer. "Everything's just fine. I'll stick around in case Sergei needs something. I'll be home after ten." She turned the phone off. "He's not feeling well."

Sergei shrugged. "I'm gonna play back the video surveillance and go for the truck. I'll be back here by seven to load."

"I already checked the video when I got here. There was nothing. I stopped the recording."

"Why?" Sergei stood with an open mouth.

"I'll turn it back on when we leave. I thought you wanted it that way," she said nonchalantly. Without waiting for a response, she added, "I'm going to stay here in case you need anything later."

He glared at her. "Suit yourself." He walked out the front

door and slammed it.

She settled back in her seat. What was important now was that Sergei stay healthy until the deal went off. After that, *skatert'yu doroga*—farewell, Sergei. Go to hell, the sooner the better. She hoped that today would be the last time she had to see that scum alive.

NINETEEN

SHORTLY after 9:00 a.m. on Monday morning, Grigor and Stacy arrived at the Hillcrest Road house and found Sergei's car parked in the garage. Grigor pulled their rented Yukon in alongside and closed the garage door. "You waited until the truck pulled out last night, right?"

"Yeah," she replied. "Don't you remember I told you that when I got home?"

"I wonder if Sergei stayed over, or drove here early this morning?"

"Who cares as long as he shot up."

They got out of the SUV and went into the kitchen. She put her finger to her lips and whispered, "Play it cool just in case." She reached into her purse, took out latex gloves, and handed a pair to Grigor.

He slipped the gloves on. "I'm going to check in the bathroom."

"I'll turn the video off."

She had just finished when Grigor yelled, "Come here, quick."

Grigor stood in the bathroom doorway looking over at Sergei, wedged between the toilet and the sink, his back up against the wall. Dried vomit covered his mouth and chin, and soiled his clothes. A hypodermic needle lodged in his left arm.

"Is he dead?" she asked.

"He looks dead." Grigor quavered. "The door was locked, and there was no answer when I knocked. I had to pick the lock." He kneeled next to Sergei and listened for his heartbeat. "I don't hear anything." He got up and waved Stacy over.

She felt Sergei's neck for a pulse. Nothing. Then touched his hands. Ice cold. "He's dead." She took a piece of paper from her pocket, crumbled it, and placed it in Sergei's left pant pocket. She removed his cell phone and slipped it into her purse.

"Let's get him to his car. Don't touch the syringe. I'll grab his stuff. You follow me to the mall. I want to be sure the police think he OD'd in his car. Leave your gloves on. We don't want any extra prints on anything."

Grigor stood and stared in space, his mouth agape.

"What's the matter with you? Move it!" she ordered.

"I won't touch him. I've had enough of this. Leave him here, and let's clear out. I don't want to do this! He wasn't . . ."

"Stop, Grigor. Get control of yourself. We agreed on a plan. It's no good to change things midstream. That's how you make mistakes."

"Why not leave him here? Why move him?"

"We want them to find the body away from the house," she said. "Then it'll take the cops longer to connect things back to us. It'll buy us time."

"So they find him here. If they want to wrap things up, they will say he broke in. We take his keys."

"Grigor, you're not making any sense. The cops will dust the house for prints. Then they'll come looking for you and for me, even if only to question us."

"I take my chances. We clean up and leave. No reason for nobody to come here. He will rot, and we will be far gone."

A feeling of resignation came over her. She wouldn't be

able to reason with Grigor. His deteriorated speech reflected his state of mind. Without his help, she couldn't move Sergei's body. "I think it's a big mistake, but I'll go along with you. Clear out your studio. Let's clean everything up and get out of here."

She pondered whether to remove Sergei's IDs but decided to leave them. No identification would be a red flag for the police. If they checked with the landlord, they'd get to Sergei since he arranged the lease on the house. Maybe she and Grigor would be lucky and the police would think Sergei's death was simply an overdose. Case closed.

She found Grigor standing in the middle of his studio looking dazed.

"I never thought I would miss this place, but now I am not so sure."

"Try to stay focused and get your things together. There'll be lots of time later on for reminiscing." *He's a basket case, and I'm letting him call the shots?* "Hurry up."

"I get my paints and brushes. Won't take long to pack them." He reached into the cabinet for two large leather cases and started piling paints and brushes inside them.

While he worked, Stacy went from room to room, carefully wiping down surfaces to get rid of fingerprints. Nothing could be left behind to help the police. She took the laptop storing the videos from the surveillance system.

When she finished her part of the cleanup and had moved everything she wanted to the SUV, she went back for Grigor. "What's keeping you so long?"

"Just one thing. I filled my flask." He pointed to a bottle of vodka. "Sergei left it for me with an apology. It's premium stuff, why waste it?"

"You promised me you'd lay off the booze."

"I'm keeping the promise. I haven't touched anything. Give me a break. Don't you realize what a strain this is on me?"

"I'm starting to think you're hopeless. No drinking now."

She gritted her teeth. *Stay calm. It's almost over.*

Grigor screwed the flask closed with a grand move and slipped it into his backpack. He placed the half-empty liquor bottle back on the shelf. "Okay, okay, let's go. You win, but don't deny me this little bit later on for a special occasion." Grigor bent down to strap up his backpack, then stood and slung it over his shoulder. "I'm ready."

"Okay, just the flask. But don't leave that bottle there." She raised her arms in exasperation. "Dump all the rest of the booze down the sink and put the empties in the car. We'll get rid of them on the way home."

Grigor grabbed the bottles and headed to the kitchen sink.

After she did a final once-over of the studio to clean up fingerprints, Stacy headed to the kitchen. "Come on. Let's get out of here."

As she followed Grigor out the door to the garage, Stacy had the nagging feeling that in doing what Grigor wanted she'd made the biggest mistake of her life.

TWENTY

ELISE carried two cups of coffee to a small table in the corner of the Clearview Hospital cafeteria. She glanced at her watch as she sat down: two-forty-five, twenty minutes since Matt called.

When she looked in the direction of the hot food counter, she spotted him standing there and waved.

He hurried over, tiny beads of perspiration on his forehead. "Hi, there." When he leaned toward her, her face warmed in anticipation of his kissing her. But then, he abruptly took the chair next to her, saying, "Coffee. You read my mind."

She felt a letdown as she moved a cup next to him.

"Black, just the way I like it. Thanks." He took a sip. "How's your Dad?"

"Not much change." After a moment she added, "You look like you've got some news. Shoot."

"Does the name Stacy Lenz and a white BMW ring a bell?"

"Sure. She's the woman who came to K&B on Thursday. She drove me here in a white BMW. How do you know her?"

"We have a stakeout on the house at seven-fifty-seven Hillcrest Road. We traced a BMW spotted there, back to a Stacy Lenz at an address in lower Manhattan." Matt took out his phone and showed her a picture. "Is this Stacy?"

Elise glanced at the shot. "Yes. Where did you get that?"

"My guys took pics of everyone who went in and out of that house in the last couple of days."

Elise's eyes lit up. "This is too much of a coincidence. What's going on?"

"Not sure yet. What do you know about her?"

"She talked nonstop when I met her. Whether any of it is true, who knows?" Elise took a sip of her coffee and put down the cup. "She claimed she loves living in NYC but needs to move closer to her new lab job in New Jersey. That's why she came to K&B, to find a place to live."

"Why pick K&B?"

"She saw a flattering article on the agency in the local newspaper."

"That true?"

Elise nodded. "The article was Laura's idea. She thought it might drum up business."

"Did Lenz say anything about having friends nearby?"

"No, but it makes sense she picked this area because she knows people here." Elise thought for a moment. "She rubbed me the wrong way."

"Why?"

"I didn't like her reaction when I told her Laura had died. She didn't seem surprised."

"Are you sure you read her right?"

Elise shrugged.

"Look, she didn't know Laura, so you wouldn't expect much reaction. You might've misinterpreted things."

"Maybe. But there's a lot about her that bothers me. I've seen enough patients with borderline personality disorder at the hospital, that I can spot a manipulative personality. She's manipulative. And she doesn't know me but told me many personal things about herself." Elise paused and played with her fingernail for a moment. She thought of her father and how he'd say he trusted his gut, and it had never failed him. She looked up at Matt. "I have to admit, though, by the time she dropped me off at the hospital, I felt sympathy for her." Elise pursed her lips. "She's charming in some ways. Quite sharp. Has a sad background."

"How so?"

"She told me about her father. He died of leukemia years ago. She's convinced it didn't happen naturally."

"What do you mean?"

"Her family's from the Ukraine. She talked about the Stasi, the East German police during the Communist days. Said they used radioactive material to mark papers and money they gave people they suspected were opponents of the State, so they could follow the distribution. Some of those people died from rare cancers and leukemia. She thinks the KGB did the same thing in the Ukraine, and her father was a victim."

"Wild." Matt scratched his head. "You know, that story worries me."

"Why?"

"People with that kind of history sometimes do bizarre things. Their sense of right and wrong can be warped. They feel they have things coming to them because society wronged their family and them." Matt cleared his throat. "Can you come up with a reason to contact her?"

"Even if I could, she made it clear she didn't want to be contacted. She said she never gives out her phone number. She's either a very private person or has a lot to hide. I'd bet both."

"Jerry's checking her out. Anything else about her I should know?"

"She's a trained scientist. Went to graduate school in the Midwest."

"Where?"

"She didn't name the school. I only know she left there a couple of years ago."

"Okay. We should be able to track her down."

"What about that Russian who Jerry spoke to? What do you know about him?"

"Name's Grigor Kuchma. Came here from the Ukraine several years ago. He's a professional artist. Graduated from the Art Institute there. He and the Lenz woman have lived together in lower Manhattan for over a year now."

Elise nodded.

"My guys talked to their neighbors. Nobody knew anything about them, or if they did, they weren't saying."

"What about the building manager?"

"I spoke to the landlady. Chatted her up a bit and then told her that Stacy gave her as a credit reference. I got the feeling she didn't like Stacy or her boyfriend much. She said they pay their rent on time and in cash. Lenz works in a lab in Hoboken, and her boyfriend has a studio somewhere in central Jersey."

"I feel like we have a stack of pieces to a liquid puzzle, but nothing fits together, and the shape keeps changing," Elise suddenly felt very tired.

"Be patient," Matt said. "We're making progress, and once Laura's final autopsy results are in, maybe we'll know more about what we're dealing with."

"You're focusing in on that house and those people, what about other leads?"

"Like?"

"The preliminary autopsy results pointed to poisoning."

"We're checking out all the places your father and Laura went. Once we learn what poison we're dealing with, we'll have a better shot at finding something out."

"What's next?"

"We're logging all activity at the house. Sometime when everyone's out, we'll get a peek inside."

"How can you do that? You're not planning to break in, are you?" Elise flinched when she saw Matt's reaction to her remarks.

"I'm going to pretend you didn't ask me that." Matt

scowled. "There are other ways to get a look inside without breaking in."

"Sorry." Elise felt her face flush. "Do you know where the police investigation stands?" She had to change the subject and distance herself from her *faux pas*.

"So far, no."

"I wanted to ask about Detective Wilhelm. It seems like he's after Jeff."

"Probably checking him out because of the insurance policies. I warned you about that."

"It's more than that," Elise said. "When Wilhelm questioned my mother and me on Saturday, he focused in on the car accident Jeff had in July, insinuating Jeff was bad news." She shook her head. "It's just not true. The accident wasn't his fault. What can we do to get Wilhelm off Jeff's back?"

"He's just fishing. If he were convinced Jeff's involved, he would've brought him in for questioning."

"What if he brings him in later on?"

"If Wilhelm makes any accusations, Jeff can volunteer to take a lie detector test."

Elise frowned. "If he were your kid, would you advise him to do that? What about false positives?"

Matt took a deep breath and exhaled. "I'd still risk it," he said. "When are Jeff and his aunt leaving for Minnesota?"

"They're still not sure. It's taking more time to do things than they thought it would."

"Tell you what. I'll talk to Jeff."

"Good." Elise pushed some stray hairs behind her ear. "Wilhelm was unpleasant when he spoke to us. He really pressed my mother. He seems to have a problem with women."

"Yep, that's Wilhelm." Matt sneered. "He comes on too strong, but he's smart. Once he finishes grilling you and is convinced you've squared with him, he'll leave you alone. Cooperate, but stand up to him. Don't let him bully you."

"Why is he such a jerk?"

Matt took a sip of coffee and lowered his voice. "He got burned in a case a few years ago. Got too close to a good-looking female suspect. She convinced him she was innocent, and he bent the rules for her. Turned out she was guilty and had pulled one over on him. He wrecked his marriage in the process and almost ruined his career too. Burt Parsons, his partner, saved his neck. Now Wilhelm shies away from personal relationships with women and goes overboard to cover his back."

"I remember Burt. He was a nice guy."

"Yeah. We go way back. You know, he's Kara's brother."

Elise touched her throat. "Isn't that awkward for you? Dealing with Burt?"

"No, it's fine. We've known each other since we were kids. We went to Rutgers together and partnered on several cases when I was with the police. We mourned together when Kara died. No issues between us, if that's what you mean. You can work with him."

"Will Wilhelm keep us informed, or will we have to go around him to Burt to find out anything?" Elise hoped for the former, but strongly suspected the latter.

"Wilhelm won't communicate. You'll do better with Burt."

"What should I do next?"

"Call the station tomorrow morning early and ask for Burt. Tell him I told you to call. He'll level with you. Even with him, don't volunteer any information."

"Why the caution?"

"Just answer the police questions. Tell them the facts. Don't speculate on anything. It can complicate things." Matt paused and rubbed the side of his nose, as if he wanted time to think. "Let's leave it at that for now. Just take my advice."

"All right. Mum's the word."

"I'm going to talk to Burt and feel him out about Jeff. Maybe things with Wilhelm aren't as bad as you think."

Elise nodded. She waited for a few moments then asked, "Who else was at that house?"

"Another guy. Shorter than the painter. He came and went in a black Lincoln. We know his name and are digging into his background."

"Are they all Russians?"

"Russian and Ukrainian."

"I thought they don't get along with each other," Elise remarked.

"These guys may be hanging around together for convenience. Who knows how well they get along?"

"If they don't live there, what are they doing in that house?"

"Good question. Last night around six-thirty a truck showed up. Jerry said some guys spent a couple of hours loading it. The license plate was obscured, so he couldn't get a make on the truck."

"What did they load?"

"Some crates and paintings. The black Lincoln left with the truck then returned to the house around midnight. Jerry's son, Chris, tailed them to Princeton, where they stopped at three pretty upscale art galleries. He got the names of the places but couldn't get in close enough to really see what was going on without blowing his cover."

"What do you make of that?"

Matt hesitated before speaking. "Could be totally legit. A small-scale art-dealing operation or one of those estate sale outfits where they peddle pricey art objects. But they could also be thieves and smugglers laundering stolen goods. We know there's no business license for the house address."

"Don't you think something's wrong here?"

"Maybe yes, maybe no. If they're just cutting corners, violating zoning and doing things on the cheap, that's not something we'd get involved in."

"It's strange to deliver merchandise on a Sunday night, isn't it? Aren't most gallery deliveries made during the hours they're open for business?"

"Galleries probably arrange deliveries whenever it's convenient for them. The bottom line is none of this matters to us unless we can prove a connection between what they are up to and your father and Laura."

Elise nodded. She rubbed her chin and thought for a moment. "Do any of these guys have a criminal record?"

"If they do, we'll find out. It'll be a good piece of info, but won't really solve anything. Their records could be clean, and they could still be bad guys."

"If this were a movie, they'd be international spies bent on getting rid of my father and Laura for some bizarre reason I can't even imagine."

"Well, it's not a movie, and we need solid evidence connecting them all, or we'll get nowhere."

"Are you going to tell the police?"

"Right now we don't have anything concrete to tell."

"What about tailing those Russian guys?"

"Let's see first what the background checks show. Otherwise, we could waste a lot of time going down the wrong track. We need to find a reason why they'd go after your father and Laura. Right now, nothing jumps out at us."

"How can I help?"

Matt stared at the next table and appeared deep in thought. A few moments passed before he responded. "I know it's unlikely, but if Stacy Lenz calls your Dad's office, arrange to meet her. I'll go with you."

"Okay. I've been wondering if you found any surprises about my father and Laura?

"Nothing yet."

"Don't misunderstand me. I'm not worried you will."

"We're looking to see if they made any enemies during the

years they were involved in local politics. We need more time to flesh that out. I'll talk with Tim to see what he knows."

Elise nodded and looked at her watch.

Matt stood. "I'm going back to my office for a few hours, and then I'll swing by for you and your mom. See you later, Kara."

Elise heard Matt call her by his late wife's name, Kara, but didn't react. She had no desire to embarrass him by drawing attention to his slip of the tongue. He was beginning to fill a void in her life. She hoped this indicated she had become an integral part of his.

TWENTY-ONE

MATT arrived promptly at Tim Dixon's office at 4:30 p.m. for their appointment. He glanced at the stacks of papers on Tim's desk and the boxes lining the office walls. "Thanks for fitting me in," Matt said. "It looks like you're pretty busy."

"I've got a bunch of deadlines coming up." Tim pulled out a chair for Matt. "If not, I would've taken a few weeks off after Laura . . ." He crumpled his forehead as he took a seat behind his desk. "Actually, I'm grateful for the work. The familiar routine keeps me going. Otherwise, I don't know how I'd get through this time."

Every few seconds there was a clinking sound and Tim glanced at the large monitor on his desk. "I'm used to that sound, but I know it bothers some people. I'm watching the activity in after-hours trading. Just a few more minutes. I hope it doesn't distract you. Please, fire away."

Matt nodded. The sound didn't really bother him, but he found Tim's divided attention annoying. "Have the police contacted you yet?"

"Yes. Detective Wilhelm stopped by this morning. He asked me a lot of questions. He's a bit rough around the edges." Tim's eyes turned to the screen. "That's it. I'm done." He powered down his computer. "Sorry about that. Now you have my full attention."

"Did Wilhelm seem to be after something specific?"

"He asked how long I've known Laura and Rick and how their business was doing."

"And?"

"My friendship with Laura and Dave, her late husband, goes back many years." He cleared his throat. "I was their accountant from the time they went into business." He rubbed his chin. "My wife died three years before Dave. Laura and Dave helped me get through difficult times."

"What about Rick Bell?"

"I met Rick through Dave . . . and we got to know each other quite well after Rick teamed up with Laura."

"How was their business doing?" Matt asked.

"As I told Wilhelm, it was doing okay. A little slow, but no real problems."

"Did Rick and Laura get on well?"

He nodded. "They were a good team."

"Were they especially close?"

"In what sense?" Tim's raised his eyebrows.

"Any sense."

"They liked each other and were supportive. Nothing more. Sharon and Laura were the close friends."

"Do you know of anyone who might have something in for either Laura or Rick?"

"You're asking because of the autopsy results, aren't you? That floored me. It must be some terrible accident. I told Wilhelm I can't think of anyone who'd want to harm either of them." He shook his head. "No one. Laura confided in me, and she never mentioned any trouble with anyone."

"Jeff said she was very upset on the Monday night, two days before she died. Sharon said Rick was upset too. Do you have any idea why?"

"The three of us had lunch on Tuesday. I didn't notice anything unusual. They were both a little skittish because we talked finances, in particular, a loan that they were applying for. But that was all business as usual. I'm baffled by the whole thing."

"May I ask what the loan was for?"

"They've been leasing their office condo and decided to buy it. I gave them the go-ahead. The numbers made it advantageous to purchase rather than rent. It also made more sense to finance than to pay cash."

Matt took out a pen and paper and made some notes. "By the way, did you speak to Laura last Monday?"

"Briefly, first thing in the morning. We both had a lot going on that day. I also had a business meeting in the evening that kept me out quite late."

"Over the last few years do you recall them ever having any conflicts or problems with anyone?"

Tim did not answer immediately. He appeared deep in thought, his eyes gazing at the window behind Matt. "There was one controversy, but . . ."

"But?"

"I doubt it's anything." He leaned forward and locked eyes with Matt. "About two, three years ago, Rick and Laura were both pretty vocal in opposing a land deal bringing a one-hundred-home-development into town"

"What happened?"

"The development was approved. The houses are up. Don't you remember the whole thing? Woodard Homes? There was a lot of coverage in the newspapers."

"Vaguely. Do you think the builders might hold a grudge against them?"

He shook his head. "If they'd managed to quash the deal, maybe they would have, but as far as I know, Rick and Laura's speaking out was nothing more than a nuisance for the builders. In the end, the builders got what they wanted."

"Why were they against the deal?"

"They were afraid it would spoil the small-town character of Guilford. Ethically, they opposed variances for big builders that undermined zoning. Woodard wanted to put twice as many houses on the tract as the zoning allowed. Laura and Rick suspected kickbacks were involved, but they couldn't prove it."

"You must have had a reason to bring it up."

Tim nodded. "It's because the town was divided on the issue. It meant jobs and increased business for local merchants during hard times. People said nasty things to Rick and Laura. Not just the builders. It took a long time until things cooled down." He shrugged. "They kept a very low profile after that. That is, until the big article about them last week."

"Hmm. Let me have some names. I'll do some quiet investigating. I doubt there's a connection after this much time has passed . . . unless something happened very recently to stir up old issues."

Tim reluctantly revealed the names. "Most likely, you'll be spinning your wheels. The police looked into it at the time and didn't find anything."

Matt moved to another subject. "Did Laura or Rick have any Russian acquaintances?"

"Russian? Not that I know of. Why do you ask?"

"Just looking for connections."

Tim appeared puzzled, but nodded.

Matt leaned back in his chair. "What are your plans, Tim?"

Tim's expression became very serious. "No long-term plans. I'm set here in Guilford for good, although I'm going to take a few weeks off later this month to go to Oregon to see my son and his family." He paused for a moment, "After I lost my wife, I was lonely for a long time until I started seeing Laura. I'm feeling lost and lonely again . . . but I'm also stronger. Laura was very sick this past summer. I went through the emotions of losing her then. I didn't think she would make it. Neither did she."

"Believe me, Tim, I can relate. I've been a widower for a year now. When I lost my wife, I didn't think I could go on but I took one day at a time and managed."

The two men sat silently for a few moments. Then Matt stood. "Thanks, for your time." He extended his hand to Tim. "Before I go, was there anything you discussed with Wilhelm you haven't mentioned to me?"

"Well, we talked about Jeff. He asked if Jeff and Laura got on well and if he ever got into trouble."

"What did you tell him?"

"Jeff's a great kid, one that I would be proud to have as a son."

"What was Wilhelm's reaction?"

"Believe it or not, he just grunted."

"I believe it."

TWENTY-TWO

CHRIS Sanders emerged from the woods onto a side street off Hillcrest Road. He slipped into the passenger seat of a dark-color Prius parked under a tree. His father, Jerry, sat behind the wheel staring into the dashboard mirror. They shared the night shift watching the house at 757 Hillcrest Road.

"It's getting cold out there." The tall, muscular twenty-six year old rubbed his hands together. "No sign of anyone. House's totally dark. Not a sound," he said. "The time's right for us to get a look at what's going on inside."

"I called Matt." Jerry checked the time on his cell phone. "It's almost ten. He'll be here any minute. He didn't want us to go in alone."

"I'm antsy for some action. I hate these watching-the-house-for-days jobs. You spend ninety-nine percent of the time on your feet, twiddling your thumbs."

"Stop complaining so much. You're getting paid. You should be grateful you have a job."

"Why don't you can that line already?"

Jerry kept his eyes on the mirror while bantering with his son. Chris was a good kid but high maintenance. At the first sign of approaching headlights, he said, "That must be Matt."

Matt parked three car lengths behind Jerry's car and got out. He looked around before approaching the Prius, checked the license plate, and then shined a flashlight into the driver's window.

Jerry rolled the window down. "Hey, cut that out, Matt."

"Sorry, guys . . . just wanted to be sure everything was cool. Ready to roll?"

"Yeah. I'll play guard and text you if anyone shows up," Jerry said.

Chris leaned in front of his father and said to Matt, "I just got back from looking around the house. Didn't spot any cameras or alarms. It'll be no problem getting in through the side door of the garage."

Matt nodded.

"I've scoped out the surrounding woods for the best way to approach," Chris added. "On the right side, just about twenty feet in, we can access the house. Everything's pretty overgrown so there's good cover."

"Okay, let's get going," Matt said.

Jerry handed latex gloves and night goggles to Matt. Chris and Jerry got out of the car and put theirs on.

There were no cars in sight as the three men slipped into the woods one by one. Once they were away from the road, they moved forward quickly, only infrequently whispering to each other. Jerry chose a lookout position on the higher portion of the lot, where he could see both the house and the start of the driveway.

Chris led Matt to the side door of the garage. He took a set of small lock picks from his pocket and whispered to Matt, "Hey, turn around so you're not a witness to what I'm doing." He worked for a couple of minutes before muttering, "You won't believe it, the door's already open. Cheap lock." He chuckled. "Some crook could rob them. Lucky it's only us law-abiding guys."

"Okay, Chris, enough with the cute remarks. Let's get in, do what we came to do, and get out."

When Matt saw the black Lincoln parked in the garage, he whispered, "Oh, crap, you said nobody's here."

"Probably all left together in that Yukon that stopped here this afternoon," Chris retorted.

"You better be right. Getting caught inside would be big trouble. Follow me. If I remember right, this door should lead into the kitchen."

"Huh. How'd you know that?"

"Laura Kirby's video."

"Oh, yeah."

Matt turned the doorknob and slowly opened the door. He slipped into the room, carefully inching forward, his back to the wall, his ears tuned for any unusual sound. Once satisfied it was safe to proceed, he motioned to Chris to follow him.

The two men walked toward the door in the far corner of the room. Matt cracked the door and moved to the side. No sound. He paused for another moment then entered the hallway. Nightlights glimmered at each end. They both lifted their goggles. Matt signaled he'd take the door across the hallway, gestured to Chris to go left. Each man moved quickly and silently.

Matt cautiously opened the door, stepped in, and surveyed the room with his flashlight. The painter's studio. Paint residues marked the floor in one section, probably where he kept his easels. With the exception of four large storage cabinets lining the wall, the room appeared empty. The shades on the windows were drawn. Matt debated for a moment about turning on the room lights to get a thorough look but decided not to. No sense taking unnecessary chances. The flashlight would have to do.

He opened all the cabinet doors and inspected every inch of the interior. Rubber bands, clips, string, and clumps of dust were strewn about on the shelves. Someone had been in a hurry clearing out. He flashed his light up and down a second time hoping to discover something of value he'd missed on the first go-round. Nothing caught his eye. Just before shutting the doors on the last cabinet, he crouched and spotted pieces of paper wedged in the corner of the bottom shelf. He pulled the pieces out one by one. Pieces of a photograph. He slipped them into his jacket pocket.

Chris came into the room and whispered, "I've found something in the bathroom. A giant cold turkey with a needle stuck in the wing."

"A tall, blond guy?"

"Nope. Short legs. Straw-colored hair, pockmarked face. He's pale as a ghost and staring into space. Doesn't look too good and smells nasty." Chris beckoned Matt to follow him.

"Guess it's not the painter your father spoke to the other day." Matt said.

"More likely the guy I followed to Princeton last night."

"Any ID on him?"

"Name on the New York driver's license in his wallet is Sergei Rimakov. Lives in Brooklyn."

"The Lincoln's registered to him. What else did you find?"

"Carrying lots of cash. All big bills."

Matt knelt and shined his flashlight on the dead man's arms. "Lots of needle marks." He stood.

"Take a look at where he stashed his stuff." Chris pointed to a towel bar, tubing, and razor blade lying on the floor. "I've heard of all sorts of hiding places but it's the first time I've actually seen this one."

Matt flashed his light on the chrome bar and nodded. He turned his attention back to the body. "Take a shot of his driver's license and the rest of the stuff and put everything back where you found it. Anything else on him?"

"Dirty tissues . . . and this crumbled piece of paper in his pants pocket."

"Any writing on it?"

"Says Bell and two-twelve."

"This guy's connected to Rick Bell? Let me see."

Chris handed the paper to Matt.

"How convenient." He returned the paper to Chris who put it back in the dead man's pocket.

"I guess he didn't leave in the Yukon."

"Brilliant conclusion, Chris, but not what I meant." Matt glanced at his watch. "Okay, leave him there. Let's check the rest of this place and get out. You finish this floor. Be real careful. Don't trip over any other bodies. I'm going upstairs."

Chris nodded and knelt next to the corpse. Matt watched him for a few seconds then headed in search of the staircase to the upper floor.

AN hour later, Matt sat in his car holding a throwaway cell phone. He punched in 911.

"Nine-one-one. What is your emergency?"

"I want to report a dead body."

"Are you in a safe location?"

"Yes."

"What is your location, sir?"

"The body's in the first floor bathroom of a white colonial at seven-fifty-seven Hillcrest Road." He hung up.

Matt sat for a moment then reached into his pocket. He took out the pieces of the photograph and fit them together on his lap. He knew the person he needed to talk to. Maybe then he'd have a clearer idea of what was going on in that house.

TWENTY-THREE

ELISE sat by the window in her father's hospital room, enjoying the warm morning sunlight while scanning printouts from an Internet search she'd run the night before. From time to time she stared out at the traffic, wondering how things were going back in Scottsdale.

A sudden knock at the door and in walked Detective Wilhelm. He gave her a limp wave and glanced at her father's bed before approaching her.

"Good morning, Detective," she said coolly. She stood and set the pages down on her chair. *What does he want now?*

"I'd like to talk to both you and your mother. Is she around?"

"No. She had to go into work for a few hours. She'll be here this afternoon." Elise waited for him to respond.

"We found Sergei's body last night." Wilhelm scowled as he spoke.

"Who?" She took a step back from him.

"Sergei Rimakov."

Elise shrugged. "I have no idea who that is."

"Are you sure?"

"Of course, I'm sure." Wilhelm's game playing irritated

her.

Without taking his eyes off her, Wilhelm reached into his pocket and pulled out a snapshot, which he handed to her. "This is Rimakov, taken last night."

"I've never seen him before." She handed the photo back to Wilhelm. "What happened to him?"

"OD'd on heroin."

"Oh." She raised her eyebrows. "Why do you think I'd know him?"

"A paper in his pocket had your father's name and room number on it."

Elise nodded. "What kind of work did he do?"

"We're checking."

"Where did you find his body?"

"In a house on Hillcrest Road."

"Hillcrest Road?"

"You know the area?"

Elise pondered what to say. "My father has a client on Hillcrest Road."

"Uh huh."

"Are you sure this man OD'd?"

"We won't be certain until autopsy results are in and we have the tox results. Why?"

"I just wondered because of Mrs. Kirby. The poisoning."

Wilhelm nodded slowly.

The door opened, and a nurse entered the room. Elise and Wilhelm watched as she greeted them, checked on Elise's father and quickly left.

Elise took a deep breath. "There's something I should mention." Her voice trembled.

"Yeah?"

"We watched a video Laura Kirby made last Monday. It was supposed to be of a new listing on Hillcrest Road. By the end of the video, Laura and my father realized they weren't actually where they thought they were."

"What?" Wilhelm grimaced.

Elise didn't like the condescending look on his face, but decided to ignore it. "It seems they may have gone to the wrong house. A number of the houses on Hillcrest Road look alike and aren't numbered in front. I wonder if they could have been near the house where you found Rimakov?"

"I'll need to see that video." He stared at Elise with piercing eyes.

"Okay. I can get you a copy."

"Yeah. It might shed light on the connection between your father and the deceased Mr. Rimakov."

"Rimakov died while my father was in the hospital, so he couldn't have seen his body, you do realize that?"

Wilhelm didn't respond to Elise's question but instead remarked, "Anything else you've neglected to mention?"

"No, but I have a question for you."

"Like what?"

"Did you find prints on the syringe my father's assailant left behind?"

"Yeah. We lifted prints."

"And?"

"They were Rimakov's. It looks like the syringe could've been his."

"So he was the one masquerading as an attendant?" Elise gasped. "What was in the syringe?"

"Potassium chloride with traces of heroin."

"Potassium chloride? So he intended to kill my father!" Elise blurted.

"Don't jump the gun, ma'am, on who did what." Wilhelm rubbed his upper lip. "Things point to Rimakov's possible involvement. We don't know for sure where he fits in yet."

"I don't understand. If his fingerprints are on the syringe, why isn't that proof enough?"

"It's like this. He could be a hired hand. Could also be he didn't do it and someone's framing him. They could've taken his syringe and used it. We can come up with lots of theories, but we need solid evidence to nail any one of them down."

"What did you find out about the wig and clothes found in the men's room?"

"We're waiting on DNA results. They take time."

"When do you expect to have the results?"

"When we get them. As I said, things take time. The lab's very busy."

Elise's lips tightened at Wilhelm's response. "Someone tried to kill my father. No matter who did it, my father needs police protection now. His life's in danger."

"Calm down. We're working on it. You've got Merano's guys until then." He grunted

Elise struggled to remain calm.

Wilhelm's cell phone chimed. He checked the screen. "I need to leave. Good-bye, ma'am." He walked out of the room.

A few minutes later he popped his head in the door. "We have an officer on the way to stand guard at your father's door. Happy now, Dr. Bell?" Without another word, he left.

The man baffled Elise. His behavior incensed her. For a moment she was tempted to go after him and ask why he made things so difficult but decided it would be a waste of effort.

Elise took out her cell phone and punched in Matt's number. He picked up on the first ring.

"Wilhelm was here. Every time I speak to the guy, I feel like smacking him," she said. "At least, he's finally assigning an officer to guard my father."

"What did he tell you?"

She related her conversation with Wilhelm. "He asked if I knew the dead man, Rimakov. His prints were found on the syringe you turned over to the police."

"What did you say?"

"That I didn't know him." Elise wrinkled her brow. "Since potassium chloride was in the syringe, it's clear he was out to kill my father." She sighed and added, "The needle jab you got shouldn't have hurt you."

"Honestly, when nothing happened to me right away, I put the whole thing out of my mind."

"I agreed to give Wilhelm a copy of Laura's video."

"Okay. I'll get it to him." Matt cleared his throat. "Just so you know, Rimakov was the Russian in the Black Lincoln we spotted at the Hillcrest Road house. I didn't have his name when I spoke to you."

A thought flashed through Elise's mind. "I may have spotted Rimakov's car near my parents' house on Thursday morning." She gave Matt the details. *Had she and her mother been in more danger than they realized?*

"It's possible he was watching your house."

She caught a ragged breath. "Matt, did you know Rimakov was dead?"

"I knew, but thought it better you find out some other way, not from me."

"Why didn't . . .?" Elise stopped mid-sentence and thought for a moment. "You're right. This way I didn't have to worry about slipping up and saying the wrong thing when I talked to Wilhelm."

"Jerry's running a background check on Rimakov. He stayed under the radar more than Stacy Lenz and her boyfriend. Because of his drug use, I think there's a chance he has a record."

"I wonder if Rimakov could've been poisoned . . . like Laura?"

"He was a heroin addict. I saw the track marks, so I'd bet he OD'd."

"You saw the body?"

"Yes. Let's leave it at that."

Elise shook her head. She wasn't going to press Matt. "They're doing an autopsy and tox tests."

"So they should nail down what happened to him."

"Wilhelm surprised me by saying Rimakov might have been framed. Does that make sense to you?"

"Maybe Wilhelm was baiting you."

"Really? Do you think his death could've been faked?"

"Anything's possible. Let's wait for the investigation and tox results. If it turns out the police have to go looking for his supplier, something tells me they won't be too anxious to put manpower on it. More likely, it'll be open and shut: another druggie OD's."

A shudder ran down Elise's spine. "It wouldn't surprise me if Stacy Lenz had a hand in this."

"Right now there's nothing to back that up." There was a clicking sound on the line. "Hold for a second," Matt said, "I've got to take another call."

Elise sat with her eyes shut waiting for Matt to come back on the line. She tried to work her way through everything that had happened.

"Okay, I'm back."

"I meant to ask you about Laura's kitchen plants. Were any of them poisonous?"

"Nope. Just common herbs."

"That eliminates that possibility."

"Look, I made an appointment in Manhattan. How'd you like to take a break and ride with me?"

"Sure. I haven't been there in years. What's going on?"

"I'll explain when I pick you up. See you at one."

Elise hung up. It would be nice to spend some time alone with Matt. She smiled at the thought.

TWENTY-FOUR

THE intercom buzzed, bringing Matt out of his thoughts about the Bell case. He reached for the phone. The receptionist's formal voice brought him to attention.

"Matt, Detective Parsons is here to see you."

"Okay. Please send him back."

Matt and Burt had been friends long before Matt married Kara, Burt's sister. Their friendship had survived Kara's death, and they had managed to find a way to interact congenially even when they were on opposing sides of a police case.

Matt shook hands with Burt. "Good to see you. Thanks for coming to pick up Laura Kirby's video."

A year older than Matt, Burt at thirty-two, a bachelor by choice, looked at least five years older. He stood roughly five-feet nine to Matt's six feet. By comparison Burt, slight-framed, with a pale complexion, and thinning blond hair, made Matt appear even more muscular and darker than he was. Every time Matt saw Burt, his strong resemblance to Kara, brought back painful memories. Losing her was the toughest thing Matt ever faced.

"Come in, have a seat." Matt gestured to a visitor's chair by his desk.

"So Burt, what did Wilhelm tell you about the video?"

"Basically, he said Elise Bell thought it might connect her father and Laura Kirby to the house on Hillcrest and to the Russian who OD'd there."

"That's reasonable."

Burt leaned forward in his chair. "Okay, Matt, let's talk. Off the record."

Matt's guard went up. Burt's expression signaled a serious discussion.

"I know the Bells hired you to investigate things before this became a police matter. It'll save both of us time if you fill me in on what you've found out."

"I'll do it if you'll be straight with me. But it has to stay between us. Wilhelm can't know."

"You've got my word." He gave a quick smile. "You know how I feel about Wilhelm. He's already badmouthing the Bells." Burt paused. "Hey, look, I'm risking more than you are. If it gets out I leaked anything to you, I could lose my job. Wilhelm's one suspicious SOB, as you are well aware."

"Then I'll cut to the chase. Even though Rimakov's fingerprints were on the syringe, I don't think he's the one who poisoned Kirby and Bell. Correction, if Rimakov's implicated, he didn't do it alone."

"Who else do you think's involved?"

"Two people: Stacy Lenz and Grigor Kuchma. Kuchma's an artist who works in that Hillcrest Road house. Lenz is his girlfriend. She went to the K&B office last Tuesday morning and met with Laura Kirby and Rick Bell. So one thing's for sure, she had an opportunity to get to them."

"So what? What makes you think she'd have any reason to?"

"Good question. Some things about her just don't add up. To start, her expensive car. Way out of the league for someone who was a student a couple of years ago. Also, she tries to be too helpful. She insisted on driving Elise to the hospital. I smell a rat."

"Sounds like a Merano hunch, huh Matt? Wishful thinking, maybe?" Burt removed some papers from the inside pocket of his jacket. He flipped through them and focused on one page. Without lifting his eyes, he asked, "Are your guys watching the Hillcrest house?"

"Don't make me lie to you."

He nodded. "I didn't ask you if you've been inside. I take it you know who's been coming and going there. And what they've been doing."

"Yeah, I know who's been to the house. As far as knowing what they were doing, the answer is maybe." Matt knew it didn't make sense for him to deny watching the house. Parsons's men must have spotted Jerry or Chris.

"What do you know about the late Mr. Rimakov?"

"Not much." Matt shook his head. "Are you guys cool with his overdosing?"

"He has tracks all over him. Definitely a user. The lab guys figure he injected himself with some bad stuff. We won't take it any further at this point. How he got hold of the heroin will be his secret, unless the Brooklyn police pursue it since that's where he lived."

"So you think he did it to himself, not that someone did it to him?"

"No restraining marks on him, no other drugs in his system, so no reason to suspect force," Burt said. "Maybe he just got some bad product on the street."

Matt nodded. "What did you find out about him?"

"He's been involved in bringing art objects into the U.S. from Russia and reselling them all across the country. Lots of charges raised but none that stuck. The guy was clever. He managed to move in some fancy art circles using different aliases. Fooled experts in the business."

"That explains his trip to Princeton," Matt said.

"What trip to Princeton?"

"My sources say he went along with a truck that made drops at three galleries in Princeton on Sunday night."

"Any specifics?"

"That's all I know now. We're working on it." Matt paused. "Did you find anything interesting when you searched the house?"

"Security cameras."

"Oh, yeah?" Matt sat up straight in his chair.

"None in the bathroom where the body was."

"Were the cameras on?" Matt asked.

"No. It was an older closed-circuit pc-based system, and the pc was gone."

"Too bad." Matt shook his head. "Find any prints you could identify?"

"We lifted several and have a make on most of them. We only got Kuchma's and Rimakov's from the bathroom." Burt looked again at his notes. "I don't see Lenz's name here. If she was at the house, she must have worn gloves all the time."

"Or did some housecleaning. It might pay for your guys to look again and harder."

"Sure."

"Any DNA results in from the wig and scrubs I found in the men's room?"

Burt shook his head. "We've put a rush on it. But the lab's backed up, as always."

"What's your take on this whole thing?"

"If a lot of time passes before we get results, I think there will be pressure to pin it all on Rimakov and close the case."

"Does that sit right with you?"

"You know me better than that, Matt. I don't quit 'til I get to the real bottom of things. No shortcuts or easy outs."

"One bit of advice. Keep Stacy Lenz in mind, and watch out for her."

"Advice taken. What do you know about her?"

"She works at some lab up in Hoboken. She's bound to have access to all sorts of stuff there." Matt stood and walked around his desk. He stopped near Burt's chair and leaned back against the desk facing him. "Get Rimakov's face plastered in papers and on TV all over NYC and down to Philly. Go heavy in the Princeton area. Someone's sure to recognize him."

"Hey, Matt. I know my job. Don't pull a Wilhelm on me."

"Sure, Burt. Sorry." He held up his hands. "I'm just a little anxious. No insults meant."

"None taken. Just don't do it again." Burt paused. "Hey, would your clients go for putting up some reward money to loosen tongues?"

"I'll check with them. They might agree."

"Elise mentioned that Wilhelm seems to really be on Jeff Kirby's case. Don't tell me he thinks Jeff tried to kill his mother?"

"You know Wilhelm. Everyone's guilty until proven innocent. I don't think the Kirby kid did anything, but he stands to come into a good deal of money. People have done a lot more for a lot less, even so-called devoted sons and daughters."

"What can Jeff do to get himself off the list of suspects?"

"Just stay available and tell us the truth when we ask him questions."

"What about a lie detector test?"

"Is he offering to take one?"

"Possibly. He doesn't want you guys wasting time going after him and letting the crooks get away."

"I'll talk to Wilhelm." Burt stood and looked around the office at the rosewood paneling and expensive furniture and smiled. "I'll keep you in the loop. Someday I might come here looking for a job."

"Anytime." They shook hands again. "Something else I meant to ask you."

"Yeah, Matt?"

"Remember the company that built a hundred homes in

town a few years back?"

"Sure. Woodard Homes. What do you want to know about them?"

"There was some talk about kickbacks. Was anything ever found out?"

"Nah. It was just gossip. We spent a lot of time on it, and nothing turned up. Why the interest now?"

"Just some speculation that Bell and Kirby made some enemies by opposing the deal, and the so-called enemies might have gotten even with them."

"Not likely. Why would anyone go after Kirby and Bell and not the other two hundred or more people who spoke out against the deal?"

"You make a good point. I was just wondering if there was some angle on this that I wasn't seeing."

Burt shook his head. He inched closer to the door and reached for the knob.

"Hey, don't forget this." Matt reached into the top drawer of his desk. He took out a thumb drive with Laura's video and handed it to Burt.

Burt put it in his pocket and nodded as he walked out.

Matt felt good about their meeting. He looked at his watch. It was time to get Elise and go to see a man about a photo.

TWENTY-FIVE

"**ARE** you sure you can trust Graiville?" Elise asked Matt as they approached the entrance to the Graiville Gallery on the ground level of a brownstone on Manhattan's Upper East Side.

"Absolutely. Don't give it a second thought, Elise." He reached out, opened the door for her, and they headed to the reception desk.

The woman on duty greeted Matt, and they chatted briefly. She gestured for him to go right back to Mr. Graiville's office.

Pierce Graiville, a distinguished looking white-haired man in his late sixties, smiled and stood when Matt knocked on his open door.

"Hello, Pierce. I appreciate your meeting with us on such short notice." Matt and Graiville shook hands.

"Always my pleasure." Graiville glanced at Elise with an approving look and back at Matt. "Glad for the opportunity to see you again."

"This is my friend, Dr. Elise Bell."

"Please call me Elise." She noticed that Graiville's dark gray suit was finely tailored, probably custom-made.

"I'm glad to meet you, Elise." Graiville shook hands with her then turned to Matt. "It's lucky you called when you did and I

160

could fit you in. I'm leaving for a two-week vacation in Italy on Friday."

Graiville motioned for them to be seated and went behind his desk.

"Pierce, rather than waste your time, let me tell you exactly why we're here. First, it's important you keep our entire conversation confidential."

Graiville reached into his desk and took out three copies of a confidentiality agreement. He filled in the blanks, signed the copies, and then passed the papers to Matt and Elise.

Once all the business details were taken care of, Matt said, "As I explained on the phone, Elise's father and his business partner may have been poisoned. The case against certain individuals is building, but we have to nail down the motive. I need your expertise to determine whether a certain lead is worth pursuing."

"I'm truly sorry, Elise. I hope your father recovers quickly."

"Thank you." The crinkles around Graiville's kind eyes validated his sincere sympathy.

"Matt, I'm delighted to have a chance to repay you," Graiville said. "Now what is it you need from me?"

Matt reached into his jacket pocket and took out the photograph he'd found in the Hillcrest house. He'd pasted the pieces to a cardboard backing. He handed it to Graiville. "Can you identify these paintings?"

Graiville reached for a magnifying loop and studied the photograph for a few moments. "The paste job, your handiwork?"

Matt nodded.

"Amateurish. Stick to your day job." Graiville shook his head playfully. "I think my assistants should be able to identify the works. What do you want to know?"

"Who the artist is and how much the paintings, if authentic, are worth."

Graiville nodded. "I see." He looked at the clock on the wall. "Have you had lunch yet?"

"Actually, no," Elise responded. She felt hunger pangs at the mention of the word lunch.

"Then, why don't the two of you go for a leisurely lunch? There's a little Thai restaurant a few doors down. When I have information for you, I'll text you. We'll need a couple of hours."

"Sounds good to me," Elise said. She reached for Matt's arm, and they headed for the door. "I know which restaurant he means. I used to go there with my parents on our outings to the art museum. I'll be your guide and point out the best dishes. In return, you can answer the questions I have for you.

GRAIVILLE handed Matt a large printout on glossy paper with sharp images of the two paintings.

"You're a magician, Pierce. This is crystal clear." He held the enlargement so Elise could see it.

"Have you identified the paintings?" Matt asked Graiville.

"Well, they're Russian, nineteenth century. Judging from the subject matter, I believe I know who painted them but need a bit more time to confirm it. How did you get these images?"

"Why do you ask?" Matt said.

"I believe these paintings are hanging in a museum in St. Petersburg, and this photo looks like it was taken in someone's studio," Graiville said. "The date imprint on the photo, if it's accurate, shows it was taken a few months ago."

"You're right on the money. Actually, I think the paintings may have been stolen and smuggled into this country."

"I know better than to pursue questioning you on how you came by this photo." Graiville smiled as he spoke. "So I won't. We've scanned it in and are checking against some databases we have access to." He glanced at his watch. "The results could be up by now. I'll need a few minutes to check."

"Please. We'll wait."

When Graiville left the room, Elise whispered to Matt. "You found that in the Hillcrest house, didn't you? When I asked you at lunch, you never answered me."

Matt nodded, but didn't say a word.

"You think the photo was taken there, right?"

"I'm sure it was." Pointing to a spot in the photo, Matt said, "See the bottom edge of this cabinet? It's the same as the one in the Russian painter's studio."

Elise looked puzzled. "When were you in the house?"

"Believe me, Elise, the less you know, the better. When this is all over, I'll give you the details. If I run into trouble, I don't want to pull you in along with me."

"Okay, we'll do it your way." She had enough to deal with and would trust Matt on this one.

Ten minutes later Pierce Graiville returned. He held several prints. "I have definite matches for you. These are by Petrov. The paintings are entitled, *A Clearing in the Woods* and *View of a Hidden Lake*. Both actually hung in Russian museums and were repatriated to the original owners some years ago. The Nazis had stolen them during World War Two. However, I believe at least one of them, possibly both, went missing from the private collection."

"That fits in with other information I have," Matt said. "How much do you think they're worth?"

"They could bring anywhere from $500,000 to $600,000 apiece, even more from a highly motivated Saudi or Japanese buyer. It's actually hard to be certain since many people won't touch this type of Russian artwork fearing it was either stolen or a forgery."

"An idea just popped into my head," Elise said to Matt.

Matt signaled her to go ahead.

"If the paintings were in the house when my father and Laura went inside, the Russians would be worried Dad and Laura might go to the police if they suspected something illegal was going on. Even if they didn't go right away, the threat would remain. The Russians could be brought in for questioning. It would put a kink in their operations, even if they weren't arrested."

"Under those circumstances it makes sense they'd try to eliminate the threat," Matt said.

Elise shuddered.

"If you're right, then the Russians must plan to sell these paintings privately," Graiville said. "No reputable art house would put them up for auction."

"Why?" Elise asked.

"Because of some big scandals in the nineteen-eighties, respectable houses either shy away from Russian artwork entirely or won't even look at a painting without seeing a well-documented history of the piece beforehand. A reputable gallery will not auction any item without provenance, written documentation attesting to its chain of ownership.

"Because of all the pillage in the former Soviet Union, there are now databases documenting the current status of Russian works. If these paintings were stolen, which I believe is a distinct possibility, they should be on the stolen paintings list. The gallery would be obligated to turn them over or face prosecution down the line. Anyone involved would be at risk not only for monetary loss but also for irreparable damage to their reputation."

"But sales do occur," Matt said, "don't they?"

"The sales are usually to private buyers, ones who are either ignorant or willing to look in the other direction in order to acquire paintings they desire. And with private sales, all parties agree not to divulge any information about the terms and participants."

"What kind of dealer would chance marketing stolen merchandise?" Elise asked.

"Unfortunately, there are more unethical dealers out there than I'd like to admit." Graiville cast his eyes down and then up at

Elise. "My dear, when big money is involved, many people close their eyes and then pretend they had no idea the works were stolen. No matter what any licensed dealer or his attorney claims, if he or she doesn't discover that a painting is stolen, it's because he or she didn't want to find it out. Unless they are totally inept." He sneered. "It's a toss-up which is worse."

"At any rate, we could be talking big money," Matt said. "If the buyers in our case didn't know the paintings were stolen, they could think they are pulling a coup by purchasing them before they can go up for auction."

Graiville nodded. "There's something else I want to tell you. Under magnification, we detected a minute amount of residual paint on the bottom corner of one of the paintings in the photograph. It appears, at one time a second coat was painted over the original painting. Most likely it was applied before the work was smuggled out of Russia. A skilled individual has removed the upper coat of paint."

"I'm flabbergasted by all this," Elise said.

A young man in a smock appeared at the door. Pierce gestured for him to enter. He handed Pierce two large rolls of paper and left the office. Pierce unrolled each print, inspected it and re-rolled it.

"Here, these copies were taken of the paintings when they hung in the Russian State Museum." Graiville passed the rolls to Matt.

"How did you get these so fast?"

"There's a database in Italy that we have access to. We simply downloaded the images, and my technician enlarged them using custom digital equipment."

Elise and Matt exchanged glances. Matt said to Pierce, "I'm amazed at what you've been able to accomplish in just a few hours."

"Amazed and grateful," Elise said.

Graiville tipped his head and smiled.

"One last thing," Matt said, "what's the chance the paintings in the photo are forgeries?"

"Now you're asking a lot. I have no idea. Without a careful examination of the actual paintings, and a battery of tests, no reputable art expert would venture a guess as to their authenticity."

Matt frowned.

"Should you ever get access to the paintings, I'll give you the cards of two individuals who could definitely verify if they're authentic." Graiville removed two business cards from his files and handed them to Matt. "These are the foremost experts in the metropolitan area." With his eyes on Elise, he added, "Good luck and Godspeed to you both. Let me know how everything works out."

"Pierce, I can't thank you enough." Matt shook Graiville's hand.

"My best wishes for your father's recovery, Elise."

She gave Pierce a warm hug.

While they walked to Matt's car, Elise said, "I just had an idea." She explained to Matt what she thought they needed to do right away.

Matt nodded. "It's worth a try." He smiled. "Now you're really thinking like a private investigator. One day you might want to come on board at Merano and Associates. We could use a medical expert on staff." They both laughed.

"Okay, hold that thought. I have a question for you that can't wait." Why is Graiville so obliging to you? He just dropped everything and had his whole crew working on the photograph. You must have done something really big for him."

Matt grinned proudly. "Let's just say, he has a daughter whom he loves, and I helped make sure she didn't make a really big mistake. Pierce had a father's intuition the man his daughter was planning to marry was bad news, and I proved it. As far as he's concerned, I saved the day. He's the type who doesn't forget debts."

Elise impulsively wrapped her arms around Matt's neck. "You're one special guy, and I'll never forget that."

"Couldn't agree with you more," he said as he kissed her softly on the lips.

Elise caught her breath in surprise, delighted by the warmth she felt all over.

TWENTY-SIX

"A tip came in that someone's trying to break into the house at 757 Hillcrest Road where the Russian guy OD'd," the police dispatcher radioed to Burt Parsons. "Wilhelm asked if you can swing by and check it out. Where are you now?"

"About five minutes away on Hazlet and Valley. I've turned around and am heading over."

"Call in when you get there. Backup's on the way."

Parsons stopped his car on a side street off Hillcrest Road, grabbed night vision binoculars and a flashlight from his trunk, and headed on foot toward the house. He made his way through the woods pausing at a spot offering an unobstructed view of the front door and the garage side of the house.

After looking around carefully and not observing anything suspicious, he started to think the tip was a phony one. He toyed with the idea of leaving. Suddenly, there were some sounds in the woods followed by signs of movement heading toward the side of the garage. He caught sight of a bobbing baseball cap. He took out his cell phone and called the dispatcher. "It's Parsons. Where's my backup?"

"Smithson just called in. He should arrive any minute."

Parsons called Wilhelm at the station. "I'm at the Hillcrest house waiting for backup. I've just spotted a white male, teen or early twenties, at the side door of the garage. He's wearing a brown windbreaker. Hold it. He just got the door open and went in. What do you want me to do?"

"Wait for backup," Wilhelm directed.

"Will do."

After a couple of minutes passed, Parsons called the dispatcher again. "Where's Smithson?"

"A minute away."

Parsons made his way around to the side door of the garage. It was unlocked. He cracked the door, looked in, and then flashlight in hand slipped into the dark garage. From there he proceeded to the door to the kitchen and crossed into the hallway. He made his way down the hallway toward a lighted bathroom.

He could hear a man cursing in a foreign language. He drew his gun, swung around to the open door and said in a loud voice, "Police. Stand up slowly, hands in the air."

The intruder, who looked to be in his late teens, sat on the bathroom floor. He gazed at Parsons with a surprised expression and slowly stood. "Hey officer, give me a break. I don't have a weapon. I'm not doing anything illegal."

"Who are you and what are you doing here?" Parsons frisked the young man and found him unarmed.

"My name's Slutsky, Viktor Slutsky. This is my uncle's house. It's all right for me to be here." He spoke in accented English.

"Let me see your ID."

"My license is in my pants pocket. Take it."

Parsons retrieved the license and glanced at it. "What's your uncle's name?"

"Sergei Rimakov. He's the guy whose body they found here. I came to get a paper of mine he promised to give me back." Slutsky grinned. "You know he's not able to now."

"How did you get in?"

"The door wasn't locked. I swear." His body shook. "Look, I don't want no trouble. I'm doing what my uncle told me to do. I'm not into drugs. I'm clean. Here, check my arms." He rolled up his sleeves while inching toward Parsons.

"Stay back."

"Yeah, sure. I got nothing to hide. I told you. My uncle gave me the okay, and I came to get my paper."

"What paper?"

"An IOU he paid off for me. I figured he hid it in here. But I didn't find it. The cops must have taken it."

"When did you see your uncle last?"

"Saturday morning. He called me in the afternoon, and we were supposed to meet here today. This morning, I find out he's dead."

"Did he live here?"

"No. In Brooklyn. Did business here."

"What kind of business?"

"Import-export."

"What did he sell?"

"All sorts of things." Slutsky snickered. "He was a resourceful guy."

"Anything else to say for yourself?"

"Just this," Slutsky roared. He hit Parsons in the mouth with a right cross, knocking him down, and then bolted.

Parsons managed to get to his feet and took off after the younger man, catching up with him in the garage. "Stop or I'll shoot!" Slutsky paused for a moment then kept moving. Parsons repeated his warning.

Slutsky dropped to the floor. "Don't shoot me, you crazy cop. I'm not armed."

"Put your hands behind your back," Parsons ordered. As he cuffed Slutsky, he heard the side door of the garage opening.

Smithson appeared gun in hand. "Sorry Burt. Traffic was heavy."

"Police brutality," Slutsky shrieked. "I'm innocent."

"If you're smart, you'll talk," Parsons said. "Burglary alone can get you three to five. And you attacked an officer on top of it. Want to end up in jail for a very long time? They'll just love a pretty boy like you in there."

Slutsky looked from one officer to the other and seemed to ponder what to do. He took a deep breath and said, "Okay, okay, you make me a deal. I'll tell you everything I know."

Parsons took a card from his pocket and began reading Slutsky his rights.

TWENTY-SEVEN

WITH Matt staying in the guest room of her parents' home, Elise felt secure, but nonetheless, disturbing thoughts plagued her dreams. She rose early and went downstairs to make coffee. Matt joined her in the kitchen a short time later, and they had breakfast together. While they ate she reached a decision.

After clearing the table, she said to him, "I'd like to talk to you about something. Let's go to the den since my mother will be coming down for breakfast any minute."

The morning sun streamed through the open Venetian blinds on the den windows, creating an inviting atmosphere. The room contained a mahogany desk, and a velvet sofa facing a brick fireplace. Oriental carpets were dispersed on the hardwood floor, and walnut shelves lined two walls. Whenever Elise wanted to think or to have a serious conversation, she liked to do it in this room.

Matt wandered over to a shelf with trophies from the time Elise's father had volunteered as a middle school soccer coach.

"I wonder if my old team's trophy is here?" Matt looked up and down a couple of times before spotting a metal statue of a youth in a soccer uniform. "Here it is." He held it up. "I remember the day we won this. We felt like world champions. The whole team carried your dad around the field." He set the trophy down and took a step toward Elise. "It was the last time I played soccer."

"Why did you give it up?"

"The next year I started high school and went out for football instead."

"Aha, where the girls were."

Matt laughed. "You've got me pegged. Me and the babes."

Elise smiled and went behind the desk and sat. She looked at Matt. "High school is supposed to be the best time of your life."

"Yeah, it was pretty good for me." Matt grinned as he moved a chair to the corner of the desk and faced her.

"Not me. Any good high school memories I had were crushed senior year on June fifteenth, to be precise, the day Jim Kelly, Frankie Castle, and Tom Williams died in the car crash." A wave of sadness overtook Elise. She rubbed her aching temples.

"That was an awful accident. It really shook Guilford. The older guys on the police force still talk about it. Only Steve Penman got out of the car alive."

"And it was all downhill for him afterwards. His body survived, but his spirit left him. Ooh," Elise said, almost moaning. "I get a dull pain in my mid-section whenever I think of Steve."

"I had hoped you were over that."

"It's not so easy." Elise started tapping on the edge of the desk. "I found Steve's body."

"I know. It's hard to get past that kind of experience, but it can be done." Matt hesitated for a moment and then asked softly, "Is that what you want to talk about?"

"Yes. I've never really spoken to anyone about it. I want to now that I'm back here. I feel you're the one person I can talk to."

Matt inched his chair closer and reached for her hand.

Elise continued. "Pierce Graiville, his daughter, and how you helped him, made me think of Steve and his father. I dreamed about them last night." Elise looked down to avoid Matt's eyes. She began to speak but then paused, biting her lip to hold back a tear. "Once I start this, I want to get it all out. Please try to listen and not ask me any questions. Okay?"

"Okay."

Elise stared ahead for several moments then started. "When I left for college that August, Steve was still in bad mental shape from the accident. I stayed away from home for three months to put off seeing him. But my parents pressured me to come back to Guilford for Thanksgiving. The day I got home I called Steve and told him I wanted to see him. I felt I had to get some things off my chest."

She took several deep breaths before continuing. "He sounded happy to hear my voice and told me he'd been counting the days. He had something special for me.

"I agreed to go to his house. When I got there, Mrs. Penman met me at the door and took me aside. I remember her words: 'Steve hasn't been himself lately. He can't cope with what happened in June. It's changed him. He barely eats and doesn't sleep well.' His mother shook her head. 'We're all changed. We barely function. Talk to Steve. I'm hoping you can help.'

"'I'm really sorry, Mrs. Penman. I understand', I said. 'I'll do everything I can.'" Elise rested her folded hands under her chin for several moments then began again.

"I climbed the stairs and walked to Steve's room. When I knocked several times and he didn't answer, I called out, 'Steve, it's Elise. Can I come in?' When there still was no response, I slowly pushed the door open. There was only a dim light in the room. Steve was on the bed with his back to me. At first I only saw the side of his head. I thought he might be dozing. I whispered to him that I was there. Then I realized there was blood on the bed quilt that covered him, lots of blood. I felt a sense of panic and began screaming. I couldn't stop. I ran out of the bedroom to the top of the stairs and shouted for his mother. She yelled she was coming. I hurried back to Steve's room and stood in the doorway, unable to move.

"Mrs. Penman brushed past me. I could tell from the look on her face she feared the worst. She ran to the bed and took one look at Steve and said in a breathless voice, 'I'll call nine-one-one.' I went closer and saw the knife." Elise heaved a sigh. "It was gruesome. I must have fainted, because I can't recall anything except Mrs. Penman holding my hand when I woke up. Her eyes were red from crying.

"The rest of the day is a blank to me."

Matt stared at Elise as she spoke. He had a sympathetic look on his face. From time to time, he opened his mouth as if to speak, but didn't.

Elise continued her soliloquy, almost oblivious to Matt's presence. "The medical examiner said Steve died from circulatory collapse due to blood loss. The circumstances of his death were kept quiet." She took a deep breath and slowly exhaled.

Elise stared into Matt's eyes. "I'm certain Steve had planned his death for some time. He'd waited for me to return, so I'd be part of what happened." Elise trembled. "His parents were devastated. While they'd seen signs of serious trouble, they didn't know how to head it off. I'm sure their guilt compounded their suffering from losing Steve.

"They haven't been able to free themselves from what happened that day, and neither have I."

Matt nodded.

"I'm still suffering." She paused. "And I know that's what Steve wanted."

"Why do you say that?"

Matt's voice startled Elise. Her mouth fell open and she gasped. "I've convinced myself it was his form of payback for deserting him, for going off to college when he'd begged me to stay in Guilford. He didn't leave a note, so I'll never know for sure."

Matt lowered his head and rubbed his forehead. When he looked up again, there was a deep frown on his face.

Elise turned to stare at the window. Once she felt more in command of herself she resumed speaking.

"Matt, when Arthur Penman called me a murderer in front of all those people at my father's party, it was the last straw. I knew I'd have to leave Guilford for good, or I'd never shake that memory."

"So you left. But have you shaken the memory?"

"No, I haven't. I've just deluded myself that I'd be able to. You know I would never have returned to Guilford if not for my father's illness. I never dreamed that at my age and a trained physician, I'd have such a hard time coming to terms with the past. But I'm determined to do so now. Laura's death, and almost losing my father, has made me realize life is too short to carry unnecessary baggage."

Matt stood and gently placed his hands on Elise's arms. He looked into her eyes as he spoke. "It's definitely time to let go of your guilt."

"How?" She eased away from him.

"You weren't responsible for Steve's life. Each person is responsible for his or her own existence. I doubt there was anything you could have done to help Steve. Even if there were, it's in the past. It's over." Matt's face hardened. "Let it go. Take it from someone who knows—that's the only way to survive. Focus on today. No more 'if onlys.'"

Elise's gaze narrowed. "I was selfish. I only thought of myself and my future. I did let Steve down."

"Even if that's true, it's okay," Matt said firmly. "If it had been any other way, two lives could've been destroyed."

"He told me he was going to kill himself. I heard his words but they didn't faze me. I didn't do anything. I just went on with my life."

The expression on Matt's face did not soften.

"I can't believe I just said that." The words had snuck out of Elise's mouth. *Maybe the truth is finally out.* Tears formed in the corners of her eyes.

Matt pulled her to her feet and wrapped his arms around her, holding her tenderly. When he released her, she reached out to him, and he took hold of her hands. Looking squarely at her, he said, "I hope you don't think you were the only one he told he was going to kill himself?"

Elise's eyes widened. Many thoughts ran through her head. "Did he tell you, too?"

"Steve had fits of depression from the time he was thirteen. He'd been seeing a psychiatrist and was on medication. His parents were ashamed and made him keep it secret," Matt said. "But all the guys knew. On numerous occasions, he told whoever would listen, that he wanted to kill himself."

"I never suspected that."

"You were young and self-absorbed. Just like every other teen-ager."

Elise's face flushed.

"The car accident probably put him over the top. It had to occur to him that if he hadn't been driving, perhaps the others wouldn't have been killed. Maybe that's true, but who knows?" Matt grimaced. "They all had too much to drink. It was an accident waiting to happen no matter which one of the four of them drove the car."

"I still feel I let Steve down."

"If anyone let him down, it was his parents. They didn't get him all the treatment he needed."

"How do you know all this?" Elise snapped at Matt without meaning to.

"When I was on the police force, one of the veteran cops told me Steve had tried to commit suicide at eleven and then again at fourteen. He'd been on medication for years. Doctors told his parents he needed inpatient treatment, but they refused."

"I didn't know." Elise shook her head sadly.

"If Steve were determined to end his life, he would have,

whether you had stayed in Guilford or gone away to school. The outcome would have been the same, no matter what you did. Believe me."

Elise's lips quivered. "I'm being self-indulgent. Now's not the time for me to tackle this. I must stay focused on doing something to help my father."

"I guess it wasn't a good idea for me to hash it out now," Matt lamented.

"Don't worry. I know you meant to help me, and in many ways you have."

"You're very strong, Elise. You can deal with this. Come to terms with what happened, and get on with your life."

"I have a very hard time deciding whether to come back to Guilford, even though I desperately wanted to see my father and be here for my mother."

"And you did it. You took the most important step, you came back."

Elise covered her eyes and exhaled slowly. "What happened to Laura and my father has been a terrible shock. One day everything was fine; the next, Laura was dead. I used to frown upon people who said you have to enjoy each day as though it were your last, and appreciate the people around you. I thought it was sappy. I don't anymore."

"You have to live in the present, Elise. It's okay to remember the past but don't beat yourself up about it. You did the best you could at the time."

"Everything that's happened, as hard as it has been, has forced me to look outward and beyond myself."

"I can't believe I'm saying this, but sometimes it's the worst events that make people stronger."

"You sound just like my father when you say that." Elise looked at Matt and hoped she hadn't offended him by comparing him to her father. She meant everything she said in the best possible way.

"No worries." Matt smiled and caressed Elise's face. "I take that as a great compliment."

"I'm trying to put this whole Steve business behind me. I honestly feel I've made progress." Elise put her hands on Matt's. "The whole Steve experience was my introduction to the real world and to a situation where I just didn't know what to do. And I didn't think my parents could help me at all." She sighed. "Too bad grief counseling wasn't in vogue in those days. I think that's what I needed. That's certainly what the Penmans needed."

"Counseling helped me when Kara died."

"I knew you were talking about yourself as much as about me. Hopefully, both of us are on the mend."

Matt wrapped his arms around Elise once again.

A shiver ran through her body as Matt drew her close to him and held her tight.

TWENTY-EIGHT

WILHELM dropped the lab report from the Kirby-Bell case on Burt's desk and stood up against the side of the cubicle. "Hairs found on that attendant's wig matched samples from Rimakov's body."

Parsons glanced at the report. "What about sweat residues? And the scrubs?"

"Nothing yet on either of them."

Parsons pushed his chair back and swiveled to face Wilhelm. "When I picked up the Kirby video from Merano, he brought up the name Stacy Lenz. He's convinced she's in the middle of everything."

"Oh yeah. What do you think?"

"It's possible. The hospital surveillance footage was very grainy but the attendant definitely looked like a woman to me. The blonde at the elevator could've been Lenz. The large sunglasses she had on and the way she held her head made it difficult to confirm. Bottom line, we need to get a sample of her DNA."

"It sounds to me like you and Merano got awfully chummy. Family reunion?" Wilhelm snickered.

"Hey, Paul. Cut the crap. We all want to solve this case." Parsons felt like punching Wilhelm whenever he picked on his relationship with Matt. From the time Matt left the Guilford police force to go private, Wilhelm began treating Matt like the enemy and expected Burt to do the same.

Wilhelm folded his arms in front of him as he faced Burt. "PIs always make trouble when they mix in police business."

"Come on, Paul. You know damned well Matt is aware of what he can and can't do. He was a good cop, and he's a good PI. He respects boundaries."

"Okay, let's drop it." Wilhelm waved Parsons off. "Any ideas how we're gonna get Lenz's DNA?"

"I'm on it."

"Run a background check on her and get a copy of her prints," Wilhelm directed. "I want to tie her to the Hillcrest house before we do anything else. Oh, yeah, and get her work address."

Parsons nodded. "Like I need you to tell me what to do," he mumbled low enough so that Wilhelm couldn't hear him. "As I said before, I'm on it."

Wilhelm stepped away. When he returned he handed Parsons a slip of paper. "Here's her apartment address in the city. Take a field trip, and see what you can find out there."

"Will do."

"Make sure you keep me informed." Wilhelm left Burt's cubicle

Burt shut off his monitor and stood. He cursed Wilhelm under his breath and walked toward the door.

TWENTY-NINE

AT half past six that evening Burt stopped by the station to pick up some files and check email. The Chief's and Lieutenant's offices were dark. Only four of the cubicles had lights on when he entered the squad room. On the way to his desk he passed Wilhelm's cubicle. Phone in hand, Wilhelm gestured to Burt he'd be over to talk to him when he finished the call.

Burt hung his jacket on the back of his desk chair and sat. He unlocked his desk and took two folders from the side drawer, and then logged into his email account.

A few minutes later, Wilhelm tapped on the top of the cubicle divider and pulled up a chair next to Burt's desk. "Whatdya get on the Lenz woman?"

Burt faced Wilhelm. "She studied biochemistry at Tarson U in Indiana. Came to New York a couple of years ago and hooked up with the Ukrainian painter, Grigor Kuchma. Moved in with him. They're friendly with a bunch of Russians in Brooklyn."

"Is she Russian?"

Yeah, but born in the Ukraine," Parsons said. "Was six when her family came to the U.S."

"Hmm. Must've had connections to get out of Russia back in those days."

"Her father was a scientist. Maybe he was spying for us and we got him out? He worked in D.C. at a government job until he died of leukemia years ago."

"Any other family?"

"Not that we know of. Mother killed in a car accident soon after the father died."

Wilhelm nodded. "Where does she work?"

"At Bantor Institute in Hoboken. Part-time as a lab assistant for the last year. Flexible hours. Affording a 530 BMW, takes a lot more than that kind of job pays. Must have another source of income."

"Prints on record?"

Burt nodded. "Yep. Had a DUI while at Tarson U. Found her AKA Ana Lenz. Ana for Anastacia. Matched her prints to the Hillcrest house." He resumed scrolling through his email.

Wilhelm snarled, "Is that all you have?"

Without turning to him, Burt replied, "I contacted Melendez in the First Precinct about her apartment. He said she and her boyfriend cleared out before dawn today."

"Melendez cooperating?"

"Yeah. He talked the landlady into letting our guys into the apartment. They took scrapings from the bathtub, hair from the sink drain and nail clippings. Forensics has doubts the samples will be good, but the lab's working them up."

Wilhelm made a face.

"We put out a BOLO for Lenz and Kuchma," Burt added.

"They're probably traveling under false identities," Wilhelm said.

Burt stared down at the worn floor carpet for a few moments, then said, "Maybe yes, maybe no. We might catch a break. They could think we're not on to them yet."

"Okay. Make sure you keep me posted." Wilhelm stood. "I'm going to reconnect with the Bells."

"Talk to you tomorrow. I'm heading out in a few minutes."

WILHELM returned to his desk, checked his phone contacts for the number of Clearview Hospital and punched it in. He asked to be put through to Rick Bell's room.

Elise Bell answered.

"It's Detective Wilhelm, Dr. Bell. We have some new information. I'd like to talk to you. I can be at the hospital in about twenty minutes."

"Okay. Matt Merano is here, too. My father's regained consciousness, and he's being moved to a room on the fourth floor as we speak."

"Good. I'll need to talk to him."

"He's not well enough for that yet."

"When will he be?"

"Too early to know. We're thankful he's started to show improvement."

The moment Wilhelm hung up, his phone rang. He picked it up expecting to hear Elise Bell's voice on the other end.

The caller said, "My name's Lloyd Gentner. I understand you're the lead detective on the Sergei Rimakov case. I read in the newspaper he OD'd the other day."

"How can I help you?"

"I own Gentner Galleries in Princeton. He called himself Serge Kharkov when he sold me some paintings. Look, am I going to have trouble?"

Wilhelm looked over at Burt's desk to signal him to pick up the extension. But his cubicle was dark.

THIRTY

ELISE and Matt stood listening to Wilhelm in the hallway outside her father's hospital room.

"We've matched straw-colored hairs found on the attendant's wig to Rimakov," he said.

"Damn," Matt said under his breath.

"Are you sure the attendant was Rimakov?" Elise's voice betrayed her disappointment. She'd hoped they'd find something to implicate Stacy Lenz.

"I didn't say that. The lab's still working on getting DNA."

"What about the surveillance footage? Didn't that help?"

"We're still studying it."

Elise mouthed to Matt that she was going to bring up Stacy Lenz's name. She debated about the right words to use. "Detective, I think it would pay to compare Stacy Lenz's DNA against any DNA obtained from the scrubs or the wig. There's a good chance she's involved in everything that's happened."

"Oh yeah? And what makes you think that?" Wilhelm challenged.

"She's definitely connected to Rimakov."

"So what? I'm asking you why you think she did something." Wilhelm emphasized the *why* and *she*.

Elise fumbled. She had to admit, she didn't have much to back up her suspicions. It was mostly gut feeling and common sense. She searched for words. "Well, we know she was at K&B last Tuesday morning, right before my father and Mrs. Kirby became ill. So she had access to them and an opportunity to poison them. If we assume somehow she poisoned them, then it makes sense she also made the second attempt on my father's life."

"She could've been the attendant I wrestled with in Mr. Bell's room," Matt asserted.

Wilhelm raised his eyebrows. "I can't do much with that. That's not evidence. Why do you think she'd do it in the first place?"

"I think it could have something to do with the house the Russians were working out of," Matt said. "Mrs. Kirby's video indicates she and Mr. Bell were inside that house and frightened by something they saw there."

"Are you keeping information from me? That's interfering with this investigation," Wilhelm snapped.

Elise was taken aback by the venom in Wilhelm's voice. She stood there with her mouth agape.

"Let me handle this, Elise," Matt said in an aside, his face flushed with anger. He spoke to Wilhelm in a controlled voice. "We've fully cooperated. We've acted responsibly and not passed on hunches and suppositions. We would've told you if we had evidence to support our suspicions."

"I'm not going to argue with you people now," Wilhelm said. He paused for a moment and then with a shrug added, "Actually, we're onto Lenz. We made the connections. Found her fingerprints and her boyfriend's in the Hillcrest house. Had their New York apartment searched."

"So you've kept quite a lot from us," Matt rebutted.

"I don't *have* to tell you anything. We release information when it doesn't compromise our investigation. You should know that, Merano," Wilhelm scolded. "On the other hand, you're obligated to tell us everything you know." Then in a calmer tone, he added, "You can help get things moving if you have something Lenz touched."

"Didn't you find anything when you searched her apartment?" Matt asked.

"She and the Kuchma guy cleaned up pretty well with bleach before they cleared out. Our guys took samples, but we don't know yet how good they'll be."

Elise and Matt looked at each other.

In her mind Elise replayed her meeting with Stacy in Laura's office. *Had Stacy touched anything?*

"Any ideas?" Wilhelm asked Elise.

"I'm thinking back to Thursday, when I met with Stacy at K&B. I'm sorry, but nothing comes to mind." She quickly added, "Did you search the lab in Hoboken where she works? You should be able to find her DNA there. And I bet she has access to all sorts of substances there."

Elise noticed the brief grin that flashed across Wilhelm's face.

"We're on it," he said. "What about you, Merano? Any great ideas?"

Matt shook his head.

"If either of you suddenly remember anything, give me a call. You have my number."

"Look, we need to keep on top of things," Matt said. "How do you want us to handle that?"

Wilhelm stared Matt down. "All right, call your buddy, Parsons. I'll give him the go-ahead to tell you whenever there's any information we can release."

"I just thought of something," Elise said. "When I was talking to Stacy in Laura Kirby's office, she gave me her empty coffee cup to throw away. I dropped it into the wastebasket. There might be enough of her saliva remaining to extract her DNA. Fortunately, the cleaning crew hasn't been in since then."

"C'mon," Wilhelm burst out. "Let's get over there."

Elise turned to Matt. "Will that be okay? I'll be right back."

"Sure. I'll stay here."

When Elise moved toward the closet to get her purse, she overheard Wilhelm speak to Matt in a loud whisper. "Don't forget I'm calling the shots. Keep out of my way."

THIRTY-ONE

THE next afternoon, Wilhelm stood next to Burt's desk while Burt took a call from the police forensics lab. When Burt hung up, he said, "They got a likely match on the Lenz woman with new hairs they found in the attendant's wig."

Wilhelm thrust his fist in the air. "Yes. That ties her to the attempt on Bell in the hospital. We've got something now."

"Not so fast," Burt cautioned. "She can claim it's her wig, but say she didn't do anything. That Rimakov swiped the wig from her and used it."

Wilhelm clucked his tongue. "Yeah, you're right. We got to get her to deny ever having a wig."

"We need to find her first."

Burt's phone rang again.

"Parsons." He listened to the caller for several moments. "When?" He signaled Wilhelm there was news. "Great. What name did she use?" He nodded. "Call me the minute you hear something." He hung up the phone.

"It looks like we caught a break. Lenz was spotted last night at San Francisco airport coming off a flight from JFK. We're waiting to hear more."

"From who?"

"San Francisco police. A flight attendant recognized Lenz's picture."

"What name was Lenz using?"

"Marie Alexander."

"What about the boyfriend?"

"No trace of him, yet. Probably took a different flight."

Burt led Wilhelm to a whiteboard on the wall across from Wilhelm's desk where three names were written: Sergei Rimakov, Stacy Lenz (AKA Ana Lenz, Anastacia Lenz), Grigor Kuchma. Burt added the name Marie Alexander to the list, and sat on the corner of the desk. "Their motive? If we assume they don't just pick off strangers for the fun of it, then these guys believed the Realtors saw something and they had to silence them."

Wilhelm stared at the names. "Rimakov's the key." He tapped his fingers on the desk. "His specialty was smuggled art. Lots of charges against him in different parts of the country, but none stuck. I say, look for the obvious, and there's a good chance it'll pan out."

"That jibes with what Rimakov's nephew, Viktor, said. The Russian painter was squirreled away in that house, and he's made out to be a big expert in art restoration. Trained in the Ukraine, certified at the Philadelphia Art Institute. Supposedly, he came up with some super-duper new techniques in restoration. There's a good bet, with his training, he's also capable of producing high-quality forgeries."

"So you think Kuchma's into forgeries?" Wilhelm asked.

"Makes sense to me. Good reason for him to team up with someone like Rimakov."

"Art theft and forgery is big business, and the Russians are the major players in the New York area."

Burt raised his eyebrows. "How much do you know about it?"

"I'm learning. My brother was over for dinner last night, and I quizzed his wife, the art professor."

"The one who teaches at Pratt?" Burt asked.

"Yeah, the brains in the family. Also, her brother is with Customs in NYC."

"What's her take on the Russians?"

"She said the mob's been smuggling paintings and religious icons out of Russia for years. They're selling them all over the U.S., Canada, and Mexico, and anywhere else where there's money to be made. They paint over the originals to hide their value and sneak them in by ship, hidden among other cargo."

"How can they pull that off?" Burt asked. "That stuff should be pretty easy to spot."

"They roll the canvases and conceal them, often in furniture."

"What about getting by Customs?"

"Supposedly, very few ships are thoroughly searched. The odds of not getting caught at Customs are fairly good." Wilhelm scratched the back of his neck. "Anyway, once the paintings get here, they're processed. The over-painting is removed. The technician has to be really good to do it without damaging the original painting. There's where Kuchma, the so-called expert, could come in." Wilhelm nodded. "Actually, the more I think about it, that scenario makes a lot of sense."

"The theory's okay, but we need evidence to back it up," Burt said.

"Look, the newspapers are loaded with articles on Rimakov. Word is out to all the art galleries, dealers, and auctioneers in the metropolitan area. Something will surface," Wilhelm said. "In fact, a few calls have already come in from people who recognized him."

"You're assuming Rimakov worked through legit channels."

"That's where the big money is. Anyway, we have no reason to think he didn't. That kind of guy has the gall. When you're brazen enough, people don't challenge you. They figure if you were a crook, you wouldn't be in their faces."

Wilhelm looked at his watch. "We've got fifteen minutes. Gentner, that Princeton art dealer who called, is coming in with his lawyer at three. I'll make sure the room is ready for the four of us."

Burt slid off the desk and stood facing Wilhelm. "I'm hoping the Bell reward money will draw some folks out of the woodwork."

"Actually, Bell's probably our best chance for finding out why the Russians were after him and his partner. That is, if he even knows."

"I'll check back with his daughter on how he's doing," Burt said.

"While you're at it, pump her for any info Merano and his guys came up with. I expect she'll open up to you more than she did to me."

"I'll talk to Merano. As you've noticed, we're still on good terms, and he recognizes we're on the same team. So Paul, you see, sometimes that comes in handy."

"Better you than me." Wilhelm curled his lip. "I can't stand that guy. The Bells are no bargains either."

Burt shook his head, turned, and walked away saying he had to hit the restroom. Under his breath, he mumbled, "Geez. They don't pay me enough to work with that SOB."

THIRTY-TWO

PARSONS and Wilhelm led Princeton art dealer Lloyd Gentner and his attorney to the second floor interview room in the Guilford Police Station. While they walked, the attorney, a baby-faced six-footer in his late-twenties, whispered non-stop to his seventy-something-year-old client.

The eight by ten interview room contained a wooden table with four chairs. The visitors took seats next to each other. Burt and Wilhelm sat opposite them.

After coffee and water were offered and declined, Wilhelm advised the art dealer and his attorney that their conversation was being recorded. He opened his notebook and addressed Gentner. "Thank you for coming in today, sir." He acknowledged the attorney with a glance. "As I understand it, you purchased two paintings from the late Sergei Rimakov and resold them to a private client of yours. You called us when you read Mr. Rimakov had died from a drug overdose."

Gentner eyed his attorney before speaking. "I dealt with a man who called himself Serge Kharkov. When I saw the picture of Rimakov in the newspaper, I realized Kharkov was Rimakov. His drug overdose placed his whole character in a different light and I thought it best to contact you."

Burt removed a photo of Sergei Rimakov from his folder and held it up for Gentner to see. "Is this the man you knew as Serge Kharkov?"

Gentner nodded. "Yes."

Burt put the photo back in the folder. "When and how did you meet Mr. Kharkov?"

"A lovely young woman, a regular at the gallery, introduced him to me about six months ago. She had told me a friend of hers was looking to sell some family heirlooms that had been stolen by the Nazis during the Second World War and only recently returned to the family. The family had incurred huge legal expenses to get the paintings back and was in desperate need of money. She thought they would be willing to sell certain paintings at attractive prices."

"And the name of this woman?" Burt asked.

"Her name is Stacy Lenz."

Burt suppressed a reaction. He reached into his folder and took out a photo. "Is this the woman you know as Stacy Lenz?"

Gentner stared at the photo for a long moment then said softly, "Yes."

"Did Ms. Lenz get paid for brokering the deal?"

Gentner looked at his attorney, who nodded to him. "She did not ask me for money, nor did I offer any. As far as I know, she was simply trying to help out a friend."

"Do you know how we can reach her?" Wilhelm interjected.

"Unfortunately, no. The address I had for her won't be of much help. She gave up her apartment in Manhattan and went to Washington DC to care for her gravely ill father. I have no idea when she plans to return."

Wilhelm exchanged glances with Burt. *Her dead father?*

"When did she leave?"

"Last week. We had lunch together the day before."

"What about a cell phone number?" Burt asked.

"She doesn't have a cell phone. She told me she can't be bothered carrying one."

"Okay." Wilhelm looked askance. "Tell us about the paintings."

"They were two landscapes by a Russian artist named Petrov."

"What proof did you get that the paintings were authentic and worth the asking price?

"Mr. Rimakov entrusted them to me for two days. I had an expert come to the gallery, authenticate them, and appraise their value."

"Can you give us the name of that expert?" Wilhelm asked.

Gentner's lawyer responded. "We'll take that request into consideration."

Wilhelm addressed Gentner. "How did Mr. Rimakov say he got them into this country? What about the import papers and the provenance? Do you have anything in writing?"

Gentner's lawyer interrupted. "I'd prefer my client not answer specific questions at this time since these were private sales. I'll only say that Mr. Gentner followed industry standards, the same procedures he's followed during his many years in the business. His reputation is impeccable."

"How was payment for the paintings made?"

With Gentner's approval, the lawyer responded and provided the name of Gentner's bank.

Wilhelm signaled to Burt then said, "Excuse us for a few moments. We'll be right back."

The two detectives left the room. Outside, they briefed their Lieutenant. He instructed them to question Gentner about any other local art dealers Rimakov may have contacted. One of them might have contact information for Stacy Lenz.

When they returned to the room, Wilhelm said, "We know you have your fingers on the pulse of the Princeton art community. Who are some of the other art dealers who may have dealt with

Mr. Rimakov?"

Gentner deferred to his attorney, who said firmly, "This interview is over for today. Mr. Gentner has answered your questions regarding his dealings with Mr. Rimakov. Any further information may be protected by confidentiality agreements. My client has a busy schedule, so we'll be on our way."

Wilhelm's parting words were, "Mr. Gentner, it would be in your interest to cooperate with us now while our investigation is getting underway. Giving us the names of others who dealt with Rimakov will certainly help. If you happen to remember anything, please call."

Burt handed Gentner and his attorney his card. Gentner asked to use the facilities and Burt showed him the location. Meanwhile, Wilhelm engaged Gentner's attorney in conversation outside the interview room. When Gentner returned, he and his lawyer were escorted out by Wilhelm, while Burt returned to his desk.

Burt suspected he'd be hearing from Gentner and soon.

MATT hurried over to the White Horse Pub after receiving a call from Burt Parsons to meet him at six o'clock. When he entered the back room of the pub, the place was dimly lit and half-empty. It usually didn't fill up until after eight. Matt spotted Burt munching on a burger at a corner table. They shook hands then Matt signaled the server to bring him a cola.

"Glad you got here on time. It's been a rough day. I stopped to grab a bite and want to get right home," Burt said.

"What's up?"

"We interviewed a Princeton art dealer named Lloyd Gentner. He bought Russian paintings from Rimakov and resold them." Burt filled Matt in on what he'd learned from Gentner.

Matt rubbed his hands together. "Let me guess. Gentner was looking to make a quick buck and now realizes he probably got taken big time. He's worried it's going to come out the paintings were stolen or forged. Am I right?"

Burt nodded. "There's big money involved. Wilhelm's sister-in-law, the Pratt art prof, said the artist, Petrov, is a big nineteenth century Russian painter, and his works go in the hundreds of thousands."

Matt couldn't help smiling.

Parsons stared at Matt. "Don't tell me, you've heard of Petrov?"

"I was laughing at the high-priced consultants Wilhelm's using these days."

Burt snickered.

The server appeared and placed Matt's soda on the table and left. Matt took a swallow and put down the glass. "Do you know who Gentner's customers were and how the payment went down?"

"We have some leads. I think we'll be able to get more information out of Gentner. Just need to be a little patient."

"I wouldn't be surprised if he's just the tip of this whole mess," Matt said.

"That's what we think. We're doing a sweep, contacting every gallery owner and art dealer in the Princeton area." He took a sip of his beer. "Guess who introduced Gentner to Rimakov?"

Matt looked puzzled for a brief moment then smiled. "Our gal Stacy Lenz?"

"You've got it. I showed Gentner her photo. He confirmed it. He thought she was a lovely young lady. The look on his face made it apparent the old guy had a yen for her."

"Bet she used all her feminine charm to up the payoff for setting up the deal."

Burt shook his head. "Not according to Gentner."

"Do you have an idea how much Gentner paid for the paintings?" Matt asked.

"Not from Gentner. He's stalling for time, claiming

confidentiality. Trying to figure out how to get out of this with the least damage to his reputation and his wallet."

"His lawyer just sat by and let him talk?"

"He didn't let him say much. The lawyer's a young guy. But maybe not so green that he didn't realize Gentner's in big trouble and not just from us."

"Unless he's clueless, he needs to be worried the Russian mob's involved. And if they have money coming to them, they'll come looking for Gentner. I bet his lawyer will advise him to cooperate with you guys in case he needs police protection at some point."

"When I talked to Gentner away from his lawyer, he admitted he'd gotten a phone tip from a woman who said the Guilford police were investigating a Russian who sold Petrov forgeries to some Princeton galleries. Gentner decided he'd better call us before we came after him."

Burt paused and fixed his eyes on Matt. "Hey, did you have a hand in this?"

"Me? No." Matt shrugged and took a drink of his soda. "If Petrovs command big numbers, Gentner probably saw big dollar signs when Rimakov offered a deal, and now he has major indigestion."

"Don't snowball me. You know more than you're letting on. If you want me to square with you, come clean with me." Burt's face reddened.

Matt looked squarely at Burt and said in a low voice, "Trust me on this. I don't want to compromise your position. I'm not trying to deceive you, just protect you. The less you know about this, the better."

Burt glared back at him. "I resent that. I can take care of myself. Just tell me everything."

Matt raised his open palms toward Burt in a gesture of conciliation. "Okay. The day I gave you Laura Kirby's video I told you my men were watching the Hillcrest house. One of them followed a truck making deliveries to three Princeton art galleries. It looked shady, but he didn't know for sure. It could've been legit. My guy couldn't get close enough to see exactly what was going on. After Rimakov died, we contacted a few of the art galleries in the area and baited them to come forward and talk to you guys."

"Who's the *we*?"

"Me and Elise Bell."

Burt sat nodding. "Where do you think her father and his partner fit in?"

Matt twisted his hands together. "The paintings could've been in the Hillcrest house when they were there. Maybe what they saw made it obvious something wasn't kosher."

"So the Russians decided they had to keep the Realtors from talking?"

"That's what I'm thinking," Matt said. "But I could be way off-base."

"Then what we need is corroboration from Bell."

Matt nodded. "His memory's coming back. Pretty soon he should be able to tell us what he saw in the house."

"It all comes down to Bell. Rimakov's dead, Lenz and Kuchma are off the scene, at least for the moment." Burt slid his half-empty beer bottle back and forth on the tabletop. "BOLOs are out for Lenz and Kuchma. She was spotted at the San Francisco Airport. If she's traveling by air out of San Francisco using one of her known identities, we'll be able to track her. That said, Wilhelm's going to push hard to talk to Bell."

"So far Bell doesn't remember anything that happened right before he landed in the hospital. We'll let you know the minute he starts talking about the Hillcrest house."

"Wilhelm's not going to wait. He'll pressure Bell's doctor for the okay to speak to him now."

"If Bell can't talk or can't remember, Wilhelm won't get anywhere. Try to reason with him to give it time."

"Reason with Wilhelm? Yeah, right."

Burt cracked his knuckles and glared over at Matt. "I'm starting to think I tell you more than you tell me. That won't work. From now on you'd better square with me or our deal is off. I'm sticking my neck out for nothing in return." Burt paused for a moment and then added, "We've been friends a long time so I've always given you the benefit of the doubt. I've overlooked your meddling in places where you shouldn't. Don't disappoint me."

Matt stared at Burt. He couldn't help thinking of Kara, his late wife. With Elise around he had thought less about her lately. Although Kara and her brother, Burt, didn't look that much alike, their expressions and behavior were almost identical when they became angry. And Burt was fuming.

"Did you hear what I said?"

Matt brought himself back to the moment. He nodded contritely. When he sensed Burt had calmed down, he said, "I know it sounds like a lame excuse, but I tell you everything that won't get you or me in trouble. Go along with me for a while longer. I give you my word I won't compromise the investigation or you personally."

Burt's grimace disappeared. "Okay, you've always come through in the past, so I'll cut you some slack. But don't push me too far. I don't want to have to deal with Wilhelm and also worry if you're keeping things from me. It's not worth it."

"I think this will wind up soon," Matt said. "Something tells me, Lenz or Kuchma, or both, are going to turn up, dead or alive. Who knows? Rimakov could've had a boss in the wings who's now looking for them and for the money."

"That's an unknown," Burt responded. "Gentner wired big bucks to protected bank accounts in Switzerland."

"And let me guess—the accounts have been emptied?" Matt frowned.

"Somebody's got the money. We found out the funds were immediately transferred after they reached the Swiss account. We don't know to whom or to where yet. Seems like Rimakov and his buddies had all the financial details nailed down."

"So if the big boys got their cut, no one's after Lenz and Kuchma," Matt said. "But, if the two of them were greedy, and ran off with all the money—"

"On the other hand, if Rimakov was an independent, with him out of the picture, we could be the only ones looking for Lenz and Kuchma."

Matt nodded.

"It's unlikely, Matt, that the Russian mob would allow a free-lancer like Rimakov to operate in their territory and reel in big money without them getting a cut. I doubt he could have pulled off such a large deal with just Lenz and Kuchma involved. He would have needed help from well-connected people."

"Maybe so," Matt said. "Either way, I'm thinking there's a good chance Lenz and Kuchma killed Rimakov. More for them with him dead."

Parsons nodded. "That idea crossed my mind." He picked up his beer bottle and finished it. "There's no way we can put extra manpower on at this point. It should all come out when we catch Lenz and Kuchma. And we will, sooner or later."

Matt doodled on the paper napkin for a moment and then raised his head and asked, "So do you have anything else?"

"You heard of a Viktor Slutsky?"

Matt shook his head. "Who is he?"

"Rimakov's nephew. Or at least, that's what he claims. I caught him in the Hillcrest house. We got a tip someone was trying to break into the house."

"Did he talk?"

"He knew about the scam with the paintings and the big payoff. He was into his uncle for a lot of money and agreed to check out Bell for him. Those are his words—'check out Bell'. On Saturday morning, while his uncle waited outside, he went into the hospital. He said he couldn't get into Bell's room because there were too many people around. Something big had happened, but nobody would tell him what. So he swears he left."

"If Slutsky was on Bell's floor between seven and eight o'clock on Saturday morning, he was there when I fought with the attendant. There was quite a commotion. What does he look like?"

"Tall, skinny guy. Over six foot, dark hair, late teens. Why?"

"Just wondered."

"You're not thinking he was the one who pretended to be an attendant?"

"Nah. Too tall," Matt said. It wasn't him.

"His account of the timing checks out, but I have doubts about the rest of his story."

"If Slutsky's telling the truth," Matt said, "and Rimakov was waiting outside, then it definitely wasn't Rimakov who tried to kill Bell. You think Slutsky was supposed to finish Bell off for Rimakov?"

"It's possible. But I don't see how we'd be able to prove it." Burt rubbed his chin. "Slutsky said Rimakov was planning to dump Lenz and Kuchma. Definitely, to get rid of Kuchma. He complained the painter was a drunk who couldn't be relied on. The kid thinks Lenz and Kuchma did his uncle in before he could finish them off."

"Whew. How do you know if any of what Slutsky says is true? He could be making it up as he goes along."

"I don't know. But one thing's for sure. He's a good-looking young guy and has good reason to be scared as hell of going to jail. He'll cooperate, if he has a brain in his head." A distressed look came over Burt's face. "Dealing with Wilhelm on this case is driving me nuts."

"Any time you want out, you have an open invitation to join me. Business is good, and I'd love to have you on board." Matt tried to lighten the conversation. "As they say in the movies, I'll make you an offer you can't refuse." He put on a tough face then half-smiled.

"I might take you up on it." Parsons grinned. "But that's a conversation for another day."

"Well, it looks like you guys have most of the pieces you need," Matt said. "Lucky you got that tip about Slutsky."

"Yeah, wasn't it."

THIRTY-THREE

ELISE answered Matt's call.

"Just left Burt," he said. "A lot's happened. Gentner, the Princeton art dealer, went in to see Burt and Wilhelm."

"He owns the first gallery I called."

"Gentner told them about a deal he had with Serge Kharkov AKA Rimakov for the Petrov landscapes. Guess who introduced Gentner to Kharkov."

"Stacy Lenz!"

"Yep."

"So the hunch my father and Laura saw the Petrovs in the house is starting to look plausible."

"Hopefully, your dad will confirm it."

"Now all the police have to do is locate Stacy and find out where the rest of the paintings went. There have to be more than two out there."

"They have men looking for the other dealers contacted by Stacy and Rimakov." Matt paused. "There's more." He related the information on Viktor Slutsky. "If Slutsky's telling the truth, it makes it clear that Rimakov couldn't have been the attendant."

"So most likely, it was Stacy. Unfortunately, finding her may not be so easy. There's a big world out there, and she and her boyfriend probably have enough money now to run. How does anyone know where to start looking for them?"

"She was spotted at San Francisco Airport traveling under an alias. They're checking there, and flights departing from there. Maybe her luck is finally running out."

THIRTY-FOUR

ON Friday morning, Elise and her mother stopped by K&B on the way to the hospital so Sharon could take care of some paperwork.

As Elise unlocked the door to the empty office suite, she reflected on how K&B would change with Laura gone. Although optimistic her father would make a full recovery, she had no idea how long it would take. In the interim, a couple of their part-time employees were handling clients. How well the business would do in the future was at question, but she wouldn't worry about that now.

They went straight to her father's office. Sharon sat at his desk and dove into the pile of papers left for her by the bookkeeper. Elise grabbed a newspaper from the mail stack, hoping to catch up on local news while she waited for her mother.

The phone rang, and Sharon flipped on the speaker. "Kirby and Bell, Sharon Bell speaking. How may I help you?"

"This is Theresa Rothe," the woman barked. "I've just read your note. I'm not selling my home on Hillcrest Road. I never talked to anyone about listing it for sale."

Elise looked up to see her mother's face flush.

"Please let me put you on hold, so I can pull up the information in my files, Ms. Rothe." Sharon muted the phone.

"Elise, we've got trouble." Her hands trembled as she logged into the agency database. She retrieved the information on the Hillcrest property and unmuted the phone. In a controlled voice she said, "There must be some misunderstanding, Ms. Rothe. I have all the data right here. It says you met with my husband and Laura Kirby on Monday a week ago, at four p.m. and they drew up a contract for the listing and gave it to you for review and signature. I have the document file in front of me. I can email it to you."

"I never talked to anyone from your agency."

"There's a notation that you called a few days ago and left a message to cancel the listing. I tried returning your call, but couldn't reach you at the number you left. That's why I wrote the note to you."

"This is absurd." Rothe's voice resonated with anger. "I've been in California visiting my daughter for the past two months. I've never met nor spoken to your husband nor anyone else from your real estate agency. It isn't as if I don't have enough trouble without this."

"Hang on for a moment, please." Sharon shook her head as she muted the phone again. She gazed at Elise. "Just what we need. She sounds almost hysterical. What now?"

"Let me speak to her." Elise took the phone.

"Hello, Ms. Rothe, this is Elise Bell. Let's see if we can get to the bottom of this. What seems to be the problem?"

"The problem is that I have never even considered putting my home up for sale. If not for what happened in my rental house next door, I'd still be in California."

"What do you mean?"

"If you must know, two days ago the police contacted me in California after the tenant OD'd in my rental house. They asked me to return to Guilford. There's no way I met with any of you last week. I was three thousand miles away."

THIRTY-FIVE

AFTER hanging up with Theresa Rothe, Elise called Matt.

"Everything Mrs. Rothe said made sense to me. She owns two houses on adjoining lots: her home under her name, and the other that she rented to Sergei Rimakov, under her business name, ATR Associates. She can prove she spent the last two months in California. She claims the person who met with my father and Laura was an imposter."

"Did she have any idea who it was?"

"She rented her home to a woman named Sara Gates. Gates moved out last week. Rothe said she has no reason to suspect Gates, but she has no idea who else it could be."

"Did she tell you what Gates looks like?"

"Average height, thin, short-hair, in her fifties. She's a teacher from the Mid-West looking to relocate to New Jersey. She rented the house to avoid staying in hotels while job hunting."

"One thing's for sure, the description doesn't match Stacy."

"But, do you think this Gates woman could possibly be the attendant you fought with?" Elise asked. "I know I'm grasping at straws hoping for random connections."

Matt remained silent for a moment. "I have no idea without seeing her. What else did Rothe say about Gates?"

208

"She's soft-spoken and pleasant. Took the house furnished, paid a month security and the two months' rent in advance. Ms. Rothe said she is keeping the security deposit, so she's not out any money. As you can imagine, she's furious someone tried to sell her home out from under her. Needless to say, she's devastated Rimakov OD'd in her rental house."

Elise heard the background sound of Matt firing up his computer. "Did Rothe run a credit check on Gates?"

"No. She liked her well enough and was glad to get a tenant."

"How did she pay?"

"Cash."

"What about her car?"

"Rothe gave me the license plate number. A blue Camry with a Jersey plate. A rental."

"Not a problem," Matt said. "Gates had to show a driver's license to rent it. There's a chance she used her real name. Let me have the plate number. I'll get Jerry right on it."

Elise read off the number from a slip of paper.

"If we're lucky, we'll be able to track down an address for Gates," Matt said. "Or for whomever she really is."

"Too much happening. My nerves are shot," Elise fretted.

"You need a break. Everything's in motion, so we can afford to take a few hours off and go out to dinner tonight."

"What a segue." Elise chuckled. "Sounds like a date, which is fine with me."

"I was thinking pasta. And it's definitely a date. I know a place where they make the best linguini and clam sauce. How does seven o'clock sound?"

THIRTY-SIX

THE trip from the Bell home to the restaurant Matt had selected took twenty minutes. Traffic was light and he drove the speed limit. As they chatted, Elise savored the feel of the breeze blowing through the open windows on the unseasonably mild evening. For the first time in over a week she managed to put her worries and fears aside, determined to enjoy an evening drive and dinner with an old friend; a friend whose company she enjoyed more and more each day. A lot more than just as a friend.

They arrived early for their reservation and sat at the bar. Although all the bar stools were occupied, the noise around them was soft enough not to interfere with their conversation. Frank Sinatra's rendition of "My Way" played in the background. The female bartender welcomed them and smiled as she placed red cocktail napkins in front of them. She took their orders and quickly filled them. Elise opted for a glass of Pinot Noir, and Matt had a dark beer.

"Hey, Merano, watch out," a man shouted from their right. Elise flinched in her seat. Matt slipped a protective arm around her shoulder as they both turned their heads in the direction of the voice. A big balding guy waved to them from several stools away. He got up and walked toward them.

210

"Barry Hamilton. How ya been?" The man chugged his beer and put the empty bottle down on the bar. He shook hands with Matt and gawked at Elise.

"Hi Barry. It's Elise Bell. It's been ages . . ." She feigned a smile. What had promised to be a fun evening suddenly threatened to become a torturous one. She hoped Barry would say a quick hello and then disappear.

With a wink, Barry eyed her up and down and whispered, "Lookin' good, girl."

Elise murmured, "Ugh," to herself, and took a swallow of her wine.

The high school buddies then spent the next twenty minutes trading stories, with Barry doing most of the talking. Elise said little. Throughout the conversation she remained on edge, fearing Steve Penman's name might come up. When the hostess arrived to escort Matt and her to their table, Barry left. Elise began to relax.

Matt's cell phone chimed the moment they'd finished ordering dinner. "It's Jerry." Matt apologized for having to take the call.

Elise sipped her wine and gazed at the Venetian murals on the restaurant walls. Thoughts of a trip to Italy crossed her mind. One of several items on her bucket list. She looked around the room searching for familiar faces. Years back she knew so many people in Guilford and the surrounding towns, it wouldn't have been unusual to run into several acquaintances at popular restaurants such as this one, but tonight she didn't recognize anyone.

Despite her apprehension, Elise admitted she'd enjoyed hearing Barry's stories about former classmates, especially since Steve Penman's name hadn't come up, and Laura's death and her father's hospitalization weren't mentioned.

Matt put his hand over the phone and mouthed to Elise, "Good news." Then into the phone to Jerry he said, "Great job. Let's grab the first flight in the morning. Call me when it's set."

Matt clicked his phone off and put it away. "Jerry's found out who the mysterious Sara Gates really is."

"Anyone we know?"

"Her name's Gwen Ferguson."

"Gwen Ferguson?" Elise shrugged. "Who is she?"

"An administrator at Tarson U in Indiana."

"How does she fit into all this?"

"Don't know yet. She's not a school teacher though. So much for the story she told Theresa Rothe."

"None of this makes much sense. Is she a Russian?"

"No."

"Stacy Lenz went to university in Indiana. Maybe that's the connection?"

"That's what we have to find out. Jerry spoke to Ferguson, and she agreed to meet us tomorrow morning at ten o'clock at a hotel in Tarson near the university. We'll take the first flight out of Newark in the morning."

"I'm going along," Elise said forcefully. "She'll be more comfortable talking with another woman."

Matt's voice sounded sympathetic when he said, "I'd love for you to come, but there could be trouble. I wouldn't want you to get caught up in it."

Elise just stared back at Matt without saying a word.

"Anyway, do you really want to leave your father? What if he starts to remember things?" Matt paused. "Jerry and I should finish with Ferguson in time to catch an afternoon flight back. If someone has to stay over, it'll be Jerry."

"No Matt. I need to go. Please have Jerry get me a ticket."

Matt sighed. "Okay. You and I will go."

At last she'd have a chance to help. Her tension eased as Matt called Jerry with the change of plans.

Once Matt hung up, Elise asked, "Is Jerry okay with this?"

"He's a good soldier."

Elise cleared her throat. "What did Jerry tell Ferguson?"

"He said we're checking for possible heirs to a large estate. Everything is confidential, and we can only divulge the details in person."

"Isn't it risky to lie to her? Once she figures out it's a ruse, she might walk away."

"That's always a possibility, but I've got a good track record for keeping people talking."

"I can attest to that." Elise and Matt's eyes met. Her heart fluttered, and her mind went blank. It took her a moment to remember what she planned to say. "Are you going to let Burt Parsons know about this?"

"Shouldn't we find out what's going on first?" Matt sounded impatient with her.

Elise nodded. She blushed.

"For now we handle it by ourselves. Trust me. It's the best way to do this."

"It's your call."

Matt reached for her hands. "No more business talk. Remember, this is supposed to be a fun evening for us."

"Then let the fun begin." She moved closer to him.

THIRTY-SEVEN

AT five minutes before ten on Saturday morning, Elise and Matt entered the Corona Hotel in Tarson, Indiana. Elise looked around the spacious lobby filled with small groups of people chatting over coffee and mid-morning snacks. The level of activity in the small-town hotel surprised her.

Matt asked the front desk clerk for Gwen Ferguson. The man pointed to a woman seated on a flowered sofa toward the back of the lobby. Matt and Elise walked over to her.

"Ms. Ferguson?" Matt asked.

"Yes." She stood.

"I'm Matt Merano, a private investigator. My assistant, Jerry Sanders, arranged today's meeting. Unfortunately, something came up last minute, and Jerry couldn't make it." He gestured to Elise. "This is my associate, Elise Bell. She's joining us in Jerry's place." They all shook hands.

Gwen Ferguson fit the description Theresa Rothe had given of her tenant, Sara Gates: slim, middle-aged, about five-five, with short graying brown hair brushed back and away from her lined face. Elise imagined she must have been quite attractive in her younger years, but now sad brown eyes and a despondent look dominated her face.

"May I see your identification?" Ferguson asked. Matt handed her his license. After a quick inspection, she returned the ID. "Please sit down. Call me Gwen." She took a seat in the middle of the sofa.

Matt and Elise sat in cushioned armchairs and faced the older woman across a narrow glass cocktail table. Elise noticed that Gwen's fingernails were bitten to the quick. The woman had to be under a great deal of stress.

"I'll try to take as little of your time as possible," Matt said in a polite voice. He glanced at Elise, who deferred to him.

"We really appreciate your meeting with us, Gwen. I'm sorry we had to stretch the truth to get you here."

Ferguson looked puzzled. "What do you mean?" She moved to the edge of her seat. "Aren't you a private investigator looking for heirs?"

"Not exactly. I am a private investigator, but we're here for a different reason." Matt leaned forward in his chair. "Please hear us out. After we've explained why we've come, if you wish to leave, we'll understand."

Ferguson glanced at her watch. "You have five minutes to tell me what's going on."

"Matt, if it's okay with you, I'd like to start," Elise said.

Matt nodded.

"I hired Mr. Merano's firm. My father, Rick Bell, is a Realtor with K&B Realty in Guilford, New Jersey. He and his partner, Laura Kirby, suddenly became very ill a week ago and were admitted to the hospital. Their doctors now believe they may have been poisoned." Elise locked eyes with Gwen hoping to see some reaction. Gwen's facial expression did not change, but she straightened up against the back of the sofa and placed her hand on her chest.

"We don't have much to go on yet, but we suspect that what happened to them may somehow be linked to a house on Hillcrest Road in Guilford. What we're trying to figure out is why they went to that particular house and if something untoward could have happened to them there. We hope you may have some information that could help us."

"Why do you think I would know anything about it?"

Elise looked pleadingly at Gwen. "We believe you know why. Please help us."

Droplets of perspiration appeared in the creases of Gwen's forehead and under her eyes. She started fidgeting then burst into tears. "Oh, my God." She began shaking. "I'm sorry. So sorry. I never imagined I'd put them in danger. I wasn't thinking straight."

Elise moved next to her and placed a kind hand on her shoulder. "Gwen, please take it easy. We don't think you wanted anyone to get hurt. But you need to tell us exactly what happened."

Gwen buried her face in her hands. Her body trembled.

"Would you like a glass of water?" Matt asked.

She nodded. "Yes, I could use some water." She bent forward, her hands still covering her eyes.

Matt got up to look for a server.

Elise handed Gwen some tissues. "It'll be okay. We'll work things out."

"Give me a moment. I need time to collect my thoughts," Gwen said.

Matt returned with a goblet of water and handed it to Gwen.

Gwen took a few sips and set the glass on the table. She looked first at Matt, then at Elise, and then down at her hands. "I'm very sorry. I never, never dreamed—."

"Please, Gwen, tell us what you know," Elise said. "It can help us find out what happened to my father and his partner."

Gwen sat wringing her hands and looking around the room. She opened and closed her mouth several times but said nothing for several moments.

"I understand your dilemma," Elise whispered, "but lives are at stake."

"Could you excuse me for a moment? I need to stop in the rest room and then make a quick call."

Elise and Matt exchanged nervous glances.

"I'll come back. I give you my word." Gwen headed in the direction of the front desk.

They watched her go. "You think she's going to skip out on us, Matt?"

"I don't know. Short of tying her up, there's not much we can do to keep her here."

"My gut tells me she's wants to do the right thing but is more afraid than anything else. She doesn't know whether she can trust us and I can understand that." Elise leaned back against the sofa pillow. "Is there any chance she could be the attendant?"

"No, I'm sure it wasn't her."

Elise shifted in her seat. "Look, I'm going to check on her."

She followed the signs to the restroom. The room was empty. No Gwen. Instead of turning left toward the lobby, Elise took a right in the direction of the exit sign and hurried down the corridor hoping to find Gwen. Near the end, next to the vending machines, she spotted her talking on her cell phone. Before Elise could slip out of sight, Gwen noticed her and raised five fingers. Elise nodded and returned to the lobby.

Elise told Matt, "She was on the phone in the hallway. She gestured she needed five minutes."

"We'll have to wait it out." A moment later he added, "We have to be really careful what we say to her. Follow my lead."

Gwen soon returned and sat down next to Elise on the sofa.

"Okay, I checked up on both of you, and I believe you are who you say you are. I'm going to take a chance you're on the level and tell you what I did. I have to start with what happened here at the university a couple of years ago. Otherwise, you won't be able to understand why I did what I did and what I've been dealing with."

"Take your time. We want to hear it all," Matt said.

Gwen took a deep breath and began. "I've been at Tarson University for over twenty years. Before becoming the graduate biochemistry department administrator, I was a research assistant to Professor James Enbright, a brilliant and generous man. Jim died suddenly two years ago. In the opinion of the doctors who treated him, he died of natural causes. I don't agree."

Matt and Elise exchanged glances.

"Three semesters before he died, Jim received a large grant to work on natural remedies, plant products used in traditional medicine. One part of the project dealt with the seeds of the plant *Abrus precatorius*."

"I've heard of the plant," Elise said.

"Various parts of the *Abrus* plant have been used for medicinal purposes, but there's a major toxicity issue. The seeds, known as jequirity beans or rosary peas, contain abrin, a toxin. The seeds can be lethal if chewed. The beans are used in ornamental jewelry and rosaries in places like India and some parts of South America. They've been outlawed in the U.S. due to deaths from accidental consumption of the beans."

"I remember reading about dogs and cats dying from eating jewelry beads thought to contain abrin," Elise said.

"Anyway, a few of Jim's graduate students worked on developing antidotes to abrin." Gwen paused for a moment. "Are you following me? Please let me know if I get too technical and say something that doesn't make sense to you."

"Yes, we will. Please continue," Elise said. "I'm a physician and have some knowledge of plant toxicology."

Gwen nodded. "Jim pulled the plug on all work on abrin after one of his graduate students accidentally poisoned herself and almost died. He later found out that student was working on her own side project making abrin derivatives." Gwen took a deep breath and frowned. "Jim should've kicked her out of the program right then, but he gave her a second chance. After she was released from the hospital, she continued her research on the derivatives behind his back, disregarding the danger to herself and to others. When word filtered back to Jim that she was selling the derivatives on the black market, he cut her funding and decided to force her to leave the university. The day he confronted her, he died."

"Oh, how awful." Elise sighed.

"It was a dreadful tragedy." Gwen stopped speaking. When she started again, her voice cracked. "I worked with Jim for a long time and knew him very well. I was the one who found him in his office gasping for breath. I called an ambulance. At first, I assumed he'd had a heart attack. He didn't do well with conflict. While I waited with him for the ambulance, I noticed an inflamed area on the back of his neck. He'd scratched it raw."

"Was the area red and blistered?" Elise asked.

Gwen nodded. "Jim died that night in the hospital."

"What did the autopsy show?"

"There was none."

"Seriously? Why not?" Elise looked wide-eyed from Gwen to Matt.

"It's partly my fault, because of my inability to demand one in time."

"What do you mean?" Matt asked.

"I became very despondent when Jim died. Although the idea he could have been poisoned crossed my mind, it took me several days to pull myself together and get the courage to ask for an autopsy. By then, it was too late. He'd been cremated."

Elise turned to Matt. "That's very strange. Hospitals automatically order an autopsy when someone dies under questionable circumstances."

"You'd think it would be the case everywhere but it isn't. This is a small town with limited resources. Here, if a physician is willing to sign a death certificate listing the death as due to natural causes, unless someone presses for an autopsy, it's not done."

"But who authorized the cremation if you didn't?" Matt asked.

"I tried to find out but couldn't. The funeral home insisted a female relative had, but they were unable to give me a name. They claimed the record had been misplaced."

"Who paid the funeral home?"

"I did. I was the executor of his estate."

Matt and Elise looked at each other.

Matt rubbed his chin. "If you were the executor of his estate, how could anyone else authorize the cremation?"

"I can't prove it, but what I think happened is someone pretended to be me over the phone and the funeral home refused to admit they'd been duped."

"Didn't Enbright have any family?" he asked.

"Not that I knew of. I was probably the one closest to him. I felt compelled to protect his interests. But, because of the cremation, it wasn't possible to run toxicology tests."

"What about blood samples the hospital took on admittance? Couldn't they have been retested?" Elise asked.

"Originally, I thought so, since the hospital normally stores blood samples for a week. But they couldn't find them and couldn't explain what happened to them. They were sorry but said nothing further could be done. I was stonewalled at every turn."

Elise shook her head. "I'm speechless." She whispered to Matt, "I wonder if there was another 'attendant' at work there?"

Matt nodded slowly then addressed Gwen. "You mentioned the raw area on the professor's neck."

"The doctors brushed that off as some kind of insect bite that became inflamed from scratching."

"But what do you think it was?"

"I think it was the spot where the poison entered Jim's body."

"Didn't you go to the police?" Matt asked.

"Yes, I did. They didn't believe me. They told me, not so nicely, that I needed counseling. They treated me like a distraught lover who couldn't accept her boyfriend's death. When I told them

I suspected his graduate student was responsible for his death, they insinuated I was jealous of the younger woman."

Elise frowned.

"An extraordinary man died, and a killer went free," Gwen lamented. "She got away with murder, and no matter what I've tried, I've been powerless to do anything about it."

"By 'she,' do you mean his graduate student?" Elise asked.

"Yes."

"Can you tell us her name?"

Gwen froze for a moment; her face paled, and then she mumbled a few words. "Her name is Ana Lenz."

"Did you say L-e-n-z?" Matt asked.

"Yes, Ana Lenz. A tall, blonde, Russian woman. She's about thirty now." Gwen glared at Matt. "You know her, don't you?" Before either Matt or Elise could respond, Gwen shrieked, "Did she put you up to this?" Fear dominated her voice. Her body trembled. "Are you trying to trick me?"

"No. Absolutely not. Everything we've told you today is true," Elise said firmly.

Gwen seemed to relax a bit.

"We do know of someone with the same last name," Matt said.

"Well, if that person is Ana, be careful. She threatened me on more than one occasion. You think she's wonderful when you first meet her but she's actually a conniving, evil creature." Gwen covered her face with her hands for several moments and then looked up. "Everything I've done, I've done to try to make sure she's punished for her crimes."

"We understand that," Elise said softly. We believe what you're saying.

"Why didn't you go to the police when she threatened you?" Matt asked.

"I did. They were less than helpful. They said it was my word against hers. I needed proof. I had none."

"I take it she's no longer connected with the University, correct?" Matt asked.

Gwen nodded. "She tried to stay on after Jim's death. Probably thought she'd be able to do whatever she pleased once he was off the scene. But she was wrong. I went to the university administration. I convinced them it was in the school's best interest to make her leave. They persuaded her to go. All her research notebooks disappeared when she left."

"Are there any samples at the university of the abrin derivatives she worked on?" Elise asked.

Gwen thought for a moment. "There should be. Samples of all material submitted for testing, are retained in the storeroom. Actually, what brought things to a head was Ana requested assays after Jim officially ended the project, and the assay lab manager informed Jim. There should be samples in storage from that last assay request."

"The police will want to get hold of those samples." Matt turned to Elise. "I'll update Burt and Wilhelm as soon as we finish here."

"Everything is on computer," Gwen said. "It should be possible to locate the material."

"I want to show you three photographs, Gwen. Please let me know if you recognize anyone." Matt handed her the first photo, one of Grigor Kuchma.

Gwen glanced at it. "I've seen his face before but I've never spoken to him. He's Ana Lenz's boyfriend, a painter. He worked in the house next door to the one I rented."

"Who showed you his picture?"

"The private investigators I hired to find Ana."

"I see. Here's the second photo."

"Yes, they showed me him, too. He's connected to the painter and Ana. They said his name is Sergei Rimakov."

Matt handed Gwen the last photo.

Deep creases formed on her face as she scowled at the

picture. "That's Ana, the monster. I'd recognize her anywhere."

"She told my father and me her name was Stacy," Elise said.

"So she calls herself Stacy now instead of Ana," Gwen mumbled. "Her name is actually Anastacia." Gwen stared at Elise for a moment. "Is your father expected to fully recover?"

"We're hopeful. Fortunately, he was very healthy before all this happened," Elise said.

"I'll pray for him." Gwen looked down at her folded hands and then up at Elise. "If you ever come face to face with Ana, watch out for your life. She'll do anything to get what she wants."

"We didn't mention this before, but Mr. Bell's business partner, Laura Kirby, died last Wednesday," Matt said.

"Oh, my God!" Gwen's face reddened, and she began rocking back and forth. "You said they suspect Mrs. Kirby was poisoned. Did they look for abrin?" Gwen breathed hard and gestured with her arms. She seemed on the verge of hysteria.

"We'll make sure they test for it."

"If Mr. Bell and his partner were poisoned with abrin, who but Ana Lenz could have done it? She dissolved her derivatives in certain solvents so they'd be absorbed by the skin and hard to detect."

Matt nodded. "That information will help."

"Under the circumstances, why is it that you are here and not the police?"

"They're on the case," Matt said. "But they're being methodical and going by the book. That's why we're still involved and why we came here. We want to make sure whoever attempted to murder Mr. Bell and killed Mrs. Kirby is caught and quickly. If Stacy Lenz was the one, we don't want to take a chance she'll be long gone by the time the police get their act together."

"I understand. The Guilford police failed me at every turn, just like the Tarson police. Even when I called telling them to check out the Hillcrest house, they didn't do the job right."

"Even then?" Elise glanced at Matt. His eyes widened at Gwen's mention of the Guilford police. "What did you tell the Guilford police?"

"I told them it was a drug house."

"And they didn't check it out? Why not?" Elise asked.

"They claimed they went out, but I know they didn't try very hard to get in. They claimed they had no grounds to get a search warrant. Can you believe that?"

Elise shook her head. "It's devastating. They could have headed off this tragedy."

"I want to scream every time I think of how long Ana's gotten away with Jim's murder."

"Did you spend a lot of time in New Jersey?" Matt asked.

"I made four trips. I stayed there after the PIs quit on me. I returned to Tarson last week."

Without warning, Gwen started sobbing again. People nearby turned their heads to stare.

Elise decided if she wanted to keep Gwen talking she'd better show sympathy and try to calm her down. She moved closer to her and handed her more tissues. "I understand it's hard for you to talk about this. But Ana needs to be stopped. It's important we gather as much information as we can to help us get her once and for all."

"I know, but I feel responsible for what happened to your father and his partner."

"What do you mean?"

"I didn't know. I didn't know."

"What didn't you know?"

"It's my fault your father and his partner went inside the house where Ana's boyfriend worked."

THIRTY-EIGHT

"**WHAT** are you saying?" Elise's hands trembled. She tried to control the rage building in her as she slowly backed away from Gwen.

Gwen wrung her hands. Her face crumpled. "I was sure something illegal was going on in that house. But the police wouldn't believe me. They said I had to file a complaint or get the owner to file one. Without evidence they couldn't do anything." She caught her breath and locked eyes with Elise. "I thought if local people, reputable people, saw something and called the police, they would listen to them."

"Why pick my father and Laura?" Elise gritted her teeth. She was starting to wonder about Gwen's reasoning.

"I read the article on K&B Realty in the local newspaper. Your father and his partner were portrayed as pillars of the community, go-getters. I thought they'd jump at a chance for a listing and go right out to the house. They'd see what was going on there. It had to be something criminal. I figured they'd report the Russian thugs to the police and Ana would be arrested."

Elise narrowed her eyes. "How could they get inside the house if you weren't there to let them in?" *And what would they tell the police?*

"Through the unlocked side door of the garage. Let me back up and explain some things to you. The painter has certain habits. He takes smoke breaks. Goes outside through the garage and leaves the side door of the garage unlocked. He's a heavy drinker and drives into Morrisville two or three times a week to get booze. Along the way he disposes of his empty vodka bottles. Probably to keep his pals from finding out how much he drinks. Before stopping at the liquor store to restock, he eats at a deli and stays away for over an hour."

Elise was having a hard time following Gwen. Certain pieces didn't make sense. "How did you know about the Russians' house in the first place?"

"The two PIs I hired traced Ana and her boyfriend first to a Manhattan apartment and then to the house on Hillcrest Road in Guilford. I paid them to watch the house. Ana and the boyfriend spent a lot of time there but didn't stay over. When the PIs told me the house next door was up for a short term rental, I felt that was an extraordinary bit of good luck and an omen. If I persevered, I would finally get Ana. I made a quick trip to Guilford and leased the house and had the PIs stay in it. A few weeks later, they threatened to quit, but I convinced them to continue working until I could fly back to New Jersey."

"Why did they want to quit?"

"They said they'd done their job finding Ana and didn't want to be paid to baby-sit. The truth is they were scared."

"Let's back up a moment," Matt said. "Okay, when you hired the PIs, what were you planning to do once they found Ana? Try to kill her yourself or hire someone else to do it?"

"No. That was never my plan. I was sure she was up to something against the law. That was her nature. Once I could find some proof, I was going to go to the police and convince them to arrest her. I know that sounds naïve, but that was my plan. As much as I hated her, I could never kill her or anyone else. I'm not a murderer. If I did anything to her, I would be no better than she is and a disgrace to Jim's memory. I believe in the law. I've never held a weapon in my hands."

Matt stared at Gwen for several moments, nodded to Elise and then said to Gwen, "Tell me again what you think scared the PIs?"

"They were small-town guys. They were afraid the Russian mob was involved. That's what I think."

"You're guessing, right? Or did you have a reason to believe someone from the mob had threatened them?" Matt asked.

Gwen shook her head. "They claimed they'd been very careful and the Russians had no idea they were being watched."

"Okay," Matt said. "Go on with what you were saying about the painter."

"The painter had a set routine. I watched him come and go, myself. I got the idea to contact a Realtor and pretend to be Mrs. Rothe, the owner of the two houses, and to say I wanted to sell one of them, but wasn't sure which one would sell faster." She focused her eyes on Elise. "I took a chance your father wouldn't know the Rothe woman."

"But what if he did? It's a small town."

"Then I would've told him I was Mrs. Rothe's sister from the Midwest."

"You said, 'two houses.' How did you know Rothe owned the two houses?" Matt asked.

"She told me. She said she had a furnished house next door that she'd rented to some Russians."

Elise nodded.

"I called your father, gave him specific directions to the Russians' house. Even tied a rope around the tree where the driveway splits and told him to be sure to go to the right."

"The timing had to be tricky," Matt said.

"I took care of that." Gwen turned her head to Elise. "When the painter left the house, I checked that the side door on the garage was unlocked and then called your father's cell phone. I said I was running late so he should just go in through the garage and look around the house. Once I saw your father's car turn into the driveway, I drove to Morrisville, found the painter's car, a beat up silver Ford Focus, and deflated one of his tires to keep him in town longer. I waited a little then called your father again. When he didn't answer, I left a message saying something had come up, and we should meet at four o'clock at my house since I'd decided to sell my own home rather than the rental house."

"Did you check if my father and Mrs. Kirby had gone to the police?"

Gwen shook her head. "I met them at four. I assumed they'd tell me what happened next door. I planned to encourage them to go to the police if they hadn't already done so."

Matt leaned forward in his seat. "So what did they say?"

"They claimed they never got out to the rental house at one o'clock. I knew they weren't leveling with me and I became convinced they had no intention of going to the police." Gwen paused, seeming to reflect on what to say next. "I became so distraught afterwards that I decided to drop the whole thing and go back to Indiana. I left a message at K&B saying I wouldn't sign the contract and they should cancel the listing." Gwen paused and wiped a tear from the corner of her eye.

Elise placed a hand on Gwen's shoulder, encouraging her to continue.

"When I left New Jersey, I had no idea what had happened." She looked down at her lap for several moments then lifted her head. Gazing at Matt, she said, "I'm a good person. Pursuing Ana has destroyed me. It's made me do things I'd never have done before. I've deceived innocent people. I can't do this anymore. I have to resign myself. Ana will never be punished. I have to finally let it all go."

"No. You can't give up. You need to tell the police everything you know," Matt said firmly. "With what we've learned and with what you tell them, they will be able to get Ana and make sure she's punished for everything she's done."

Gwen sighed. "You're right." In a weak voice she added, "How much trouble am I in?"

"I think you'd better get yourself a lawyer right away."

Elise stared at the broken woman and momentarily felt sympathy for her. "Matt, if Gwen didn't purposely try to hurt anyone, won't that work in her favor?" As soon as her words were out of her mouth she regretted saying them.

How could she feel compassion for Gwen? Even if unintentional, Gwen's actions were responsible for Laura's death and for almost getting her father killed. When Elise looked at Matt he gave her a cold stare. She bit her lip and kept still.

Matt took a deep breath. "Gwen, it's in your best interest to hire a lawyer before you contact the police."

"I need some time to decide what to do."

"Don't delay." Matt curled his lip. "Let me ask you something." He barely concealed his disgust.

"Haven't I told you enough?"

Elise patted her hand. "With what you've told us, we stand a chance of getting justice. We need a little more information, and we'll be there. Please answer Matt's questions." Elise had decided it served her purpose to be the good PI to Matt's bad PI.

Gwen rubbed her eyes with a tissue. "I can't tell you how sorry I am for what's happened. I promise I'll try to answer all your questions."

"To start, tell us everything you know about Ana Lenz and her previous illegal activities."

THIRTY-NINE

WHEN they left the hotel, Matt reproached Elise for showing sympathy toward Gwen. She tried to explain to him that Gwen was nearing the breaking point and she did it to keep her talking,

They said little to each other during the taxi ride to the airport. He stared out his window. Matt was right. She had let her emotions get the better of her. She couldn't blame him for being angry with her.

A couple of hours later, after Matt contacted Burt Parsons and updated him, they were waiting in the airport terminal to board their flight, when Matt's cell phone rang. He answered it then handed the phone to Elise, his expression distant. "It's Gwen Ferguson. She wants to talk to you."

Elise took the phone. "Hello, Gwen."

"I have more information for you. First, I want to apologize again. I never meant to harm anyone."

Elise squirmed in her seat. She didn't want to talk to Gwen right now. All she wanted to do was to return to New Jersey, mend things with Matt, and help her father get well. She was not cut out to be an investigator. The police could handle Gwen, Stacy, and whomever else was responsible for Laura's death and her father's illness. "Okay. What do you want to tell me?"

"Elise, I mean to do everything I can to help get Ana, even if I end up in jail." Elise heard what sounded like quiet sobs. "It was very hard for me," Gwen continued, "but I dug out my personal diaries from two years ago. That was an awful time. I suspected Jim was having an affair with Ana, even though he denied it and said he loved me. Reading the pages of the diaries made me relive the pain I experienced. But I wanted to tell you what Ana said she planned to do once her boat came in, her expression, not mine."

Elise's ears perked up. After allowing Gwen to drone on for several moments, she asked, "So do you have an idea where Ana could be now?"

"Quite possibly somewhere in the Hawaiian Islands. She talked about going there one day when she had money. I guess I blocked that out along with all the unpleasantness surrounding her. Jim's death paralyzed me. It took over a year of therapy for me to even begin to function again."

She doubted Gwen had recovered, given her behavior and poor judgment. Elise's heart pounded. Maybe Gwen's information would lead the police to Stacy. "Thank you Gwen. This may help." A thought occurred to her. "Have you contacted the police yet? It's better if you go to them before they come looking for you."

"I called a lawyer. He's arranging a meeting with the Tarson police as we speak."

"Please hold for a moment." Elise muted the phone. "Gwen says Stacy could be in the Hawaiian Islands. Do you want me to ask her anything?"

"No."

Elise unmuted the phone. "Thanks Gwen. We will be in touch."

"I knew you'd understand, Elise. You know how you'd feel if Ana had come between you and Matt, the way she came between Jim and me. And then Jim died before we could repair our relationship." Gwen began crying.

231

Elise was taken aback, both by what Gwen had said about herself and also, that she'd recognized Elise's feelings for Matt. Elise ended the call as quickly as she could and handed the phone back to Matt. He immediately looked away from her.

She had to clear the air. "Matt, I know I goofed badly with Gwen at the hotel. I'm very sorry."

He faced her and sighed heavily. "It's my own fault. I shouldn't have taken you with me."

"I pressured you, and you tried to be nice to me. I let you down. It won't happen again."

Matt nodded.

"I mean I'll follow your lead from now on, never blurt out my feelings." She narrowed her eyes. "Did you mean you'll never take me along again when you're working?"

He broke into a smile. "I'm afraid you're right about that."

Elise pouted. "I've learned my lesson." She looked into his fiery brown eyes and made the best contrite expression she knew how to make. "You forgive me, don't you? And you'll give me another chance?"

"This is serious business. No place for amateurs."

Elise looked away. She felt her eyes tear up and didn't want Matt to see. The stress of the last week had gotten to her. She wasn't acting like her normal self. She'd better pull herself together.

"Since Jerry had checked out Gwen, I figured it was a low risk situation. Chances were a meeting with her in public would be safe, so I took you along. But there could be times, when if you moved the wrong way or said the wrong thing, you could get into a lot of trouble. You can't go off on your own."

"Advice taken. I won't make the same mistake, twice. I promise you."

"Out there, we're up against bad guys." Matt stopped for a moment and stared at her with a stern expression. His mouth slowly crinkled into a smile. "You know you're real cute when your feelings are hurt. Come here." He put his arm around her and drew her close. "I'm sorry. I'm really tired and mouthing off. To be honest, the real reason I'm upset is that I could never forgive myself if I put you in any danger. You're too important to me to risk your safety." He looked at her with soulful eyes and gave her a warm kiss. "We make a great team," he said. "It's so good to have you back in my life. And I want to make sure you stay."

FORTY

ELISE called her mother.

"Thank God it's you, Elise. I've been watching the clock waiting for your call. Are you okay?"

"Matt and I are fine. I've got to make this quick. We board in ten minutes."

"What did you find out?"

"Plenty." Elise gave her mother a brief recap.

"If the real Theresa Rothe hadn't gotten back to me," Sharon said, "we might not even know about Sara Gates . . . and Gwen Ferguson. I'm amazed the Ferguson woman could afford to hire detectives, rent a house, travel . . ."

"She was willing to spend every cent she has to see that Stacy Lenz gets the punishment she deserves. She's convinced Stacy murdered Jim Enright and she's the only one in the world who even cares."

"I can understand her frustration, but she is a criminal. She caused Laura's death and she should be held accountable. She also broke the law when she pretended to put someone else's property up for sale. Did she think she could simply cancel the listing and by doing so undo the crime? For a supposedly smart woman, she did some very stupid things. Do you think she'll go into hiding?"

"I honestly don't think so. She wants to make amends."

Elise could hear her mother mumbling about a lousy twist of fate and the monsters that walk among us.

"Matt contacted Burt Parsons and Detective Wilhelm. They'll arrange things with the Indiana police."

"I hope nobody gives you guys a hard time for meddling in police business. Somehow, things always turn against innocent people. Especially, when all they're trying to do is the right thing."

"Mom, enough. Matt will work it all out—trust me. Look, we have to go."

"Before you hang up, Elise, I've got some wonderful news for you. Dad is awake. He's started to regain his memory. I don't think it'll be long before he can tell us his side of the story."

"Have you told him about Laura?"

"Not yet. I'm dreading his reaction."

FORTY-ONE

WHILE Matt waited in the lobby of the toxicology building on the State University campus, Elise went to Dr. Patel's office to speak with him. She knocked on his door.

"Please come in and have a seat," Patel said, with a wave of the hand.

Elise entered the small, unpretentious office furnished with a computer desk, armchair, and two visitor's chairs. Patel and Elise adjusted their chairs to face each other.

"Thanks for agreeing to see me on such short notice," she said. "I only need a few minutes of your time."

"Please, go ahead."

"Matt Merano and I just returned from Indiana where we met with a woman from Tarson University's Graduate Biochemistry Department. Based on what she told us, we think my father and Mrs. Kirby could have been poisoned with an abrin derivative." Elise waited for Patel's reaction.

Patel nodded. "Abrin poisoning would fit the pattern we've seen. I believe I've mentioned to you, there was a series of highly notorious crimes in India in the 1950s, dubbed the 'Handshake Street Assassinations'. Two very highly poisonous plant toxins were used. One was ricin, the other abrin."

"Yes, I recall." Elise massaged the back of her neck to relieve the tension she felt. "How likely is it that abrin caused the damage to my father and Mrs. Kirby's hands?"

"It's possible. That occurred to me when I saw the condition of Mrs. Kirby's hand. The 'handshake' assassins used potent chemical derivatives of both abrin and ricin, topically active derivatives. They wore special gloves permeated with solutions of the material to administer the toxin." Patel placed a paper in front of them on the desk and began sketching. "The thumb of the glove was embedded in this way with miniature-sized sharp particles. Compression with the glove abraded the victim's skin and the toxin permeated the skin and entered the blood stream. Victims usually were unaware of the attack."

"How did the assassins avoid poisoning themselves in the process?"

"They used gloves lined with an impermeable material that shielded them from the effects of the toxin. There were occasions when the would-be assassins were careless. That is how the police got the upper hand and eventually stopped the assassinations. By threatening to withhold all treatment, the police were able to extract confessions from criminals who had accidentally poisoned themselves."

"Do all exposed victims die?"

"In poisonings with abrin, unlike ricin, victims have a chance to survive, dependent on how much of the substance they have absorbed. It's very destructive to skin and organs. Without immediate medical care, there can be severe local and internal damage."

"I ran a quick search of the latest scientific literature hoping for new information on abrin antidotes. I didn't find anything."

"I'm not surprised. I continually monitor the literature and haven't encountered anything new on the subject. A colleague of mine in India mentioned something about a collaboration with an American professor in the Midwest who was working on antidotes, but I've no idea where the research stands."

"Did he tell you the professor's name?"

"I don't recall, but I can fire an e-mail off to India and let you know what I find out."

"I suspect it could have been Professor James Enbright at Tarson University in Indiana."

"I'll include that name in the email."

"What about differential diagnosis in suspected poisonings?"

"Radioimmunoassay is used to confirm the presence of abrin. We'll alert the police we have serum samples from your father and Mrs. Kirby and suggest they have them tested for abrin."

"How long does it take to get the results?"

"I know of only one lab in this county that does those assays, and it's always backed up. I expect the police have additional resources." Patel coughed twice. "But, keep in mind, in your father's case, the identity of the poison is probably academic at this point since your father is recovering."

"It's vital from the criminal standpoint."

"While I certainly agree, my focus is medical. If abrin is responsible for your father's illness, the supportive treatment we gave him was the proper course of action. The rest is up to the police."

"I understand. Since my father is recovering, my primary concern is that the police identify the poison and find whomever killed Mrs. Kirby and tried to kill my father." Elise's voice strengthened. "Whoever did this must be brought to justice."

FORTY-TWO

AFTER Elise's meeting with Patel, she and Matt went straight to the hospital. They found her father sitting up in bed when they entered his room. Although he flashed a smile when he saw them, his tear-stained cheeks and morose expression revealed his deep sadness. Elise had never seen her father cry and was glad not to have witnessed it. He'd always prided himself on his strength and his ability to control his emotions, but understandably, this situation was too much for anyone to bear.

Her mother sat next to the bed, with her back to the door. She soon turned her head. "Oh, I'm glad you're both here. I've broken the news to Dad about Laura, and we've discussed his hospital stay. We haven't talked about anything else yet."

Elise leaned over and hugged her father. He spoke to her in a weak voice. "It's wonderful to see you, sweetheart." He took a labored breath. "Laura's gone. I can't believe it." He paused. "How are you holding up? I can imagine how hard this has been for you."

"I'm okay Dad." She haltingly added, "We're all devastated by Laura's death and your illness." She heaved a deep sigh. "I'm so glad to see you're getting better. That's the most important thing." She gestured toward Matt, "Dad, you remember Matt Merano? He's been helping us."

The two men shook hands and exchanged a few words then Rick said to Elise, "Your mother said it's likely Laura was murdered. Can that be true?"

"We believe she was poisoned, and I'm afraid, so were you, Dad."

"Poisoned? Are you sure? That doesn't make any sense. Who would do that? Why on earth?"

"Everything points to a woman named Stacy Lenz. She came to K&B on Tuesday."

"Who?" Rick's eyes jutted from Elise to Sharon to Matt and back.

"Stacy Lenz. Do you recognize the name?"

Rick shook his head. "No, should I? Who is she?"

"An attractive blonde woman about my height and age." Elise recounted that Stacy Lenz had met with him and Laura at K&B on Tuesday morning and that she had kept a scheduled follow-up appointment on Thursday.

"I'm sorry. I don't remember her." He closed his eyes.

"What's the last thing you do remember before waking up this morning?"

Rick did not answer immediately. He slowly opened his eyes. "I don't know. I can't think clearly with the way my head is buzzing."

"It's the medication," Elise said. "Things will get better as the effects wear off."

Sharon's lips quivered. "Let Dad rest now. Today's been tough for him."

"Yes, we will, but . . ." Elise rubbed the back of her neck. "We can't afford to lose more time." To her father she said, "We're hoping you remember something that will help the police." She weighed her next words. "I've been thinking, since time is of the essence, we could try to stimulate your memory, Dad. There's a simple process using word association that might help. Would you be willing to try it?"

Sharon held up her hand. "Enough for now." Elise heard an uncharacteristic edge in her mother's voice.

Elise glanced at Matt. He signaled her to back off.

"Okay, Mom, we won't do anything right now. We can think about calling in a neuro specialist later on, if necessary."

"It's all right, Sharon," Rick said in a soft voice. "I'm okay. I have to rejoin the world." He addressed Elise. "If it's urgent that I do it right away, I'll do anything you need me to do."

"I'm sorry I jumped at you," Sharon said to Elise. "Dad was devastated when I told him about Laura. I want to spare him any further stress today."

Elise touched her mother's shoulder. "I understand. Believe me. I wouldn't press this if time weren't critical. The police have to act quickly to catch the people who did this. It's important to find out whatever Dad knows with the least delay."

Sharon nodded gingerly. "Forgive me, but I can't help being emotional. My best friend died, and I almost lost my husband."

"What we want to do won't harm Dad. It might possibly help him regain his memory faster. We can stop if it becomes too much for him."

Rick patted his wife's hand. "It'll be fine, Sharon. Don't worry. And all of you, please stop talking about me as if I weren't here."

THE hospital neuropsychologist came out of Rick's room and walked up to Elise and Sharon, who waited for her near the nurses' station. Matt was elsewhere calling his office.

Dr. Jill Ammond, a tall, imposing African-American woman in her late-forties, summarized her impressions from her first session with Rick. She finished by saying, "We've found most patients who regain their memories post-coma do so within twenty-four to forty-eight hours after awakening. So far, it appears

Mr. Bell may need a bit more time."

"Elise mentioned using word association to stimulate her father's memory. Do you think it would work?" Sharon asked.

Dr. Ammond took a few moments to consider the question. "Most of my experience has been with trauma patients, unlike Mr. Bell who endured a metabolic coma. Generally, I've found you can't rush things. But on occasion, we have had some success with word association in situations similar to this one."

"Is there any reason not to try?" Elise glanced at her mother for approval.

Sharon offered no opposition.

"We can do it if you wish. In my opinion, your father already shows signs he'll regain his memory in time. Be patient. My suggestion would be to wait a couple of days, see how things go. But if you want me to try word association now, I'll just take a few minutes to check in with my service and come back."

"Given the circumstances, I think we need to give it a try." Elise whispered to her mother, "Rest assured, if there's even the slightest indication that Dad's in trouble, I promise we'll stop immediately."

THEY began a half hour later. Elise and Matt had provided Dr. Ammond with a word list. The doctor sat down next to Rick's bed and paged through a small notebook. Addressing Elise, Sharon, and Matt, who all stood off to the side, she said, "Normally, I prefer to work alone with the patient, but in this situation, your presence may prove helpful. Please don't say anything unless I ask you something." All three nodded.

"Now, Mr. Bell, I'd like you to tell me the first word that comes to mind in response to the word I say."

Rick nodded and whispered, "I will."

"Remember, there's no right or wrong answer. Are you ready?"

"Yes."

"Here we go. Sunny."

"Day," Rick responded.

"Sharon."

"Wife."

"Daughter."

He smiled briefly. "Elise."

"Road."

Rick shook his head. "Nothing. I didn't think of anything."

"Okay, let's go on. House."

"Home."

"Listing."

"Commission."

"K&B."

"Laura." Rick's eyes teared.

"Paintings."

Rick cleared his throat. "Nothing."

"Okay." Dr. Ammond jotted something in her notebook. She looked up at Rick. "Secret."

"Hide."

"Danger."

He shook his head.

"Theresa Rothe."

There was a long pause before Rick answered. "Woman."

"Russians."

Rick began coughing. Dr. Ammond offered him a glass of water. He took a long, slow drink, then handed the glass back. His face flushed. In a halting voice he said, "I want to stop, now."

"Is something making you uneasy?" the doctor asked.

"I don't feel comfortable doing this any longer. I'm tired."

Elise joined in. "Dr. Ammond, would you mind if I ask my father a couple of questions?"

"Go right ahead. Our session is over."

"Dad, do you remember my calling you on your birthday?"

"Yes, I do."

"Later that day you met with a new client. Do you remember that?"

"Yes."

"Does the name Theresa Rothe sound at all familiar?"

"Yes. Yes. Now I remember. She wanted to put her house up for sale . . . I think. Am I right?"

"Do you remember her house?"

Rick bit on his upper lip. "I drove with Laura to see the house."

"Good. What happened there?"

A look of distress came over his face.

"It's okay, Dad. Tell us. We know part of it already. We found Laura's video."

"You found the video? Laura said she was going to destroy it."

"Something must've made her change her mind. Do you—?" Elise stopped mid-sentence when she noticed her father's pinched mouth and sour expression.

"Not now, Elise. I need to rest. Send in my nurse when you all leave."

FORTY-THREE

ELISE huddled in conversation with her mother and Dr. Ammond in the corridor outside her father's room. From the corner of her eye she spotted Detective Wilhelm heading in their direction. "I'm here to talk with Mr. Bell." He waved to them as he passed by.

Elise caught up with him. "This is not a good time. My father's resting now." She tilted her chin in Dr. Ammond's direction. "His psychologist had to interrupt her session with him because of his fatigue. Perhaps you can come back later this evening or tomorrow morning."

"I'm afraid it has to be now," Wilhelm continued on his path.

Elise followed him.

Wilhelm stopped in the doorway and extended his arm to block Elise from entering her father's room. "Excuse me, Dr. Bell. You'll need to wait in the hallway. I'd like to speak to your father alone."

"I'm not leaving."

Wilhelm made a face and turned to address Elise's father. "Mr. Bell, it's Detective Wilhelm of the Guilford Police. I'm investigating Laura Kirby's death. I've come to speak with you."

Rick opened one eye. "Who . . . are . . . you?"

"Detective Paul Wilhelm. Guilford Police Department." He elevated his voice and enunciated each word. "I'm investigating Laura Kirby's murder and your poisoning."

"Not now. I can't talk now. I'm too—"

"Mr. Bell, don't you want us to find out who did this?"

"Detective Wilhelm, can't you see he's exhausted?" Elise fired. "I'll have to ask you to leave immediately, or I'm going to call his physician."

Wilhelm ignored her. "Mr. Bell, you need to talk to me now."

Rick did not respond.

Elise picked up the phone. "For the last time, Detective Wilhelm, I insist you leave right now."

"Okay, okay. But how do you expect us to do our job if you don't cooperate?"

"I give you my word. When he's able to talk to you, we'll contact you."

"You make sure you do that." Wilhelm handed Elise his card and walked out.

ELISE sipped coffee from a paper cup as she gazed out the window of her father's room. When she heard him stir she went next to his bed. The sparkle in his eyes lifted her spirits. "You've been asleep for almost two hours. How do you feel now?"

"My head's finally clear." He smiled. "Believe it or not, while I was sleeping, I remembered what happened."

"I'm not surprised. As the medication wears off, you'll find your memory will rush back."

"Well, I've got a lot to tell you already. Are your mother and Matt here?"

"Mom went down to the cafeteria. Matt is nearby. I'll get him."

A few minutes later Matt stood next to Rick's bed. "Elise

tells me you have some information for us."

"It's about Theresa Rothe."

"Yes."

"We drew up a contract to list her home. Initially, she wanted to sell her rental property on the adjacent lot. We went out to see it." He stopped and took a breath. "She was supposed to meet us there but told us to go in if she was late." He lowered his voice. "What we saw inside scared the hell out of us."

Matt leaned over the bed so he could hear Rick speak. "Like what?"

"Jewelry, and paintings. Really expensive stuff. On tables and in crates. At first it looked to us like it could be the stash from burglaries."

"So that's what frightened you? Seeing all that stuff? Your wife said something was troubling you on Monday and Tuesday nights."

"There's a lot more to it." Rick took a deep breath and pushed it out. "Soon after we went into the house, I felt something was off and wanted to leave. Laura insisted we stay and go through the entire place."

"Why didn't she want to leave?"

"She insisted it was okay for us to be there. Mrs. Rothe gave us permission to go inside if we got there before she did. Maybe what we saw wasn't stolen merchandise. The tenants could be into something like estate sales or run a consignment shop." He stopped and rested. "That could have been true, but I felt the tenants wouldn't want anyone in the house with all that stuff around. But Laura didn't want to risk losing the listing and miss out on a big commission."

Elise glanced at Matt. He stood poker-faced. "Did something in particular scare you, Dad?"

"What we saw in the artist's studio. The large paintings. Someone had removed a covering layer off several of them."

"How could you tell?" Matt asked.

"From photos on a bulletin board showing the work in progress. Also, open books with pictures of the same paintings hanging in museums. And enlarged prints of the paintings."

Matt nodded.

"There were a number of copies of each painting. You couldn't tell if some were originals and others copies. We figured someone might intend to pass them all off as originals."

"Why did you think any were original?" Elise asked.

"Well," Rick exhaled loudly, "if they weren't masterpieces, why would they be painted over and then the top layer removed? I've seen lots of movies where that kind of thing was done, and it was always part of a scam."

"So you guessed at least some were originals?"

"Yes, after we saw Russian packing slips. We figured the paintings were stolen in Russia and smuggled into the U.S. Maybe our imaginations ran loose, but that's what we both thought."

"You have a funny look on your face. What's on your mind, Elise?" Matt asked.

"Some of the things Graiville said. To make the whole scheme work, Rimakov had to have originals. With large amounts of money at stake, buyers would insist on having the paintings authenticated. Rimakov could make an original available for authentication then substitute a copy at the time the actual delivery took place."

"Who is this Graiville you're talking about?" Rick asked. A moment later he added, "Do you already know most of what I'm telling you?"

"Why don't you finish Dad, and then we'll fill you in on what we know."

"The whole thing looked like a well-organized racket. Before we left, Laura was almost hysterical. She spouted that the Russian mob could be involved and we better not mess with them. That they'd come looking for us. And kill us."

"Where did she get that idea?" Matt asked.

"From stories she'd seen on TV and newspaper articles. Once Laura saw the packing slips with Cyrillic lettering, she was afraid we'd stumbled on to an illegal Russian mob activity."

"Why didn't you go to the police?"

"We were too scared, Elise. I know, we were told we could go into the house, but Mrs. Rothe might not have known what was going on in there."

"The police wouldn't have charged you with anything if you had the owner's permission to enter the premises," Matt said.

"Rothe could always back track and say she hadn't given her okay. But that wasn't our biggest fear." He paused. "We were worried the police wouldn't be able to protect us. They could bungle things, and the Russian mobsters would find us." Rick ran his hand over his forehead. "We were also afraid our reputations would be permanently damaged, no matter what we did. Maybe—"

"Maybe, what?"

"Maybe if we had more time to think it out, we would've taken our chances going to the police, but it all happened so quickly. Things appear a lot different now from the way they did then."

"The bad guys found out who you were and did come after you," Matt said.

"Yeah?" Rick sighed. "I still can't believe all this happened to people like us. To Laura, especially." His voice caught. "We were just doing our jobs. We didn't intentionally do anything wrong."

Elise glanced at Matt. What her father had just said was becoming a familiar refrain. Gwen Ferguson had used similar words. She didn't intentionally do anything wrong, either.

Matt looked sympathetic. "You got mixed up in the wrong people's lives through little fault of your own."

"Who actually tried to kill us? Were they Russian mobsters?"

"We don't know if the Russian mob per se was involved,

but things point to a Russian woman named Stacy Lenz playing a major role. Either she acted alone, or did so with the help of her boyfriend, the painter whose studio you were in, and another man. And possibly additional people." Matt caught Elise's eye and she nodded. "Whether they were acting independently or were connected to a so-called mob, isn't clear yet." Matt paused. "Do you remember the woman now? She was at K&B on Tuesday morning."

"Maybe I would if I saw her again."

"Hold on a sec." Matt reached into his pocket for some photos. He held the first one in front of Rick. "Have you ever seen this before?"

Rick scrutinized the photo. "Yes. I think it's one of the paintings in the studio."

"How can you be sure?"

"It reminds me of Candlewood Lake, where we once kept a boat. I immediately thought of the lake when I saw the painting."

Matt looked over to Elise, who smiled.

"Take a look at this, Mr. Bell. Do you recognize this woman?"

Rick studied the photo. "Yes, I do. She came to K&B on Tuesday morning. Said she was starting a job in New Jersey and looking for a place to live close to work."

Matt turned to Elise. "Everything is falling into place."

"I don't understand. How does that woman fit in with the house?" Rick asked.

Matt summed it up. "She lined up the art dealers who resold the paintings. We believe her boyfriend, a painter by the name of Grigor Kuchma, was the one who did the restorations and forged the copies. He worked in the studio in the rental house you were in."

Rick appeared to have trouble processing what he'd just heard. When he spoke again, his voice cracked. "I guess they wanted to get rid of us so we couldn't go to the police and squash their business." He placed his hands on his chest.

"That's what we think," Matt said.

"Do you suppose they might try again to kill me or get to Elise and Sharon?"

"No, we're pretty sure you're safe now. The paintings are gone. They've already changed hands and have been paid for. The woman, Stacy Lenz, and her painter boyfriend, have fled. Their accomplice, a man named Sergei Rimakov, is dead, and his face has been in all the newspapers. Everything's out in the open. And there's a police guard at your door. My men and I are guarding Mrs. Bell and Elise."

"Has anyone tried to hurt Sharon and Elise?" Rick asked, wide-eyed.

"No. I've had someone watching over them twenty-four-seven."

"Oh boy. This is unbelievable." Rick shook his head back and forth several times. "But how did that Stacy woman poison us?" He directed his question to Elise.

"Based on my conversations with Dr. Patel, a toxicologist, she could have done it if she wore gloves permeated with a toxin. When she came to your office, did she insist on shaking your hands and lingering?"

Rick scratched his head. "But she wasn't wearing gloves."

"Are you sure, Dad?"

"Let me think. I know she didn't have gloves on when she came in because she rubbed her hands together when she first spoke to us. She remarked about how chilly it was outside, and she was trying to warm her hands up." He thought for a moment more. "Wait, wait. I remember now. Just as she got ready to leave, she reached into her purse and took out a case containing her gloves and maneuvered them on. I should have realized something was fishy. Nobody keeps gloves in a case in a purse. Eyeglasses, yes, gloves, no way. It just didn't register with me at the time."

"I bet she set it up for you to focus on her cold fingers upon arrival so that you wouldn't take much notice when she put gloves on before she left," Matt said. "She had everything planned."

"Oh, Dad, no normal person would even imagine someone could be so evil."

"Yeah. She shook hands with us, while thanking us profusely. I remember pulling my hand away as soon as I could, but she did a job on Laura." He sighed. "It blows my mind she could smile so sweetly and at the same time try to kill us."

"Unfortunately, the evil in someone isn't reflected in their face," Elise said sadly.

"But why would she use poison?" Rick asked. "There are easier ways to do someone in."

"That's true, but with the kind of poison she used, she stood a good chance of getting away with it. If not for Dr. Patel, the consulting toxicologist brought in by Dr. Fletcher, the poisoning might not have been detected." Elise quickly added, "We think Lenz may have used the same type of poison to kill her university professor in Indiana a couple of years ago."

"Laura didn't like that woman from the start. She was suspicious of her."

"Why?" Elise asked.

"Her expensive clothing and expensive car. Laura thought they were too pricey for a relatively young woman who claimed to be on a tight budget and starting a new job. Also, she told us she didn't have a cell phone, so she couldn't be contacted. But Laura swore she spotted her talking into one in the parking lot. Laura was a good judge of character. That's what made her so effective in sales." He took a breath. "I still don't understand how they knew we were inside the house."

"There were surveillance cameras in the studio and all rooms except the kitchen, bathroom, and hallways," Matt said. "Fortunately, it was an old system, and it appears they couldn't check it remotely, or the outcome could've been even worse."

"We could have been killed on the spot." Rick's jaw fell.

"Once they saw our faces in the surveillance video, though, it was easy for them to find out who we were. Our pictures are on our website, and there was that newspaper article on us. The Lenz woman mentioned the article when she called our office to make an appointment."

"Something's puzzles me," Elise said. "Did Laura use her camera in any room other than the kitchen?"

Rick tilted his hand and appeared to consider the question. "Only in the kitchen. I upset her by what I said there, and she tossed the camera into her purse."

"It looks like the Russians didn't know she had a camera, since they didn't come looking for it. I shudder to think what else could've happened if they had," Elise said.

Matt put his arm around her and drew her close to him.

"It's in police hands now, Mr. Bell," Matt said. "I'm going to call Detective Parsons and let him know what you've told us."

"Oops," Elise said. "I had promised to let Wilhelm know when my father was ready to be interviewed."

"Okay, I'll handle that when I talk to Burt." Matt addressed Rick, "Mr. Bell, either Detective Parsons or Wilhelm will stop by to get a statement from you."

Seeing her father mouth the name Parsons, Elise explained, "Detective Wilhelm is the lead on the case. Burt Parsons is his partner. While Wilhelm's been tough to deal with, Parsons has been very helpful. I bet you'll recognize him from years ago." She chose not to mention that Burt Parsons was the brother of Matt's late wife.

"Do you think I'll need a lawyer?" Rick asked.

"I'll make a call and get some advice," Matt said.

FORTY-FOUR

LATER that evening, Elise sat in a fourth-floor meeting room at the hospital waiting for Matt. She thought about the conversation she needed to have with him. Her stomach rumbled. *Nerves.* She popped an antacid into her mouth. Conflicting thoughts ran through her mind. She wanted to tell him she loved him in a romantic way but feared he might not feel the same way about her. They had been friends for so long, could they move on to a different type of relationship? Was it too soon after his wife's death to expect him to want to or be able to commit to another woman? While she risked getting hurt, if she didn't speak up she could lose this chance at love. She had wasted too much time already.

Matt wore a relaxed smile when he entered the room. *He's so handsome. Even more than he was years ago.* He touched her shoulder then sat next to her.

With a few sentences he brought her up-to-date on his conversations with the police and assured her everything was under control.

She turned to him, her leg touching his. "Dr. Patel just called me," she said. "He heard back from his connections in India. They confirmed Professor Enbright was the academic they collaborated with. He had a large grant to develop abrin antidotes. When one of his female students had to be hospitalized for an extended time and almost died, he decided the work was too dangerous and ended the project before making any real progress. That corroborates what Gwen Ferguson told us."

"I bet Stacy familiarized herself with hospital procedures during the time she spent in the Indiana hospital and put that knowledge to use later on." Both nodded. "Anything else?"

"Patel said the police have my Dad's and Laura's serum samples and will submit them for abrin analysis, but not to expect any results for several weeks."

Matt stared at her. "From the look in your eyes I think you've got something else weighing on your mind. What's up?"

Elise chose her words carefully. "Now that the docs assure me my Dad is expected to make a full recovery, I have to think about going back to Scottsdale." She took a deep breath, glanced down at the floor for a moment, and then studied Matt's face to gauge his reaction. "I had hoped to stay here until Stacy Lenz was in police custody, but it doesn't look like I'll be able to. The head of Internal Medicine at the hospital was sympathetic at the beginning and allowed me time off. But now he has the departmental secretary calling me every day to ask when I'll be back." She paused. "You look surprised. What's wrong?"

Matt was slow to speak. "To be honest, I hoped you'd stay. I guess that was unrealistic. I've gotten used to you being around and seeing you every day. I actually thought we had something going for us."

Elise's eyes begin to mist. Her heart throbbed. She wanted to shout that she was going to chuck everything and remain here with him. But it wasn't possible. At least, not now. Her voice trembled. "Matt, I have no choice. If I did, I would want to stay here with you, but I'm obligated to go back and finish out this year."

His expression turned sad. "I realize that. When do you

have to leave?"

"Monday, at the latest. I've been away from work almost two weeks. They're short-staffed at the hospital and have had to juggle schedules to cover for me."

Matt took her hands in his. "I know we've been good friends for a very long time. I've always loved you. But it's different now. I'm in love with you, Elise."

Elise's pulse quickened. She looked into his warm brown eyes. "I've been searching for the right words to tell you how I feel. Probably, down deep, I've always loved you but was too dumb to realize just how much. I was afraid you might not feel the same way about me." She chuckled. "It's ironic, I'm deeply sad over Laura's death and my father's illness, but at the same time I feel a kind of happiness I've never experienced before." She wrapped her arms around his neck, and they held each other tightly.

After several moments, Matt cupped her face in his hands and kissed her lips. "Well, what are we going to do about it? You in Scottsdale, and me here?"

Her shoulders slumped. "I have to complete my residency. I've worked so hard to get to this point. After that, I can go anywhere I choose. I love living out west and considered staying in Arizona permanently, but I don't have to." She thought for a moment. "You know, Phoenix is a growing city. A good private investigator like you could find lots of clients out there. Would you ever consider moving to Arizona?"

"Here I am professing my love for you, and you sound like an employment agent. You got a lot to learn about timing, girl, and I mean that in a good way." He took a deep breath and smiled. "Actually, I have vacation coming up and had no idea how to use it. I guess I'll be buying a plane ticket to Phoenix."

Their eyes met. Any lingering doubts she had disappeared. The tension in her body dissipated. She laughed with joy.

"Tell you what," he said. "I know a much nicer place for us

to continue this conversation. Hungry?"

"Famished."

"It's a great restaurant with just the right atmosphere. I've been itching to take you there."

ELISE and Matt stopped by her father's room and said a quick good night to her parents before heading out to The Chateau, an upscale continental restaurant about fifteen minutes away.

They arrived at the elaborately decorated eatery for a late dinner. Matt had called ahead and reserved a corner booth, which afforded them privacy.

The moment they sat down, the server arrived at the table with a small basket of breads and olive oil. He took their beverage orders and left.

While they waited for their drinks, they held hands and planned what they'd do in the time before Elise had to leave. Within minutes they'd also agreed Matt would fly to Phoenix so they could spend Thanksgiving together.

"Now that that's settled, something's been bugging me for years," Matt said.

"What?"

"Remember, just before you left your father's party, we kissed each other good-bye. I held you in my arms and felt your response. And there definitely was a response. Much more than a good-bye between old friends. I couldn't accept the idea that we would never see each other again. I gave it a little time then got up my courage and wrote to you. You never answered. Three letters. I waited and waited. I even called your mom a few times to see how you were doing. After a while, I gave up. I went on with my life, started seeing Kara. Pretty soon we were engaged then married. I loved her . . . but not the way I've always loved you." He took a deep breath. "Why didn't you answer me?"

She fought back tears. Thoughts raced through her mind. "I

never got your letters. When did you send them?"

"Two weeks after you left."

"Oh, Matt. I think I know what happened." She took a tissue from her purse and wiped tears from the corners of her eyes. "I was in bad shape when I arrived back at medical school in Philadelphia and needed a change of scenery. Since I planned to do my residency in Scottsdale, I did a two-month rotation there. I didn't tell my parents for a number of reasons."

Matt nodded.

Elise continued. "I gave up my apartment in Philly, and when I got back I roomed with classmates until medical school graduation. Your letters never reached me." She shook her head. "I'm so sorry. Why didn't you call me?" As the words left her mouth, she regretted saying them. "I'm so sorry. You must have been very hurt."

Matt reached for her hands. "I guess I can be philosophical about it now. Maybe we both needed time apart in order to recognize it was right for us to be together."

"It's unlikely things would have worked out between us back then even if I had received your letters. I wasn't in a good place at the time."

The server brought their drinks. Once he left the table, Matt kissed her.

He raised his glass and toasted, "The past is past. To us, to the future."

Elise touched her glass to his. "To our future *together*." They sipped their drinks.

Their eyes met. In unison, they said breathlessly, "Food can wait. Let's get out of here."

FORTY-FIVE

EARLY Monday morning, Elise folded her navy pantsuit, placed it on top of her other clothes, and zippered her suitcase. A sudden twinge of sadness overtook her. She sat on the bed and looked around her childhood bedroom. The feelings she had now were different from what she'd experienced four years earlier when she sat in the same spot and contemplated what it would be like never to return to Guilford. Never to see her childhood home again.

So much had happened over the last two weeks: Laura's death, her father's poisoning and recovery, encountering Stacy Lenz and cohorts and their evil machinations, and ultimately, finding love with Matt. Guilford no longer frightened her. Although she hadn't been tested, she felt she could even handle running into the Penmans. She had a better understanding of her guilt and had made steps toward overcoming it.

There would always be a hole in her heart for Laura. The impact of her death was indescribable. At the same time, Elise marveled at her father's recovery. Released from the hospital yesterday afternoon, one of his first actions upon arriving home had been to call Laura's sister, Deanna, to ask her to consider relocating from Minneapolis to Guilford to join him at K&B.

Falling in love with Matt was the crowning event, an

unexpected blessing, something she had never anticipated. She hated to admit it, but she had almost given up hope of finding someone with whom she'd want to spend the rest of her life. And there he was, Matt, someone she'd known since childhood. How could she have been so blind?

She would see him again at Thanksgiving, and they would be together in a new environment for him. Yet, her training as a physician made her question whether her heightened emotions over the last two weeks had made her unusually receptive to a chance at love. Would her feelings for Matt survive her return to everyday life in Scottsdale? Would he be willing to leave his familiar surroundings and start a business in a new location? A lot of questions remained. She slapped her cheeks. *Go with the flow. Stop analyzing everything. Let things happen. Enjoy being in love.*

Her cell phone chimed. Matt was a few minutes away. She finished getting her belongings together and brought them downstairs, setting them by the door.

The bell rang. Elise opened the door to a beaming Matt. He reached out to her, and they hugged and kissed.

"Boy, you're looking amazingly well-rested," Matt said. "No one would guess how much you've been on the go the last couple of days."

"Okay, Romeo." Elise felt herself blushing.

"I'm a little early. I wanted to spend time with you before your flight."

"I'm ready. Come with me to the kitchen to say hello to my folks."

Elise's parents greeted Matt warmly and thanked him for all his help. After a few minutes of chatting they walked with Elise and Matt out to his car where they said their goodbyes. Once Elise's parents had gone back into the house, and she and Matt were seated in the car, Matt reached into the glove compartment and took out a small package covered with gold foil paper. He handed it to her. "I'd like you to have this."

"Thank you. What is this?"

"Go ahead, open it."

Elise began to undo the wrapping paper. Her fingers trembled. *A black velour box.* She read the embossed words on the top of the box. "Scott's Jewelry. My favorite in Guilford."

Matt smiled. "You see, I don't forget the important things."

Elise's mind raced. She proceeded carefully, knowing that Matt's eyes were focused on her, watching for her reaction. She opened the box and beamed. Inside was a delicate chain with an exquisite gold locket, a small diamond in the center of the face. "It's beautiful. I love it." She removed the chain and locket from the box and opened the locket.

"No pictures, yet," he said. "But please look at the back."

Elise turned the locket over and read the engraving. "You're always in my heart. Matt."

She swallowed hard. Her eyes teared. "Please help me put it on."

Matt opened the clasp and tenderly placed the chain around her neck, then kissed the nape. "You mean everything to me."

Elise smiled and said without any reservation, "I love you so much."

THEY stood at the security gate saying last minute goodbyes when Matt's phone rang. Elise watched as he answered and listened to the caller. She loved the way he looked and remembered how exciting and secure it had felt to be in his arms. Once he hung up, he said to her, "I have some good news courtesy of Burt."

"Fantastic. Let's hear it."

"First off, Gentner gave them the names of other dealers who bought paintings from Stacy and company. Wilhelm and Burt are taking statements from all the involved parties. The next part is big."

"Have they caught Stacy?"

"Not quite, but things are looking up. The Hawaiian police have located packages Marie and Stan Alexander, aka Stacy Lenz and boyfriend, left in a storage facility in Waikiki. The 'Alexanders' said they were moving to one of the other islands and made arrangements for the boxes to be shipped to them once they're settled. When their forwarding address comes in, the police will nail them."

Elise wrinkled her brow. "That doesn't sound like a certainty. They could decide to abandon the stuff."

"That's true, but I bet they think they're safe and will send for their belongings. It may take a little while, but the police expect it to happen. People like Stacy think they can outsmart everyone."

"No wonder. If Gwen is right, Stacy's gotten away with murder for over two years. That alone can make someone smug, I guess. And careless, I hope."

"Her time will be up. The police are searching for her and her boyfriend all over the Islands."

Elise said forcefully, "They're murderers. They need to be locked up. They can't be allowed to hurt anyone else." She inhaled deeply and blew out a long breath to calm her frustration. "Now that I've said that, I don't want to think about them right now. Let's enjoy the rest of our time together before I have to leave."

"You got it."

Elise fingered the chain Matt gave her. "I was just thinking. When you are in Scottsdale, we can . . ."

EPILOGUE

One month later

MARIE Alexander emerged from the crystal clear blue ocean, spread her arms, and watched water droplets slowly slide down her oiled body. Although evening was approaching, it was still warm, and a delicious breeze filled the air. She contemplated what an amazing day it had been, capped by a luxurious swim.

She walked out of the water onto the sand and picked up her towel. After blotting herself dry, she draped the towel around her waist and on a whim quickly whirled around savoring the feel of the wind in her hair. Out of the corner of her eye she spotted a young woman snuggling an infant in her arms. She imagined what it would be like to walk on this beach holding a baby of her own. Maybe one day. There were things she wanted to accomplish before then.

This was a second chance at the life she wanted for herself, and she was going to make the most of it. It had been easier than she anticipated to settle into living here. Trekking to some of the less-populated spots allowed her to explore the rich plant life. She had already collected a large number of exotic specimens and had begun cataloguing them. She was a scientist once again. While she had anticipated she would have a career elsewhere, this beautiful island was a wonderful place to be.

Grigor was happy. She gave herself a gentle slap on her cheek as his name ran through her thoughts. In public she had gotten used to calling him Stan, but in her mind and when they were alone, he remained Grigor. He always would. She had never seen him so serene and at the same time creative. He was calm, able to sleep at night, and off the booze. He'd sworn to her his drinking days were over. With Sergei out of the picture, life had become less stressful for him.

A sudden strong wind sent a chill through her body. She picked up her blanket and headed toward their cottage. She waved to Grigor who sat on the second floor deck watching her. He blew her a kiss. Earlier in the day he had driven to the UPS in the center of town to pick up the last of their shipped boxes, ones that contained items from his studio. When he started unpacking she left for a swim.

She felt safe. Safe from everything left behind in her former life. The old life was just that—left behind—a previous existence. They didn't read newspapers. They didn't care about anything outside the island. Sergei was dead. He no longer mattered. He had been relegated to the past where he belonged.

It had all gone smoothly: getting to Hawaii, boating to this island, and finding a cottage. She had planned quickly, but well. The few belongings they had brought with them were easy to manage. Whatever else they needed right away, they had acquired. One really didn't need much here, and besides, with money, it was possible to get anything they wanted. The money transfer had been easy to arrange. Marie Alexander had excellent credit and a sizeable bank account. The fact that the original Marie died two years ago, made no difference to anyone. No body, no death, no one the wiser. Just one more woman disappearing, but with one difference: her identity had now resurfaced, far from her former life.

Marie really owed Sergei for her happiness. He'd made it all possible. She smiled when she thought of the irony. She hoped he was turning over in his grave. He thought he had outsmarted her, but he was so wrong.

She stopped outside the front door and called up to Grigor. "Stan, I'm going to shower and change. I'll be up in a few minutes."

She stepped inside the cottage and walked through the living area to their bedroom. She removed her swimsuit, dropped it on the floor, and popped into the shower where she lulled for several minutes under the strong warm spray. Afterwards, she dressed in a short, vibrant red, blue, and orange gauze dress and went upstairs to where Grigor waited for her.

"You look beautiful, *Dorogaya*. Come, let me kiss you," he said.

She delighted in seeing the glimmer in his eyes. His once sad, listless look had disappeared. She sat in his lap, wrapped her arms around his neck, and they enjoyed a relaxing embrace.

"Let's have a drink to celebrate this moment," he said. "I have some vodka."

"Vodka?" She pulled back and glared at him. "Don't tell me you went and bought vodka after all your promises." *Control yourself.* She bit her lip. "Why did you break your word to me? This is not good."

"No, I haven't. I didn't buy anything. I have my flask."

"What flask?"

He pointed to the table. "It was in the boxes I picked up today."

She looked with disdain at the flask and two glasses next to it. In an instant all her good feelings evaporated. Grigor's scent became unbearable. She stood and took a seat on the other side of the table.

Grigor reached over and took the flask in his hand. "This was in my studio. I almost forgot I'd packed it. It's from the bottle Sergei left for me to celebrate the end of the deal. It would've been a sin to waste such good stuff. You remember. I told you when I filled my flask. You didn't object." He poured a shot and placed it on the table in front of her. "Please, one drink with me. It'll make today perfect. Once this is gone, there will be no more." Sadness settled in his eyes.

Was the glimmer she saw before a buzz from booze? She stared at him. She hated when he begged for anything. Instead of making her feel sympathetic, it hardened her. He could be so child-like. *But you said I could.* "If you drink, you drink alone."

Grigor gingerly filled his glass and waited. He looked at her with imploring eyes. "*Dorogaya*, just this one time. Never any more." He waited then slowly raised the glass to his lips and shouted, "*Na zdorov'ya*," gulped the drink down in one swallow and threw the glass against the wall.

Stacy turned away and stared at the ocean, quietly seething—furious at him, angry at herself for believing he had changed. A wave of despair rushed through her. One slip and he could fall back into his old patterns. She would not put up with it.

She turned to look at him. He sat there beaming at her. Just as she opened her mouth to warn him, his face contorted, he shrieked and clutched his midsection.

"That's not funny. Don't think you can smooth things over that easily, Grigor."

He squirmed and moaned, gasped for air, then collapsed onto the floor.

This was no pretense. What was happening to him? Should she call 911? Was there even a 911 if she dared to call? *CPR?* She'd give him CPR.

From the street below came the sudden sound of tires screeching. Car doors slamming. Pounding on the front door.

She resisted the urge to look down at the street. *Concentrate on Grigor.* She pressed his neck for a pulse. *Nothing.*

More pounding on the door. Shouts of "Police. Open up." Sounds of the front door being kicked in. The thunder of feet rushing the stairs.

She stared at Grigor's still body. Her eyes filled with fury. *This can't be happening.* She shook her fists. "Don't you leave me!"

Then it all became clear.

Sergei.

ACKNOWLEDGMENTS

The author would like to thank many people for sharing their expertise and providing advice and feedback. Any mistakes that are present in the manuscript are solely the author's.

Extreme gratitude to Merle McCann and Sally J. Smith for their unwavering encouragement, inspiration and for investing the time to serve as beta-readers.

Huge appreciation to Deborah J Ledford for her insight on so many aspects of writing and publication, and to Timothy W. Moore, Phoenix Police Detective (retired), for patiently responding to countless questions related to police procedure.

Thanks to past and present critique group members: Maria Grazia Swan, Suzanne Flaig, CR Bolinski, Rose Gonsoulin, Arwen Kemp and Phyllis Ciarametaro for their valuable suggestions.

Thanks also to the membership of Sisters in Crime Desert Sleuths Chapter for generous support and sharing their knowledge and experiences.

Last and utmost, a tremendous thank you to my husband John, and daughters, Adriane and Leila, who helped in ways too numerous to list.

ABOUT THE AUTHOR

Susan Budavari has always been an avid mystery reader. After years as a scientific writer and information specialist in the pharmaceutical industry, she traded the New Jersey seashore and winter snow for the amazing skies and dry heat of Arizona, and turned to writing fiction. Many of her short stories have appeared in award-winning anthologies. *Deadly Listing* is the first novel in the Merano & Bell Novel series.

More about the author: www.susanbudavari.com
Information on the series: www.ferventpress.com